PHOENIX

SHONA BLASS

GOLD CROW BOOKS

Published in 2022 by Gold Crow Books

ISBN 978-1-8382554-2-8 (paperback)
ISBN 978-1-8382554-3-5 (e-book)

British Library Cataloguing in Publication Data
A CIP catalogue record for this book is available from the British Library

Cover design and typesetting by JD Smith Design

For Paul

CHAPTER 1

Benjamin

Something's wrong. It's too quiet outside. My laptop screen is bright but my room's grown dark. Why didn't I notice before? It's too dark. Rising quickly, I go to the window. No lights are on in the houses opposite, not even Mrs Singh's, and her lights are never off. No cars driving by. No bins out for tomorrow's collection. It's Sunday night, and none of this is right.

Fear slinks like ice down my back. Dad. He's downstairs. He's hardly ever here, his visit's unexpected, but that doesn't mean it's safe. A black car pulls out of a side street. It's got tinted windows. There's no number plate.

I stop breathing. It may already be too late. There's another car and I bolt from my room.

'Gil, run! Now!' I yell down the stairs. 'They're coming.'

The longest second of silence. Then the back door bursts open and he's off. They crash through the front door, the wood splintering; the lock's a joke. There's a charge of bodies below, and my mother's screaming. I race back to my room and crawl under the bed. I've practised this but never thought I'd do it for real. Clawing at the floorboards, I raise them enough to see the cavity beneath.

Gunshot. The sound explodes through the house – once, twice. Then silence. I cannot hear my mother, her voice has gone. Shaking, I crawl into the cavity and rearrange the floorboards above me. I'm crying out inside. *They've killed her. I'll kill them. Gil, run.*

More shots. A volley of bullets. I close my eyes and will my father to have made it to the end of the garden, to have vaulted the fence, to be weaving his way down side streets, elusive, defiant, alive.

A triumphant voice. 'He's down. He's down, stand back.'

A sob escapes my lips, but I swallow it. I can't do that, can't be heard.

Feet clump up the stairs. I lie still like I'm dead and they enter my room. They'll see the computer on, the textbooks open, and maybe smell my fear.

'Benjamin.' A male voice, officious. 'Benjamin Turner, we know you're here. Come out with your hands raised.'

Dust tickles my nose. The wires from the lights of the room below press into my back. It's hard to breathe.

'We're not going to hurt you.' Another voice, female. 'But we do need to speak to you.'

Somebody crosses the room. The wardrobe doors creak, then they pull out the drawers of my bedside table. The old chest is kicked. Each step they take, the floorboards shift.

I will not let you kill me. I will not let you do what you want.

Somebody else comes into the room. 'The bathroom window's open.'

'He can't have got away.'

'It's unlikely, but … possible.'

They're silent. I sense them contemplating the worst: I've already gone. My eyes smart with tears. The bathroom window's open, which means Dad took a shit and wanted to clear the air. It drives Mum mad if he doesn't – some hang-up she's had for years. The irony of it almost chokes me. When Dad's here we keep all the windows shut, can't risk anyone hearing or knowing anything, but this one time … the bathroom window …

'Search the place,' the first man orders. 'Take it apart. And bag everything – every phone, computer, tablet. Any photo, ID or document. I want it all.'

I'm cramped and uncomfortable and the space is airless, but I'll be here for hours. I don't know what it is to be brave, but I've got to manage it now. Gil taught me how to control fear and pain. Focus, he said. Focus on an image and don't let your mind wander from it. Let it calm you and keep your breathing even. I grasp at the memory.

Four years ago, I was fourteen. My shoulder was dislocated; I'd been crying and then shock set in.

'I can't stop shivering,' I told him.

'Yeah, it's your body reacting. We'll get you home soon and then Gemma will take you to hospital.'

He'd thrown me too hard when I wasn't experienced enough in martial arts. He'd been proving to everyone I wasn't getting preferential treatment for being his son, but he'd gone too far. I should have hated him. I half did, except that he was upset too.

'I'm cold,' I said, all snot and misery.

'Hey, can somebody get us a blanket?'

Somebody did, but I needed him to make me feel better. That was when he told me to focus. To take deep slow breaths.

'I can't think what to focus on.' My body was rattling. 'I'm cold.'

'Then imagine …' he said, 'imagine you have wings of fire keeping you warm.'

And I saw them, quite clearly, wings of fire. Rising around me, enveloping me, keeping me warm. I grew calmer. He stroked the side of my face, his fingers gentle; he'd not done that since I was a child.

'You see,' he whispered. 'You can do it.'

Focus. They've killed my mother, they've killed my father but they can't get me. The darkness is unbearable, the hole claustrophobic, but I must survive. I will not betray myself: no tears, gasp, or sob.

The floorboards creak. It sounds like there are still two of them in the room. They're taking their time, not trashing anything yet.

'Got the kid's ID card here.'

'I thought he was a student.'

'Yeah. Imperial College. Apparently good at science, worked hard.'

'Poor fucking sod. He might be innocent.'

'And we might come from Mars.'

I'm sweating. My mouth's dry. If they find me will they take me in, interrogate me and torture me? Or will I just be shot? One of the guys is huffing and puffing – I guess they're not finding what they want. The plug on my computer is wrenched from the socket, books are thrown off the shelf, and the bed pushed aside. It scrapes across the floorboards and I freeze. Can't even let my chest rise and fall. Then the mattress is overturned. I try to gauge where exactly they are; the bed's legs might be directly above me. That means they've fixed the floorboards in place – they can't find me with the bed on top. Shit, I might not be able to get out. I could suffocate in here. The bed's legs scratch across the floor again. It must be back where it was.

Hours pass. My body is stiff and sore. Every sound I hear I try to work out where they are in the house, what they're saying, what they've found. I know all they'll get on me: a stack of university assignments; emails and texts; banal social media posts. All it will prove is how ordinary my friends are, and the only family shots will be of me with Mum. Is it possible I'm safe? In a court of law there won't be evidence to convict me. But what do they care about courts of law? They've just shot my father: summary justice. And Gemma … what did she do wrong?

Noise outside. A helicopter above, and soon the press below. I visualise the police cordon, the click of cameras, and guess tomorrow's front pages. A government triumph: 'Gil Zimmerman, leader of the Disciples, is dead. The eco-terrorist mastermind has finally been neutralised. Britain is a safer place.'

And suddenly I feel so tired, exhausted. Make it go away. My body is floating …

I wake with a jolt. Panic. I'm in darkness, entombed. Then I remember. How could I have fallen asleep? The house is quiet now. It's possible they've gone, but it will only be for the night. Some police officer, wishing for a different shift, will be on guard outside. I've got to get out but they mustn't hear me. I slowly push back the floorboards. The dust that hits me makes me sneeze. Shit. I freeze and wait to see if there's any sound from outside, then emerge slowly into the room. I dig around the cavity for the leather pouch that's hidden there – it's got everything I need: cash, notebook, revolver and memory stick. The bag is heavier than I remember because the revolver is loaded with its six bullets. But if I have to use it, it'll mean I'm cornered and everything is already too late. And if I'm picked up, it'll be evidence against me. My hand shakes slightly as I take the gun out of the bag and gently place it back in the cavity; with the floorboards over it, it'll never be found.

Gil's voice echoes in my memory: 'If I die, and it's not during an active operation, then take it I've been betrayed.'

What do I do? I retrieve the gun and return it to the bag. My clothes are scattered across the floor, thrown from every drawer, but my old backpack is still at the bottom of the wardrobe. I withdraw it carefully then, without taking more than a step or two, I stretch over to pick up a few items: another pair of jeans, underwear, some T-shirts, and although it's summer I pull on a hoodie. I put the leather pouch in the front pocket then tiptoe out of the bedroom.

A gust of fresh air. The bathroom window's still open, but

the drop down is too big; can't risk twisting my ankle or worse. Instead, I creep down the stairs, heading for the back door. Every step feels perilous. The wood creaks. If the guard outside is paying attention they'll hear. From the hallway I make for the kitchen. Blood. I'm stepping through blood. My legs weaken and I might faint; it's my mother's blood. I focus ahead and think of the door beyond. Focus, breathe, control. She'd want me to live. I have to survive.

The back door's gone. There's just police tape, and I ease my way round it. The garden is long and the grass needs cutting. I gasp. Near the back fence is a mound. Gil. They haven't removed his body. Oh, Jesus, no. But the mound rises and stretches. It's the dark shadow of a fox. It scampers over the fence, its claws scratching at the wood.

Footsteps behind me. I've made too much noise. Seeing the outline of the police officer, I race down the garden and vault the low fence. He calls after me. A shot is fired, but I'm out of range. *Run.* A police siren wails in a street nearby. I can't afford a chase; even though I'm fit, they'll outrun me. I need somewhere to hide.

Olivia Hamilton – her place is half a mile away. Posh girl, rich parents, she liked to hang out with me to wind her father up. She said she loved me; I didn't love her. Still, I remember the summerhouse at the back of their garden. I couldn't believe anyone would have a fridge and a cooker in a summerhouse. I don't remember it being alarmed, and I should be able to pick the lock.

I find her place before the police find me, but the wall around the garden is high. Metal spikes are placed at regular intervals across the top. No wonder the summerhouse wasn't alarmed; I forgot about this wall. I stand back then take a running leap and throw the backpack. One of its straps loops over a spike and I haul myself up. But straddling the wall is the most awkward thing, and I need to release the backpack; I can't leave it behind. Then I'm hurtling down on the other side – and the pain in my left arm is excruciating. There are long nails sticking out of the bricks – I couldn't see them in the dark. They rip my flesh, tearing back the skin, and my mind fills with white light; it takes everything not to scream. I crawl to the summerhouse, winded. My fingers fumble picking the lock but I get inside. There's a long futon sofa and I collapse onto it. I can only rest for the shortest time.

CHAPTER 2

Benjamin

A light goes on in the Hamiltons' house. A door opens and someone comes into the garden. They're a silhouette in the dark. I'm not ready to run, and I don't want to use the gun, but I might have to do both. They draw closer, using their phone as a torch. It's Olivia. She stands outside the summerhouse looking in. I'm not sure if she can see me in the dark, but then she opens the door and we stare at each other.

'I thought I heard something,' she says quietly.

I can't answer, my voice is trapped in my throat.

'I saw the news before I went to bed and …' She exhales; I think she's afraid. 'Benjamin *Zimmerman*.' She stresses the surname.

There's no point trying to tell her I've never been called that because I know what she's saying.

'Your picture's on TV, I … couldn't believe it.'

'Have you called the police?' I ask, almost inaudible.

She shakes her head.

'Are you going to?'

'Not unless you try to shoot me.' Her face is serious but then she says, almost teasing, 'Are you going to try and shoot me?'

'Of course not,' I say gently.

'Then what are you doing here?'

'I needed to rest a while. It's the only place I could think of.'

She glances briefly behind. 'How did you get in? The door's undamaged.'

'I picked the lock.'

'So you're a criminal like your father.'

'No. I can just pick a lock.'

'You're such a liar,' she says, but not aggressively.

'I think I've hurt my arm,' I say because I don't want to talk about the rest.

She comes closer and sits beside me. The sleeve on my hoodie is ripped. There's a deep gash on my upper arm. The blood is beginning to congeal but both of us can see it won't take much for it to get going again.

'That needs stitching,' she says matter-of-factly. 'You need to go to hospital.'

I shrug, that's not an option.

'Is it sore?'

'Everything's sore right now,' I say, and to my horror my eyes fill with tears.

Silence spreads between us. Then she whispers, 'I should hate you, Benjamin. We were getting close and then you dumped me like a shit.'

'I'm sorry. It wasn't personal.'

She laughs. 'You know, Benjamin, for a while I thought you were something special. The smartest kid in school, way ahead of everyone else, except of course for Mo. I was stupid enough not to realise you're just a geeky nerd. Except you don't look like one with all that hair and your big dark eyes ...' She pauses. Her gaze feels hot on my skin. 'I never made the connection with Gil, but then who would, although I can see it now. He was handsome, your father, which is kind of sick. A major threat to national security and I'd look at his picture and think, hmm, he's kind of cool.'

I swallow but can't speak.

After a while she asks, 'Are you a Disciple too?'

'No.'

'Then why are they after you?'

'Because they're fucking MI5, agents of the State with nobody to stop them.'

She watches me closely. 'You are political, aren't you? I never realised that before.'

'They've killed both my parents.'

Her expression alters, shocked.

'I thought you'd seen the news.'

She looks down, flicks across her phone then tries to show me something. 'They don't say anything about your mother.'

'No, well …' I try to hold my voice steady. 'Why would they? It's murder.'

'Gemma's dead?' she asks, like I haven't already told her.

All I can do is breathe and hope that she stops.

'I liked your mother,' she says, as though that could possibly have anything to do with it.

'So maybe now you can start to understand,' I say through gritted teeth.

'Shit, Ben. But she … why?' She shakes her head. 'I still remember her chilli, she made a great veggie chilli …'

My throat is so tight, like I'm being strangled. We're silent for a while.

'What are you going to do now?' she asks quietly.

'I'd like to rest a little, and then …' I shrug. I know the notebook in my backpack contains a list of names. People to potentially contact. People Gil trusted. 'I'll figure something out,' I say softly.

'Is there anything I can do to help?'

I'd never thought of Olivia as kind, but maybe she is. 'Don't think so.'

'Let me at least get something to clean that wound. I'll go

in, get you some paracetamol and something else to wear – that hoodie's wrecked.'

'No. Don't wake your family, the risk's too great.'

'My folks are away and Freddie sleeps through anything.'

I think of her brother in bed, oblivious.

'Okay. Thanks.'

Olivia walks back to the house. I rest my head on the futon; my arm aches, and I feel so sick. She isn't away long and returns with a small stash.

She sits beside me. 'I'm going to use this neat.' She moistens some cotton wool with antiseptic. 'It'll probably sting but it'll be more potent than diluting it.'

It hurts but I look away and manage to hold my arm steady.

'It really needs stitching,' she says, examining it, 'and when did you last have a tetanus jab?'

I shake my head. She gives me a pack of paracetamol and takes a can from the fridge. I swallow a couple of tablets.

'Keep the rest,' she says.

She passes me a hoodie and an old denim jacket. 'Good job Freddie's a similar height.'

'What are you going to say when he notices they're missing?'

'I'm going to pretend he gave them to the charity shop but just can't remember.'

Somehow, that's almost funny; I'm not sure why. We're both quiet.

Eventually, I say, 'I won't stay long, I promise. When you get up in the morning, I'll be gone.'

She waits a while before responding. 'You know what will save you, Benjamin, don't you? Your big puppy-dog eyes. 'Cause right now …' She wavers, her lower lip trembling. 'You look so fucking sad and beautiful, all I want to do is hug you and …' She stops.

I take a deep breath. 'I'm sorry I hurt you before.'

'Well, at least you won't forget me now.'

'No. I won't.'

She leans over and kisses me gently on the cheek, then stands to go. 'Don't let them get you. Please, I couldn't bear to read it.'

'I won't, and thanks, Livie.'

She half smiles and leaves. After a while I turn to the backpack, unzip the front pocket and remove the leather pouch. I flick through the notebook. There are code words, contact addresses, names. But my heart slowly sinks. I know each person mentioned, and they've all been, or are currently, Disciples. It's possible my father was betrayed, and I've no idea to what extent the Disciples have been infiltrated. I can't go to any of them; my life may be over. There is no help. What if I go to Livie and ask her to call the police? She can let them know I'm here. I don't think they'd shoot me in front of her, and I'd be handing myself in. Perhaps, then, I'd survive. I go through the notebook again starting from the back. There's one name and address on the final page. I missed it before but my father's writing is clear: Adam Faber and then, in brackets, Adam McKenzie, followed by an address in Scotland. I've never heard of him and I've no idea how I'll get there, but he's the answer. A warm trickle of blood trails down my fingers and wets the page.

CHAPTER 3

Jess

The sound of my alarm clock is piercing my brain and I pull my pillow over my ears, but that doesn't make it go away. Of course not. It's six thirty. The start of another day in the McKenzie household.

I get up, dress quickly and run some toothpaste across my teeth. Downstairs, I go into our large kitchen where every morning during the summer, my grandad and I make breakfast. We're catering for the guests in the B&B part of our home. We're at full capacity right now: three couples and a six-year-old child. It's a clear, bright day – our guests will be happy. They love the views and scenery. 'You're so lucky to have grown up here,' I've been told more than once. I just smile back.

Greg's voice greets me. 'Good morning, Jess.'

His head's in the fridge as he retrieves the sausages and bacon and he motions to the loaves that need slicing.

'And the rolls in that plastic bag are for Mrs Connick. Guaranteed gluten free, no cross-contamination.'

I cut the bread into thick slices and pile them up by the industrial-sized toaster. The newspapers are in a stash at the side. Mum gets up particularly early to get them. 'It's always good to give our guests that little extra.'

All the papers are leading with the same story. Gil

Zimmerman – the Disciples' leader – is dead. Shot last night on a residential road. No one else hurt. A cold sensation forms at the back of my head then creeps down my spine.

'Have you seen this, Greg?'

'What's that?' he asks, counting out eggs.

'The news.'

He pauses, looks over and eventually nods.

'Is … is Dad alright?'

Greg doesn't answer immediately. 'Put it like this, your mum went out without him.'

Dad's not alright. This is meant to be a normal day. I was hoping to focus on writing a song, or at least preparing for Thursday's audition. I don't want to be thinking about the Disciples.

Last year, I read a big piece about how the eco-terrorists were a spent force. No major attacks for ages – not after their attempts to disrupt the country's digital infrastructure. I'd been relieved; my father's past seemed increasingly irrelevant, but now … it never goes away.

I get through breakfast, ensuring our guests get what they want and chatting a bit about this and that. But I'm thinking about Dad. I finish clearing up and go to find him. The door to my parents' bedroom is ajar. The light's off and the curtains are closed, but I can see his silhouette on the bed. I knock gently. He doesn't respond so I open it carefully.

'Dad, are you okay?'

He's lying on his front, his face hidden in the pillow.

'Dad?'

'Migraine,' he mumbles. He sounds terrible.

'Have you been sick?' When he's really stressed he'll vomit.

He doesn't reply but I think he nods.

'Is there something I can get you? Have you taken any tablets?'

'No point, I'll only bring them up.'

I move closer hoping in some way I can comfort him. 'I'm sorry,' I say, although I'm not sure why.

He's still. I should go and leave him to recover. Yet there's something about his intense sadness – I see it like an aura around him. I stand by the bed and gently place my hand on his back. 'I'm sorry, Dom,' I whisper, then fear I've crossed a line.

I never call him Dom, although sometimes my mother does when they're talking softly and in private. Dad was born Dominic Minster, and he lived with that name for eighteen years. But all the years of my life he's been Adam, Adam Faber, and then when my folks got married he became Adam McKenzie. He took Mum's surname because he loved her. Adam is my father, but Dominic knew Gil Zimmerman.

He turns to me. His eyes are puffy and it's an effort for him to speak. 'Dominic Minster's dead.'

I might cry. I leave him to sleep and rush to the attic; it's my private room, separate to my bedroom. I close the door and sit at my desk. Okay, this is just an upset. Something that's happened today but Dad will feel better. I gaze out the window, down the length of our garden and into the hills beyond. I know we're safe. The attic is always safe. There's a bed for friends when they stay over, and most important is my desk. It's scattered with my songs and improvisations. My guitars are at the side.

Above my desk, I've pinned up cool shots of my favourite singers, and family photos. Pictures of me with my cousins and Aunt Emma and Uncle Theo. My aunt has the same colour hair as Dad, and blue eyes. Sometimes I can really see how they're twins. Yet they look so different now to the photos that were published when they were sixteen. When Dad was Dominic and Emma, Charley. The authorities were after them. They were younger than me then; I can never get my head around that. Uncle Theo's not changed much from those days (when he was called Flint) except he's heavier. His soft afro hair is short and his dark skin contrasts with Emma's.

I smile at the pictures of my cousins Xavier and Tommy. They both take after Flint, although Xav's more handsome. I love them with all my heart. Xav is nearly the same age as me (Tommy's eight years younger), yet we've only spoken about our family's past once.

We were at their home in France, and I was staying in Xav's room. 'Don't you sometimes wish they'd just talk about it,' I whispered, 'and tell us everything that happened?'

'Sometimes Dad talks about things,' he said, 'like when he first met Mum, but all the stuff that happened with the Disciples, I think they want to forget it. It wasn't like it was their choice. I mean even their names. The Disciples just gave them new IDs and documents. They didn't ask what they wanted – Dad hated Theo at first.'

'I like the name Theo.'

'Yeah, me too, obviously, but that's just because we've only known our folks by those names. And they *never* want to talk about what happened with your dad. It feels like … I don't know, they're trying to protect him or something.'

'Protect him?'

'Yeah, 'cause when Grandad Minster died it affected your dad most. Look at that declaration he made, that video the Disciples put out after everyone thought he was dead, and it's pretty obvious how much it affected him.'

'But don't you find – when you think about what happened – that it's all like some crazy dream or film? It doesn't seem real *because* they never talk about it.'

Xav shrugged. It didn't seem to bother him as much.

I dropped my voice even lower. 'Our parents played a key part in exposing LifeStar Corporation and their involvement in trying to develop a weapon of mass destruction. That was a huge, major event. That whole branch of the company got closed down. And they weren't a lot older than us. I can barely think about that stuff, let alone imagine being caught up in it.'

'Me neither.' Xav sighed. 'I guess part of their silence is because of the Disciples. Dad said when you're dealing with a bunch of terrorists, it's best to keep your mouth shut. It's the safest thing.'

Now, what Xav and I know has never felt more inadequate. I open the drawer at the top of my desk. There are pens and highlighters, my Falcon Taylor concert programme, and my private notebook. I pull back the elasticated tie and at the back is an A4 printout from the internet – a black and white image. I rarely look at it because I find it so compelling. It's not the greatest photo because it was taken from a police helicopter and it was raining.

There are two figures on a motorbike. They've stopped near a cliff edge, the sea beyond. It's the end of a chase; they look exhausted. The person sitting at the back is Dad – he was eighteen. My father always seems old to me with his well-trimmed beard and moustache, but he was young and clean-shaven then. He's looking at the camera and his eyes are full of difficult emotions. He's holding on to the man in front who's older and clearly in charge. His long dark hair and dark eyes have never changed – Gil Zimmerman. His left hand is raised in the victory sign.

I know from what I've seen and read that, after that picture was taken, a shot was fired and Gil lost his hand. Then he drove the bike over the cliff edge and they plunged into the sea. Nobody, in theory, can survive that. The world believed Dominic Minster was dead. My father has never told me how he survived, and I don't expect to ever hear the truth.

Gil Zimmerman. It's hard to believe he's gone. He was accused at the time of ruthlessly manipulating my father, a naïve young man. Yet Dad survived, and it's Gil now who's dead. I stare at Gil Zimmerman, a whirlwind of wild, dangerous energy.

CHAPTER 4

Jess

The glare of the light makes the garage feel hostile. Everything's up close and too personal. There's a whiff of petrol and a large freezer in the corner, but it's obvious they like to rehearse here; the drum kit looks ensconced. Logan, Seth and Kamal watch me. I'm auditioning for their band Talisman and complete my song by strumming three chords. I've done the best I can but I wish Kamal didn't look so distracted. I should have sung better at the beginning.

'So, Jess,' Seth says, 'thanks for coming over. 'pretiate it. We're seeing a few people, so we'll let you know soon.'

If they liked me surely they'd sound more enthusiastic? I need to say something. 'Just so you know, I'm available to sing whenever you need me.'

'Yeah. Thanks, Jess.'

I pack up quickly, putting my guitar in its gig bag. Logan nods at me on the way out. I know him from school, not that he goes there anymore. He's always been good looking, and is definitely a popular guy. If they pick me … has he got a girlfriend?

I head home on my bike, through the housing estate, and then there are fields on either side. It's past ten but the setting sun provides enough light. I pedal faster. The guys probably won't pick me. I've got a sinking feeling in my belly.

When I get in, Dad's playing the piano in his study. During term time he gives music lessons in the evening, but now he's just playing for himself. He wanted to be a musician once, and helped me get my grades.

I give him a big hug from behind.

'Hey, what's that for?' He stops mid-bar.

'I don't know.' I release him.

'How was the audition?'

'I got too nervous at the beginning but then I was okay.' I shrug. 'They'll let me know.'

The doorbell rings. Nobody rings this time of night. The guests have their own keys and entrance. We wait a few moments. Mum's deaf so won't hear it but Greg should. It rings again.

Dad sighs and gets up. 'One of the guests must have forgotten their key.'

'I'll go.'

I open the front door. There's a man standing there I've never seen before. The porch light illumines his face. There are dark circles around his eyes, his cheeks look gaunt, and his hood is up covering his hair. What does he want? I shiver but he doesn't move. His jeans are dirty and his denim jacket is the wrong size, and although it's not that cold, he's wearing a hoodie beneath it. Has he got mental health problems? He looks like he's been sleeping rough.

'Does Adam Faber live here?' he asks softly. He's got an English accent.

I swallow hard. Nobody calls Dad by that name. Not for years.

'I'd like to speak to Adam Faber,' he says a little louder.

I have to call Dad. He needs to deal with this but the words won't come.

'Adam McKenzie?' He steps back.

'Dad,' I call, but he's already behind me and takes over.

The sunken eyes stare at him. 'My father gave me your name,' the man says slowly. 'You … knew my father.'

Dad doesn't appear to know what's going on either.

'You knew my father,' the guy repeats, and there's something desperate about his voice. 'He's dead now. Please …' His lower lip trembles. Maybe he's not much older than me.

'Oh, Jesus,' Dad says. 'Benjamin?'

A sob leaves his lips. He says, almost inaudible, 'Gil said you could help.'

Oh, God, no. Now I understand. Something of the past is hurtling into the present. Dad leans forward and grabs him, dragging him inside. I step back quickly but still I catch his smell. The rank stench of sweat, a slight whiff of piss, and there's a grubby backpack over his shoulder.

We don't have a hallway, just a front room so I can stand at a distance. But he is clearly, undeniably, in our home.

He looks around and then his eyes roll back in his head. 'I'm sorry …'

His legs buckle and he's falling forward. My father goes to catch him but struggles under his weight.

'Jess, get Greg. And some cushions, a blanket.'

I can't move. Dad tries to lay him down but it's awkward. He looks at me for help but I'm frozen to the spot. 'Greg!'

My grandad comes quickly; it's clear that something's wrong.

'Jess, cushions and a blanket,' he repeats. Then to Greg, 'He's fainted, help me get him out of this stuff – he needs air.'

They take his denim jacket off and slide back the hood. That's when I see his thick, dark curls. That's when I realise. He's not Gil Zimmerman, that man is dead, but this one looks more like him than I could have imagined. What did Dad call him? What did I read? I feel sick. I'm staring at Benjamin Turner. The Disciples' leader's son. The one person the authorities want to interview; his picture was on the news. How has this happened?

I charge out to find Mum. She's reading in the living room oblivious to what's going on. She turns to me. Still, I can't speak. Normally, we communicate by her reading my lips, but now I just sign, 'Trouble.' I don't know a lot of sign language but I know that word because she's used it on me. But whatever trouble I've caused it's nothing compared to this.

She follows me back to the front room. There's a cushion under his head now, and a blanket at his side.

My mother's quiet, taking it all in, then she says, 'Call the police.'

My father stops and looks across at her. 'What?'

'Adam, please. Not this. Call the police.'

My grandfather grows still. He doesn't look at either of them. It's like I'm watching a film, the scene before me unfolding like fiction; it's not part of my life.

My father says slowly, 'If I call the police they'll want to know why he's here. And once they start asking that …' He shakes his head.

'Why is he here?' My mother's voice is sharp.

'Christ knows, Mary. Gil must have given him my name.'

'Even after death he finds you.'

I need to speak too. 'Dad, please, get him out of here.' Maybe I sound cruel, the man's flat out on our floor, but that's what needs to happen.

A weak voice interrupts. 'I'm sorry.' He's conscious again. 'I think I'm going to be …' He turns to the side and vomits; Greg just gets out of the way in time. He doesn't vomit much, maybe he's not eaten for a while, but still, sick is sick. I hate the smell of it. I turn and run to my bedroom. I shut the door hard and then realise I'm shaking.

I sit there feeling terrible. I might throw up myself. Downstairs, my parents' voices are rising. They don't fight much but they're fighting now. I cover my ears, but then Greg's voice intervenes. Everything hushes and there are only murmurs. I wait a while wondering what they'll do. I wait for what feels like forever until there are footsteps on the stairs. Greg is huffing and puffing.

My father says, 'Shit, I wish this staircase was wider.'

I realise with horror what's happening. They're taking that man up to the attic.

'Jess,' my father calls out, 'can you come up here and take your things down.'

I rush from my room, furious and afraid, charge up the stairs and glare at them. He's laid out on the bed. He's not under the covers yet, my father and Greg are in the process of helping him out of his clothes, but it's clear where he's spending the night. I grab my other guitar and charge back down, put it in my room then go up again. I gather together my music and pick up my laptop. I don't look at them but hear the guy murmuring, and then he cries out. I turn and see his left arm; my father's just released it from his hoodie. It's a mess of torn flesh and congealed blood and yellow bits of pus.

'That needs a doctor's attention,' Greg says firmly.

He and Dad look at each other and their mood alters.

'I'm sorry,' my father says softly, turning to the terrorist's son. 'We can't do this. You need to go to hospital.'

'They'll kill me,' he says starkly.

'No. You're not well. We can't look after you here, your arm needs proper medical attention. I'm not going to stand by and watch you potentially—'

'I'd rather die here than let them kill me.'

'They're not going to kill you,' Greg says.

But the man keeps his eyes on my father. 'You don't believe that, do you? I told you, they killed my mother. Two bullets in the hallway. In her own home.'

All the time I'm standing there it's like I don't exist. Then his eyes focus on me. They're dark and defiant but I can see he's also afraid. I turn and leave the attic.

CHAPTER 5

Jess

It's very late when my father comes to my room. They've settled the intruder for the night. I helped a bit, getting disinfectant for his arm, but mostly I watched from the doorway. His clothes were dirty and smelly so Dad insisted I get a pair of his pyjamas. I brought them up just as they were sliding off his jeans. The movement pulled at his boxer shorts and I briefly saw his groin – a thick mass of dark hair and half of what I'd no right to see. I was shocked but couldn't look away. Dad took the pyjamas and I went back to my room.

The bed shifts as Dad sits beside me.

'I don't know what we're going to do, Jess. Okay? We'll talk about it in the morning. I'm trying to think it through.'

'We should hand him in, Dad. The police want to interview him.'

'It's not that simple. He's here, which means … it's just not that simple.'

'Dad, he's dangerous.'

'No, he's in more danger than he's actually dangerous to us.'

'The authorities are looking for him. We have to hand him in. Surely there isn't anything to discuss?'

'Jess, you have no idea,' he says gently. 'Not about the police or MI5. If we hand him in they'll also start asking questions

23

about us. *That* would be dangerous. If they ever found out who I was, I … it can't happen.'

'Because you were once a wanted man. A Disciple.' The words taste like grit. It doesn't feel right to even say them.

He doesn't reply but nods. 'Tomorrow, we'll talk. All of us as a family, and then with him. We'll decide what to do.' He glances at my clock. It's two thirty in the morning. 'You should get some sleep now.'

'What are you going to do?' He doesn't look ready to sleep.

'I'm going to check him out, read what I can online.' He gets up to go.

'Dad,' I say, urgent, 'why did he come here?'

He's still. 'I found a notebook in his backpack, full of names and addresses. Gil's writing. My name was the last one in it. I don't know why Benjamin didn't contact any of the others, and it's obvious he doesn't really know who I am, so … I can only think Gil believed I would give him shelter if nobody else could. He knew that was a possibility.'

'Why would he know that? You haven't had contact with him, have you?'

'No, of course not. But Gil knew me. I mean *really* knew me.'

I don't like that answer. I think of them on that motorbike. The grainy image of Dad holding Gil. I love my father, and have always been close to him, but right now it's like I don't know him.

'I'm scared,' I whisper.

'Me too.' He half smiles and goes.

I lie back and try to sleep, tossing and turning and watching the minutes tick by on my bedside clock. The attic room is immediately above mine but I hear nothing from it. Mum and Dad's room is down the other end of the house. I rarely hear anything from them and I can't hear anything now. I wonder if Greg, whose room is on the ground floor, is still awake too.

I get up and go down to Dad's study. He doesn't seem surprised to see me.

'What have you found?' I ask, standing behind him and looking at the computer screen on his desk.

'There's not a lot to find. Just that he's a student who's studying biomedical engineering, and he's only eighteen.' Dad glances at me. 'Not much older than you.'

I stare at the photo on the screen. Two schoolboys in uniform smiling at the camera. 'What's that?'

My father reads the caption. 'Benjamin Turner and Muhammad Qureshi. Bishop Down's Academy. Apparently, they put the school at the top of the league table. Both of them got their A levels early and went straight to university. This picture's from the local paper. They're a state school triumph.'

'He must be clever.'

'Yeah. They're both at Imperial College now. The Qureshi boy's put out some kind of appeal.' Dad clicks on the clip.

It's hard to watch. Muhammad Qureshi looks like a distraught schoolkid.

'Benjamin, please come back. Everyone's missing you. The police just want to talk. They know you're good. Everyone here knows you're a good guy. They don't want you caught up in this stuff. Just give me a call, please. You know I'm here for you.'

Dad says, 'Some professor from his college has put out a similar appeal.'

'Can't he just go back then?' Surely this is good. 'The police just want to question him. They know he's done nothing wrong.'

'He may not even have seen this. It's not like he's got a phone on him.'

'Tomorrow,' I say, 'when we speak to him, I think we should get him to go back.'

Dad doesn't answer but I'm relieved. It's obvious now that he can go back. He'll sleep here tonight, and then we'll put him on a train to London. I turn to leave.

'What's that?' I ask, spying a leather pouch on the floor. It looks like it belongs to another age – something a highwayman might use to hold gold coins.

'I found it in his rucksack.'

I'm shocked. My father's been through his things. I didn't think he'd do that. 'Aren't you going to put it back?'

'Not immediately.'

I watch him, again feeling that I don't know him like I thought I did. 'Have you looked inside?'

He nods. 'There's a notebook. Some cash. A memory stick.'

'So it's proof he's a student. That's good.'

'And,' Dad says slowly, 'a revolver.'

I'm light-headed. Nothing is making sense anymore. I leave the room. I just want to sleep and make it all go away.

CHAPTER 6

Benjamin

I wake in an unfamiliar room. Flowers on the curtains, a glass of water on the desk, my clothes folded on a chair. Am I dreaming? The smell is real. Clean sheets and something else I can't describe, except that it's feminine. There was the girl last night, gathering up her things. Maybe it's her scent?

A throbbing pain. My arm hurts too much for it to be a dream, and my stomach feels hollow. I vomited on their carpet – I can't do that again. The room spins as I sit up; it takes a while to stop.

'You're safe,' he said. Adam. I've no idea if that's true.

The door is slightly ajar. The room is small with a sloping roof, and I open the curtains a fraction. There are hills beyond. No other houses and not a person in sight. I really am in the middle of nowhere. What a relief: no CCTV cameras, no surveillance. The photos pinned above the desk are mostly of the girl with what looks like family, two boys in particular. Glancing at the door, I listen. No one's on the stairs and I open the drawer of the desk. I need to find something that shows me who these people are. There are brightly coloured pens, and a Falcon Taylor programme. Why do girls like him so much? I pick up a notebook and at the back of it … a sheet of paper. A grainy image, one I can never forget. My father and Dominic

Minster. They look young, cold and tired. It was taken seconds before my father lost his hand. I wasn't even a year old then, yet I almost lost him. I watched the footage online – Gil's hand being blown off and then the motorbike plunging into the sea. I couldn't watch it again.

'Did it hurt?' I asked him. It was the maddest question, but I couldn't understand why he didn't scream, or how he ever survived. But he wouldn't answer my questions.

'Benjamin,' he said softly, 'it's better you don't know.'

'I'll never be as brave as you,' I said, anguished.

He shrugged. 'You don't have to be.'

I put the picture back, close the notebook and then the drawer. I don't understand. Dominic Minster died. His body was never found but the remains of his clothing were. The Disciples put out a video after his death: his final testament. Yet now … I look at the girl's photos. Wasn't there a sister and a cousin involved too? Are they the older man and woman in the pictures? I take a few sips of water and lie back again, exhausted.

Later, when I wake, Adam comes into the room. Is it possible that, behind that beard and moustache, he's Dominic? How well my father and the Disciples hid that truth. But of course they would.

'How you feeling?' He looks at me, concerned. 'You may have a fever.'

My mouth is dry. 'I just need a shower.'

His manner is gentle. He gives me a towel and shows me the bathroom.

'Can we put your clothes through the wash?'

'Yes, thanks. But I need my backpack.'

When I get out of the shower there's a clean pair of jeans, underwear and a top on the bed. Why didn't he bring up all my stuff? I understand. He's gone through it and found the pouch. So Adam was a Disciple; no one else would go through my private things like that. Yet my father wanted me to believe

Dominic was dead, and if I hadn't found that photo … I can't say anything.

I dress slowly. My arm looks bad; it's swelling around the makeshift bandage and now that's wet too. I go downstairs as Adam instructed and find the old man in the kitchen.

'Can I get you something to eat, Benjamin?' he says gruffly. 'You can call me Greg.'

I smell bacon and sausage; it must have been cooked earlier. My stomach turns.

'I'm not sure I can eat,' I say. 'I haven't for days.'

'What about a boiled egg then? Something light.'

'I don't know. Mostly, I'm vegan.'

'Avocado?'

I nod. He slices up some vegetables, stones the avocado, and finds a carton of hummus. I sit at the table and he puts the plate in front of me; it's like I'm a small kid. I burst into tears. Shit, what am I doing? I cover my face with my hands. The shame of crying feels terrible.

'Poor lad. You've really been screwed over, haven't you?'

That only makes me cry more. When I'm a little calmer, I ask, 'Did you know my father?'

He takes his time responding. 'Not personally.'

I wonder how much I can ask.

'We'll talk about these things later,' he says, and motions to my plate.

I slowly pick up the fork and try to eat – I know I've got to keep food down. As I finish the others come into the kitchen.

Adam introduces his wife. 'Mary's deaf so when you speak to her make sure you're facing her so she can read your lips.'

She's got dark hair and dark eyes but something about her gaze unnerves me. She says nothing.

'I'm Jess.' His daughter looks a younger version of Mary except for her blue eyes. 'It's my room you're sleeping in. And as we're sharing a bathroom, I'd be grateful if you could put the toilet seat down when you're finished.'

They all sit.

'We need to discuss what happens next,' Adam says. 'An open, honest discussion.'

Their eyes fix on me. My mouth feels dry again. 'Okay.'

'When did you join the Disciples?' The question drops lightly from his lips but his face couldn't be more serious.

'I'm not a member of the Disciples,' I say slowly. Then after a pause, 'Were you?'

'No,' he says firmly.

So, we're both going to lie. 'But you knew my father?'

He nods. 'I'm an old family friend.'

I glance across at Greg. He's watching me.

I turn back to Adam. 'They never spoke of you. Not Gemma or Gil.'

'Obviously not,' he says carefully. 'Yet your father sent you here because he thought you would be safe. And in order to keep you safe I need to know the truth. What information or links you have.'

'I'm not a member of the Disciples,' I repeat.

'Then why do you have a gun in your bag?' he asks softly.

I try to keep my voice even. 'My father always knew that something might happen to him, and he gave it to me in case it did.'

'Do you know how to use it?'

'He showed me how to fire it. But I've never used one. Not on anyone.'

'And the notebook? He gave you that too, in case something happened?'

I nod.

'And the memory stick?'

'I've no idea what that's about.'

'Benjamin, do you really expect me to believe that?'

Shit. I'm trying to judge what's going on but I'm struggling. 'I don't know what you will or won't believe,' I say slowly. 'All

I can do is tell you the truth. The first time I saw that memory stick was when I retrieved the pouch. We kept it under the floorboards in my bedroom. I knew the gun was in it, and the notebook, but the memory stick …' I shake my head.

A brief period of silence.

'Benjamin,' Adam says, 'I've been looking at your profile online. You're obviously very clever, a student at Imperial College, and there's a friend of yours and a professor both appealing for you to come forward. If that's all you are, then perhaps you should hand yourself in.'

My breath quickens. 'No. I told you, they'll kill me.'

'Why?' Mary says. Her voice is distinct, you might know she was deaf. 'The police just want to speak to you. They're not calling you a terrorist or a Disciple. Surely you could contact Professor Atholl? Speak to him and get him to help you hand yourself in.'

'Professor Atholl?' I say, shocked.

'He's the one who made the appeal.'

'And your friend Muhammad Qureshi,' Jess says. She puts her phone in front of me and presses play.

I hear Mo's voice and see the way he gestures. It's so familiar and the pain of seeing him pierces me like a knife. They've got him. Fucking MI5 have got him. And probably Atholl too. I close my eyes; I hate what's happened. He's my best friend, Mo.

When I open them again, Jess is watching me intently, yet it's Mary who speaks.

'You're very upset,' she says softly, 'and you're also a liar. What I can't figure out is what is upset and what's a lie. Possibly all of it is both.'

She's a witch. A real-life witch who can slice right through a man and see inside him. I don't answer because I can't. A tense silence follows.

'Why would anyone want to kill you?' Jess asks. 'You're not your father. You're not a Disciple. I don't get it.'

'Because they won't believe that,' I say. 'Even your father's having trouble believing it.'

'The secret service doesn't just shoot people,' she says.

I wince. She's naïve and stupid. Even that picture in her desk is a sign of how much she doesn't understand – she should never have printed it off. I say slowly, 'If they don't shoot me, they'll certainly hurt me. They've wanted my father for a long time and it suits them to have me an enemy. They shot my mother. They found that very easy to do.'

She keeps looking at me. 'Did you love your father?'

Of all the questions. I don't think I can answer but they're waiting. 'He wasn't around much,' I say, almost inaudible. 'It wasn't like he was a regular father, but yes, I loved him.'

Adam watches me. 'If you didn't see him often how come he was in your home that night?'

I'm tired. Adam isn't going to let anything go. 'Because he'd just turn up sometimes.'

'Was your mother … was Gemma still an *active* member?' he asks.

How much does he know? I shake my head.

He raises his eyebrows, sceptical.

I feel a wave of nausea. 'She's not been active for years,' I say. 'She's been building up her own business – recycled and vegan leather products, the pouch bag, that sort of thing. She sells them at markets and music festivals. She …' I'm shaking. I'm talking about her in the present tense.

Adam says softly. 'Benjamin, I'm sorry for your loss, but please, I need to know the truth. Tell me why your father was at your home that night.'

'Because I'm his son, and he still loved Gemma. We had a meal together, and then … the usual pattern would be he'd stay a while, but he'd be gone by the morning.'

'Are you really telling me that they didn't discuss anything about the Disciples?'

'I never heard them discuss the Disciples. He came because he loved us.'

Adam doesn't take his eyes off me. 'When did you last see Gil before that?'

Should I be answering any of this? I don't know. Right now, I really don't know but I've nowhere else to go. 'It was about three, four months ago.'

'In your home?'

'No. We met outside. We went for a bike ride in the country. Just the two of us.'

'Yet that night, MI5 knew he was in your home?'

I want this to end. 'Yes.'

Our eyes meet. Does he realise my father was probably betrayed?

'Somehow, MI5 knew,' I say, stronger. 'And they shot Gil, and they shot my mother. No questions. No interrogation. No attempt even to capture him. And if they'd found me, I truly believe they'd have shot me too.'

There's nothing else I can say to defend myself. I'm exhausted.

'We need to make a decision,' Greg says slowly. 'Please go back upstairs while we talk.'

CHAPTER 7

Jess

Benjamin has gone back up to the attic. I've no idea what happens now.

'What do you think?' Dad asks.

'He can't stay here,' Mum says. 'He's a liability whether he's innocent or not. And if he doesn't want to go back that's his choice, but we've got to get him out of here.'

'I agree with Mum,' I say quickly.

'He's not innocent,' Greg says. 'Some of what he said is probably true. I doubt he's shot anyone or blown anything up – the Disciples haven't done much of that for a while – but he's a clever kid. Gil Zimmerman would never let that pass him by.'

'No, I don't think so either,' Dad agrees.

'He's not our responsibility,' Mum says. 'Gil's dead. You don't owe him anything now, Adam, and you don't owe his son anything either. I'm sorry he's in trouble, and he's suffered a loss, but that doesn't make him our responsibility. You've had nothing to do with the Disciples for ages. They're not relevant now.'

'I'm not sure that's the point,' Dad says. 'My concern is what happens if they get hold of him. They'll question him, and they'll want to know exactly where he's been, and that will lead them here.'

'Dominic's been dead for years,' Mum says calmly. 'Benjamin doesn't even know who you were. Adam McKenzie's just an old friend of his mother's, somebody he turned to in extremis. Beyond that, we don't figure.'

'Mary, we can't know that. And MI5 are not going to buy some "friend of the family" story. They almost destroyed my father. If they get hold of him, he'll tell them everything. He won't be able to hold out.'

'Adam's right,' Greg says. 'We can't risk MI5 coming anywhere near us. That would be the most dangerous thing.'

'What are you suggesting then?' Mum asks, her voice tight. 'That we should let him stay here?'

Greg shrugs. 'It's a possibility. He'd be safe.'

'No,' I say. 'No!' They're making me afraid.

Greg turns to me. 'Jess, MI5 were once after Dominic Minster. I may have been naïve and foolish to shelter him – I certainly had moments when I thought so – but I've never regretted it. It was the best thing I ever did.'

'Don't talk soft, Dad,' Mum says aggressively. 'Keep to the facts. I loved Dom and we hated LifeStar Corporation, that's why you sheltered him. We take risks for love. I'd do anything for Jess – we all would. But we don't owe this young man anything, and all that was a lifetime ago.'

Dad says softly, 'I loved Gil.' The words hang in the air. 'He saved my life. And I know if our daughter were ever in trouble and had needed his help, he'd have given it to her. No question about it. So his son's come to me, and I want to help him.'

We're all quiet. Dad's made up his mind and I feel sick.

'Adam,' Mum says, 'there must be other people he can call on. Let us help him find them.'

'Yes, Dad, please. Don't let him stay. I won't feel safe with him around.'

'I hear you both, but I don't think there's anywhere else he can go, because if there was he'd be there now.'

How can this be happening? We don't need to do this.

'I have a suggestion,' Greg says. 'We let him stay here, but on our terms, and not for long. The news is already changing. There will be a moment when he can go, when he can reinvent himself, go abroad, whatever. It's what Dominic did, after all. Until then, while he's here we keep him occupied. There's always plenty to do around the property. He's got to pay in some way for staying here. And we keep his things locked up: the revolver, notebook and memory stick. Maybe we even destroy them.'

Silence.

'That could work,' Dad says. 'It keeps us safe, and it keeps him alive.'

Mum's eyes flit between the two of them. She's not happy. 'I don't know if it keeps us safe, although I concede it's one way forward. But he can't stay here. That's not fair on Jess. We put him in the cottage. It's been on the market with Culvers for months and we've had all of two viewings. I say we take it off and put him there.'

Finally, someone's thinking about me. My family have a small old cottage some miles from here. Grandad used to rent it out to holidaymakers, and Mum and Dad lived in it when I was a baby. But it needs a complete renovation now so they've been trying to sell it rather than do the work.

Greg nods. 'I'm happy with that.'

'So am I,' I say. 'It's not exactly comfortable. Nobody would want to stay in it for long.'

Dad's quiet, but then he says, 'Good, we're agreed.'

Greg and I have driven to the cottage to check it over. I shiver as we step inside. Although it's summer, the place is freezing. It feels miserable. Nobody's lived in it properly for years; I wouldn't want to live in it now. The electricity is still connected and we plug in the fridge, but the gas cooker's stopped working.

We make up the bed in the larger of the two small bedrooms, but it feels damp. Water comes out of the shower, but it's not hot.

When we get back, Dad's spoken to Benjamin. 'He thanks us and hopes he can repay us in some way. He knows we're taking a risk.'

'Aye,' says Greg, 'and he understands our rules?'

'Yes. He doesn't leave the property or switch on any lights. I told him it gets dark late so he shouldn't need to. I also stressed that everyone round here knows the property's uninhabited – he can't risk drawing any attention to it.'

'Where's Mum?' I wonder what part she'll play in all of this.

'She's upstairs looking at his arm. That's my biggest worry – that we'll have to take him to the doctor or even hospital.'

I watch Mum quietly from the attic doorway. She doesn't like him so I'm surprised at how caring she is. She's bathed his wound in disinfectant and Benjamin is silent as she dries it. Picking up a jar of honey, she carefully scoops some out and spreads it across the wound.

'Honey?' he says. 'I don't understand.'

'It's wonderful for healing wounds and it reduces infection.'

'I'd no idea.'

'No. Most people don't realise how useful honey is. And this is manuka honey, which produces the best results. We need that to heal.'

She gently covers the wound with gauze. 'We'll need to check on it.' She gets up to go but his eyes don't move from her.

'Hey,' I say, aware he's not noticed me. 'Dad and Greg are getting some food together and then we'll go.'

I'll get my room back. He's been in it one night, and that's already too long.

CHAPTER 8

Benjamin

Their car drives off. The cottage is cold and quiet, except for the low hum of the fridge. They've left me food – some meals they prepared so I don't need to cook. Looking around, it's not as bad as they said. There's an old, tired sofa, and the bed when I lie on it is half comfortable. But it's desolate. Did somebody die here? I didn't ask that question, but I think they did.

I'm completely alone. No connection to the outside world. My phone and computer will be sitting in some MI5 office being trawled through by an agent. Will it ever be safe to contact my friends again? Mo. Shit, what will they have done to him? I spent hours in his home. There were meals with his family; they accepted me. I can't imagine what they're thinking now.

'We'll find something for you to do,' Adam said. 'In the meantime …' He pointed to the small bookshelf. 'We're trying to sell the place and we left them. It makes the room look less empty.'

No, I think, *it's empty.* There isn't a book on that shelf I'd want to read, but then there's nothing I want to read but the news. How much damage has been done? Have any Disciples' cells been infiltrated? Who else has been betrayed?

Out the back, the garden is overgrown, and beyond that there's empty landscape. I'm not to turn on the lights, but who in the world would see them if I did? It's possible I really am safe. I should feel relief, but I don't. I lie down upstairs and hope for sleep. Instead, I remember.

'Guess who's here?' My mother's voice, just as it was.

She woke me with a kiss, her breath tickling my cheek.

I was three years old. It's my earliest memory. I followed her to her bedroom and found Gil there, asleep, his dark curls on the pillow. Because this was how it happened: he'd suddenly be there. Gasping with excitement I bounded onto the bed.

'Gilly!' I shouted, waking him. He tickled me with his right hand while I squealed and wriggled like an octopus; we all laughed. Later, I sat quietly on his lap and touched the stump of his left arm. He didn't have a hand but I didn't understand why. He hugged me and kissed my head. Sometimes he hugged me so tight I could barely breathe.

I was five years old when for an entire week they both belonged to me. We were a family, day after glorious day. Mum rented a cottage in the country and we went to the beach when nobody else was around. The wind howled and the water was freezing, but that didn't stop us running into the sea. Gil splashed water at Gemma and she just laughed. I loved my mother so much, and her laughter made me feel special. She was happy, he was happy, I didn't want it to end.

When the week was over and we were driving home, I slept in the back of the car. His voice roused me. 'I'll come in with you.'

'No,' Gemma said, 'it's better you don't. You'll only wake him.'

But he got out and unstrapped me. I was wearing pyjamas; they must have got me ready for bed before the journey. His arms were strong as he lifted me, and then I was lying against his chest, my head on his shoulder. He held me, standing in the hallway.

'He's exhausted,' she said, 'he needs to go to bed.'

'Yeah.' Gil's breath was on my cheek. 'But I won't be here in the morning.'

I kept my eyes open for as long as I could, for as long as he held me and stroked my hair.

I was six when Gil turned up again. We were living in the flat then. The living room was small but we all squeezed onto the sofa. We were watching a film and sharing a big bowl of crisps, and I had a packet of chewy sweets; that was the best. Mum got up and I heard her in the kitchen then Gil went too. Suddenly I was alone. Where were they? I went to look for them. They weren't in the kitchen but the door to Mum's room was closed. I stood outside it, silent. They were in there but they weren't talking. Instead, a laugh and a sound like moaning. I stood back quickly. I didn't know what they were doing but I did know I had to keep away; it was the strangest sensation.

I wasn't going to watch the film alone. Gil's jacket was hanging near the door. I went and put my hands in its pockets, pushing them in deep, my right hand searching for whatever he kept there. Something hard and metallic. I withdrew it slowly – a gun. But it wasn't like those I'd played with; this one was heavy. Would it make a loud sound if I pulled the trigger? I pointed it at the front door then glanced at the bedroom behind. I could pull it, and that would get their attention.

But something stopped me – some fear that it wasn't really a game. Back in the living room, I hid under the sofa. They could look for me now. I fell asleep.

'Benjamin, come out of there.'

I opened my eyes and my father was gazing at me. He was kneeling on the floor.

'No,' I said, 'what were you and Mum doing?'

'Benjamin, just come out.' His hand closed around my arm and he dragged me towards him. 'Fuck,' he said, seeing the gun. 'Jesus fucking Christ.' He took it off me quickly and I laughed because he'd used that word.

'Fuck,' I said back.

'Benjamin, don't ever take anything like that from me again.' His expression was frightening.

'Why do you have a gun, Gil?'

He answered slowly. 'Because there are bad people out there who'd like to hurt me. And if I have this, I can defend myself.'

'Why would they want to hurt you?'

'There are some things I'll explain when you're older.'

I wanted to kick him.

'Benjamin,' Mum said gently. 'It's part of the rules. Okay?'

Gil put the gun back in his jacket. We sat down and tried to watch another film, but I couldn't enjoy it. I knew he wasn't happy; he was angry with me.

After that, he went away for a long time. I didn't know if I'd see him again, he was that angry with me.

When I wake, I'm lying on the bed with all my clothes on. The curtains are open, the sun is setting. My body feels like lead. There's no one to remember those things with me. No one to share details of that holiday cottage, or the film we watched or even how we felt. Gil and Gemma are gone. Did any of it even happen?

I remember the rules. Even at six they were ingrained, swearing me to silence. I had to call him Gil but not Dad. I was never to talk about him outside home or with anyone but Mum.

'He's our secret,' she said. 'Just your and my secret, and we protect secrets by keeping silent.'

So I told people I didn't have a dad. Mum concocted a story: she broke up with my father before I was born, and she'd not seen him since. Nobody questioned the lie, but sometimes I'd feel it burning the back of my throat. Now, both of them are gone, and they were my only witnesses.

I try to remember details, proof that it was real. Houses and flats Mum and I lived in. They were part of our history. But the details blur. Old musty sofas, once a new bed, and cheap flat-pack furniture. Mum tried to keep me in one school, but we moved too many times, until she got that inheritance. Then she bought the house they murdered her in. I'd been happy there, but never again. It's empty and growing colder. The wooden floors are stained with blood. The solid door smashed. None of us will return.

'Try to think of something good,' I whisper in the darkening room. There were the summers Mum and I spent together, going from festival to festival, setting up her stall and selling her bags. We took the turquoise camper van. Yeah, I loved that van. It was cool.

It was the weekend Storm Ann was due to hit south-west England. Normally, we slept in the tent and kept our stuff in the camper, but it was too wet for that. We were both in the van. I laid out my sleeping bag on the makeshift bed. She pushed back the passenger seat but it didn't look comfortable.

'Mum, don't sleep like that.'

I squeezed over on the bed and motioned for her to join me.

'You're too old now for me to get on there.' She smiled.

'I'm scared of the lightning,' I lied, wanting her to come.

She walked over and leaned down. Her hair fell around my face; it smelt sweet, like vanilla. She whispered in my ear, 'No you're not. You're not scared of anything, Benjamin Zimmerman.'

She never called me that, but it had slipped from her lips, and I felt how much she still loved him, even though he'd not been around. I didn't say anything back.

During the festivals I'd wander off for hours, finding and losing friends. I always kept the rules. 'I don't have a father. He died before I was born.' I loved that embellishment. People treated me like a stray dog, a kid who needed looking after. They'd buy me food and treats along with those for their own children. I got to have burgers and ice cream although I never told Mum. She just wanted to eat veggie so when she bought me chips, I never confessed to eating fish elsewhere. She'd have freaked if she knew.

Sometimes, grungy blokes joined us. I didn't like them. I hated the way they let their hands fall on Mum's thigh, or their fingers slipped through hers and they kissed.

'Do you love Angus?' I asked her, trying to sound cool and like I didn't care.

'No,' she said easily.

'Then why are you hanging out with him?'

'Because I like hanging out with him, but that doesn't mean I love him.'

I lowered my voice. 'So, what, you only love Dad?'

She didn't answer that.

''Cause don't you think he'd mind?'

She threw back her head and laughed. She almost cried laughing. 'Oh, sweetheart.' She motioned for me to come for a hug. 'I can assure you,' she whispered, 'your father isn't sitting around thinking of me. He's not alone, and I don't need to be either.'

'That doesn't mean you've got to be with Angus.'

'We're just enjoying some time together, Benjamin. It's no more than that. And … don't I let you go where you want? You're enjoying yourself, aren't you?'

There was only one guy I liked, but he was already close to

Gil. Tom. The Disciples' second in command. He stayed over sometimes. When I was very young he let me sit on his lap and joined me painting. There was lots of water and colour on the kitchen table, but Mum didn't mind. He ruffled my hair. 'Hey, kid.'

Then, when I was older, we'd play frisbee. I felt his affection.

'One day, Tom,' Mum said, 'you need to have your own kids. You're a natural.'

'I don't know.' He shrugged. 'It's enough to borrow yours.'

I sit up quickly, gasping. Tom. Shit. Have they got him too? I need Tom to be safe. Someone must've survived. Then we can retaliate for what's been done. We can hit them hard, but I don't know if he's safe. He might be lying in a pool of blood and I'll never read about it. He'll just be gone. All the witnesses to my life are gone. I look out the window and the sun has set. There is only darkness.

CHAPTER 9

The cottage is freezing. I can't stop shivering, and get under the covers. I don't bother taking off my clothes. The curtains are still open; the moon's my only company. Sadness sits in my chest and it's lodged in my throat. I wrap the blankets around my head, and feel the silver chain and pendant on my neck. It's still there. A gift from my mother and the only thing I have left of her. She gave me it when she was afraid of what Gil might do to me – and she was right.

I'll never forget it. I was thirteen years old and nearing the end of Year 8 at secondary school. Without warning, Gil was back in our lives. At school I worked hard, but outside of it I'd picked up some bad habits: got good at shoplifting and smashed a car window. Still, it was nothing compared to him. I knew what he was now. Leader of the Disciples. A terrorist. Recently, his picture had been linked to an explosion near a nuclear power station. It wasn't to take out the plant – that would've been too dangerous – but to draw attention to just how vulnerable and risky its existence was.

I was nothing compared to him, but the police picked me up and cautioned me. Mum freaked out. If I pushed it too far, I could end up endangering him. At last, I'd got his attention. It was the first time I'd seen him in nine months.

We stood in the living room and he told me off, his voice tight and angry. He didn't even say he was glad to see me, I just got a mouthful from him.

'Fuck you!' I shouted back. 'You can't tell me what to do, you're never fucking here. You're not my father.' Our eyes locked. I was getting to him. 'You're nothing but a terrorist,' I hissed. 'I could destroy you. I could betray you to the police.'

He slapped my face so hard my brain rattled. I stood there stunned; he'd never hit me before. He struck me again, quick and brutal. I was too winded to speak. Even his gaze felt punishing.

'There are some lines you never cross,' he said quietly.

Something about the softness of his voice, compared to how much he'd hurt me, was terrifying. He was a very dangerous man, a powerful force.

I burst into tears, all bravado gone. I was just a child.

'I'd never betray you,' I sobbed, shivering. 'I promise, Gil, I'd never betray you.'

There was a moment's pause, then the tension in his face lessened. He took me in his arms and held me, but I couldn't stop crying.

'What am I going to do with you?' he said, hushed. 'Hey, Benjamin?'

I didn't want him to let me go, I wanted my father. Slowly, he released his embrace.

'Dad,' I said, wiping the tears on my cheeks. 'Let me join the Disciples.'

Mum gave me the necklace the first weekend I went to him, my first time with the Disciples. I opened the gift box and there it was – one of Mick Munro's creations. He'd run a stall opposite Mum's. I loved his stuff with its medieval and mythic motifs, but it was expensive.

'A phoenix.' The silver was cool and smooth. I touched its long wings and eagle body, all feathers of fire. The chain felt solid too.

'It's a great image.' She smiled.

'Yeah. Fantastic.' I couldn't believe she'd bought it for me. Some of Mick's clients were rock stars. He loved boasting about that.

'Mum, I … thanks.' I undid the chain to put it on. I might never take it off.

'It'll probably get physical this weekend,' she said. 'Best to leave it here until you get back. You don't want it to break.'

I couldn't see it breaking but something in Mum's voice told me she needed me to leave it. I put the box in my room, then gave her a big hug. 'It's the best present you've ever given me.'

'Yes, I think it is.' She squeezed me.

'And, Mum, I'll be fine.'

Two days later, we were sitting in A&E because he'd dislocated my shoulder. She was furious, her anger bristling on her skin. We got back home and I crashed out on my bed, gutted. I'd been a shit Disciple and she was seething. I'd failed and nothing could make that better.

Then Gil turned up. I didn't think he'd do that. I held my breath listening to them in the kitchen.

'We agreed,' she growled, 'you promised, you'd never hurt my son!'

There was the sound of a plate smashing.

'Gemma, stop. Stop!'

Shit, were they physically fighting? They'd never done that before – and it was all because of me.

'My son, *your* son,' she said, crying.

'Gemma, shush. Please,' he said, almost tender. 'I'm sorry.'

Her voice grew muffled and I sensed they were hugging.

'I'm sorry,' he said. 'Okay, but we both know, sometimes … to protect them.'

After that, there was mumbling then silence. They'd made up, but that didn't help me.

It was very late when he came to my room – the man who'd dislocated my shoulder. He'd caused me extreme pain. I'd cried and the shame of it stuck in my throat, yet he was only coming to my room now. He stood in the doorway and I hoped my gaze pierced his skin.

'I don't think it's going to work out,' he said softly.

'No. I hate you.'

He paused then said carefully, 'I did warn you.'

'Some people have a father.' My voice cracked; I didn't want to cry. 'I don't. I tell people you died before I was born. A great lie except it feels like the truth. But anyway, it doesn't matter because I hate you. I hate the Disciples. You can all fuck off.' I lay back on the pillow and stared at the ceiling.

He came over and sat on the edge of my bed. He whispered, 'I'd like us to find a way, Benjamin, of having a relationship that doesn't feel so … difficult.'

I wasn't used to him being close to me. That weekend, being near Gil, I'd felt a new kind of anguish. 'Then you should show up more.'

He was quiet for a while. 'You've not had a fair deal from me, have you?' His dark eyes held mine. 'But you're still my son. I don't want to see you mess up your life. Not for me. Not for your own future. You don't need to be involved with the Disciples, and certainly not now.'

'You hurt me. You made me cry in front of everyone.'

'There's no shame in crying. It's just a human response.' Then, a little quieter, 'Everyone else has forgotten it. You and I are talking, but they're getting on with the rest of their day.'

I grew calmer. He was paying me attention. 'Mum said you were proud of my school report.'

He nodded. 'Very.'

'I think I'm better at maths and physics than being a Disciple.'

He almost smiled. 'Let's agree, shall we, you're going to forget about the Disciples for now. Okay? There are more important things for you to focus on.'

'Okay.' I breathed. 'But then, will you come round and see me more?'

'I'll try and do that.'

I think we both believed what we were saying.

'Benjamin.' Someone's calling my name. 'Benjamin!' The voice is louder, female.

I try to sit up. Somehow, I'm on the sofa but I don't remember coming downstairs.

'How you feeling?' It's Mary. She walks towards me.

I shrug.

'You don't look great.'

I shiver. 'Cold. I just feel cold.'

She sits beside me and puts her hand to my forehead. 'You're very hot.' She looks at my left arm. 'Is it throbbing?'

'A bit.'

'You've hardly eaten anything,' Jess says. I hadn't realised she was here too. 'If you don't eat this food it will just go off.' She's standing in the kitchen with the fridge door open.

'I've not been hungry.'

Mary checks my arm. 'This is not good.' She walks back into the kitchen, takes a glass bottle out of a bag and places it on the table. 'I've prepared a herbal brew. I meant to give it to you earlier but … anyway, it might help.' But she doesn't sound hopeful. She turns to Jess and signs something. I wonder if they often communicate like that. Then she goes to the door. 'I'm just popping outside.'

Jess slowly draws closer. She hovers near the arm of the sofa. 'You need to eat,' she says more softly. 'If not you won't get better, and you've got to take Mum's potion with food. Believe me, I've had them. They taste horrible.'

'Maybe I don't want to get better,' I say, although I'm not sure why.

'Then what are you doing here?'

Our eyes meet. A part of me is aware that, in other circumstances, I might care that she dislikes me so much. I might also see that she's pretty, but none of that matters now.

'So what is it you study?' she asks.

'Study?'

'Yes, you know, at uni.'

I sense she's making an effort. Perhaps she's been instructed to talk to me.

'I'm doing a master's in biomedical engineering.'

'Which is what?'

'Well, it's a variety of things.'

She raises her eyebrows. 'Like what?'

I sit straighter and try to think. It's alright to talk about this. 'An example of what I'm working on, of what I hope to make my main project, is an artificial eyeball.'

'An eyeball?' she says, incredulous.

'Yes. There are some bionic eyeballs out there, but with this one the aim is to restore as much vision as normal sight. Maybe one day it could even take vision beyond human capabilities. There are animals out there that have much better sight than us.'

She watches me, her expression curious. 'Are you saying you've enabled a person who's lost their sight to see again?'

'No. It's not at that stage yet, and I'm just one person out of many working on the project. The company that funds us deals with the patients. They manage the therapeutic side.'

'It's sound like it's important – what you're doing.'

'Hopefully. If we pull it off.'

'So you really *are* smart.'

I shrug.

''Cause we read that you went to uni early.'

'I found school easy.'

She shakes her head. 'Lucky you. I don't like school. I'll go to uni, but I don't like all that academic stuff. I'm not clever like that.'

I feel a wave of nausea. 'Anyway, I'll probably never finish that project now.'

Mary comes back into the cottage. She's brought a first-aid kit and changes the dressing. She doesn't speak. I don't think she likes me either. Jess hangs back, ready to go.

'I've texted Adam,' Mary says, closing the kit. 'You might see him later – you might have to see a doctor.'

I want to tell her no, I can't possibly go to a doctor, but the words won't come.

'Ready, Jess?' She stands up.

'Coming.' Jess walks to the door.

'These are the instructions on how to take the medicine,' Mary says, putting a note on the kitchen table. 'But you've got to eat first.'

I nod because I want them to go, and it's the quickest way to make that happen. The door closes behind them and I am alone again.

CHAPTER 10

Jess

I get the email Sunday evening.

Hi Jess,

Loved your singing but the decision wasn't mine alone. Sorry we've not picked you. Hope you don't feel too cut up. See you. Logan.

A pit opens in my stomach. I won't admit how gutted I am but who did they pick? And I don't get him. Why bother telling me he loved my singing? This feels like it did when Ellie started going out with Fraser; I'd fancied him too. Why does nobody want me? I stare at the screen. Okay, it doesn't matter. I don't need to play in a band. I'll be a star one day in my own right.

Outside, the sun is setting. The sky's a beautiful rose pink, but that doesn't change anything. Things feel like shit. Logan's email is just part of it. Benjamin is another part. He won't go away. Mum insisted I went with her to see him today.

'Speak to him,' she said.

'Why, because you don't want to?'

Now Dad's involved again. He went to check on him after us.

'I'll phone Dr Lee,' he said when he got back. 'He'll have to take a look. We can't let his arm get any worse.'

'What will you tell him?' Mum asked.

'I'll say he's a relative up from London. He had an accident in the garden, we hoped it would heal but it hasn't. I'll offer to pay, of course.'

Although Dr Lee's helped with guests in the past, this is different. 'Dad, Dr Lee reads the news.'

'He also knows us, Jess. We're part of this community and we're people to trust. He won't make any connection with what he's seen on the news. I promise you, it won't cross his mind.'

Dad drove off hours ago. It's been the longest day, but I won't go to bed until he's home safe. I hear his key in the front door and rush downstairs.

'You took so long I was getting worried.'

'Well, I did text your mother to let her know,' he says, like I should have checked with her.

'How did it go?'

Dad looks tired but calm. 'With Dr Lee? It was fine. There was a brief moment when he asked Benjamin for his name and I realised we hadn't planned for that, but he just said Josh. Quick thinking. Then Lee cleaned up the wound and stitched it. It looked pretty unpleasant, but Benjamin was a good patient. I'm just glad they do minor surgery there – if not we'd have had to go to hospital and that *would* have been tricky.'

'So he's back in the cottage now?'

'Yes, with ten stitches, a course of antibiotics, painkillers, and a couple of sleeping tabs to help his disturbed sleep.' He yawns.

'Well, it took enough time.'

'I had to pull off the road for a while, coming back. I think the reality of his situation is hitting home.'

I watch my father. 'You mean he got upset?'

Dad nods.

'Like crying?'

He nods again. How bad must you feel to cry in front of strangers? I go upstairs, lie on my bed and glare at the ceiling. I hate that man – Benjamin. He just turned up in our lives. My dad's pulling over because he's crying; he gets that much of my father's attention. Am I supposed to feel sorry for him? Because he had ten stitches and it probably hurt? I turn on my side and try to sleep. Who did Talisman pick instead of me? Logan loved my singing.

The following week, I've plenty to focus on. Ellie's party's coming up and our exam results. If I get the right grades, I've got a place at Glasgow to study music. I'll finally get away from home. But I can't escape the current situation. On Thursday, Dad wants me to go to the cottage with him.

'I'm kind of busy,' I lie.

'Come. I want your opinion.'

As soon as we pull up in the car, I have a bad feeling about it. The cottage looks more neglected than it did five days ago. Is it changing with its occupant? Going inside, we're not sure where Benjamin is. Perhaps he's had enough and gone; that would be good. Dad calls out but there's no reply; he's not lying on the sofa this time. I follow Dad upstairs and Benjamin's lying on the bed, his clothes on and his face in the pillow. He's so still I shiver.

'Benjamin,' Dad says softly.

He slowly turns his head to us. His eyes look swollen and bloodshot, and his face is gaunt; he's lost weight.

'I think this place is haunted,' he says.

'No,' Dad says calmly. 'It's not. I lived here for years and it's not haunted.'

'I'm seeing things. I think they're ghosts.'

Dad is very still.

'I know about eyes and I'm definitely seeing things.'

I stand motionless behind Dad. I really don't want to be here.

Dad changes the subject. 'Have you eaten? If you're hungry it's not going to help.'

'I'm not hungry.'

'Benjamin, you need to eat. We're trying to help you here.'

He raises himself a little but doesn't reply. Something about his misery is defiant.

'I'm going to go downstairs,' Dad says slowly, 'and check something, and then I'll be back up.' He motions to me and we both go down.

'What do you think?' he whispers when we're in the kitchen.

'What do I think? I don't want to go near him. He's not alright.'

'No,' Dad agrees. 'I don't think we can leave him here alone.'

A sick feeling turns in my stomach.

'He's not eating and he's too upset to be left alone.'

'Dad, he's not our problem.'

He gives a sad half smile. 'We need to take him back with us.'

The sick feeling in my stomach gets a whole lot worse. 'That is not a good idea. No way.'

'We can't leave him here alone.'

'I think we have to,' I say. 'We've got guests in the B&B, there's nowhere for him to stay.'

'There's the attic room.'

I don't understand how this has happened, why my father would even say that when he loves me. 'I really don't want him in my room. And if he's not alright, if he's losing it, that's even more reason not to bring him back.'

'Then what do we do?'

I suddenly see how all the times I've insisted my parents treat me like an adult has led to a question like this. But I don't feel like an adult right now, just very upset.

'Mum will freak it,' I say, trying to build a wall between me and what I know is going to happen.

'I've already discussed it with her,' he says. 'She thinks that now he's a greater risk here than with us.'

None of this is fair. I've no choice. 'If you've already made up your mind,' I say, my voice rising, 'why are you asking me?'

'Because I'd like to give you the opportunity to agree too.'

'I don't agree,' I say aggressively, but I know I've already lost.

'I wish it wasn't like this either.'

I leave the cottage and get back into the car. When they come down, I won't look at Benjamin. I hate him. It's a horrible feeling; I don't want to be like this.

Back home, I clear the attic of my personal stuff. I don't wait for him to come up or listen to what my parents are saying to him. Instead, I find Greg at the bottom of the garden. He's checking on the vegetables we're growing.

'I suppose you approve of it too?' I half shout. 'Benjamin in my room? I don't have a say in this family. But I live and work here too. It's not fair.'

'It's not fair at all, Jess,' Greg says. 'But at this precise moment it's necessary.' He stands up straighter. 'But we're going to keep him busy. There's no way he's staying here and not putting some effort into these here vegetables, or fixing the fence or painting that outhouse.' He indicates the wooden stable behind us. We've kept delaying working on it, but with the right attention it could be something. 'Who knows, Jess, we could turn it into a practice room for you. How about that?'

My rage lessens. What if we fixed it up with recording equipment? But there seems a catch in what he's saying. 'How are you going to get him to do that without someone realising who he is?'

'A jacket and a baseball cap will prove an adequate disguise. Nobody's going near him.'

I almost laugh.

'A bit of hard labour never hurt anyone,' Greg says with a smile.

I lie in bed and listen. Benjamin's in the room above. I think he's crying, and that's the second time in six days. Six long days and then this at night. My parents think he's improving because he eats with us each evening. I barely look at him; that would be accepting the situation and I'm not ready to accept it yet. Still, I sense how being in a kitchen with other people has enabled him to eat. He doesn't talk much, but I heard some mumbled conversation with Dad about ordering some other clothes online. He's stopped talking about seeing things, and I reckon he made that up; he just didn't want to stay in the cottage. At least Greg's not letting him off the hook. He's given him an earful on the dos and don'ts of weeding and vegetable cultivation. He's hoping to get him chopping wood, although only when he's sure he can handle an axe. I wouldn't trust him with an axe. And this is what I have to put up with: crying at night. It's just not right. I'm going to speak to him.

I walk up the stairs, letting the floorboards creak so he'll know I'm coming. I'm allowed to go in there, it's my room. I stop outside and listen. He's quiet now. I open the door slowly and it brushes over the carpet.

The room is not as dark as I expected. The curtains are open and it's almost a full moon. Benjamin is still and silent, but he must know I'm there. The smell gets me. It's different now. A male scent, that's the only way I can describe it. A boy's smell: sweat, deodorant, and maybe his hot tears too. I tiptoe to his bed. He doesn't turn or speak but lies there motionless. I'm silent too. His eyes are closed but his eyelashes are glossed with tears. One streaks his cheek. And then I remember the deer we found wounded at the side of the road, and how it had the longest eyelashes too. I cried over it. My anger shrinks.

The moon outside is large and bright. It's bigger than either of us; it doesn't care about my petty emotions. It shines on his pale skin.

'Please don't cry,' I whisper. 'You don't need to cry.'

He doesn't stir or give any sign that he's even aware of my presence. But the tension in his face lessens and then his eyelids flicker. He's fallen asleep, and I didn't notice before what he really looks like. His dark curls, his face smooth and unblemished. None of that I noticed. Only now, standing in the light of the moon, I realise that he's beautiful.

CHAPTER 11

Benjamin

Jess has gone now. Or was I dreaming? Opening my eyes, something has changed. I feel different. Outside, the moon is wearing a crown of fire. I had no idea there was an eclipse tonight. I stand by the window; I've never seen anything like it.

'Amazing, isn't it?' A soft, familiar voice. I turn. It's Gil. There's no blood on his clothing or bullet wounds in his chest. There is nothing to tell me he's dead. Yet, I know he must be.

'Don't worry,' he says, 'you're not as mad as you think.'

'Then what are you doing here?'

He doesn't answer immediately. 'Dry your eyes, Benjamin,' he says gently. 'You need to focus. I was betrayed.'

I'm silent.

'They killed Gemma, and they wanted to destroy you. *We* were betrayed.'

I swallow, but still can't speak.

'You did well, Benjamin. You hid as planned. You survived. But now, you need to plot your revenge.'

His eyes glisten like pools of dark water. I didn't think a ghost could be so lifelike.

'Phoenix,' he whispers.

No. This isn't the conversation I want to be having.

'Phoenix,' he repeats.

It takes me a while before I can speak, my voice low. 'Forget it. Adam's got the memory stick. They're controlling everything I do. I can't even look at the news online – they won't let me near a computer.'

'You can't get it now, but you will.'

'Gil. He's a good man. That's why you sent me to him – I get that. Don't ask me to go against him, to do anything that could hurt them.'

'Benjamin, you're in a place of safety but you can't stay here forever.'

We're standing in the light of the blazing moon. 'The girl likes you,' he says.

I shake my head. 'She doesn't. I promise you. Most of the time, she's as mad as hell with me. I'm invading her life.'

'I've never understood, Benjamin, why you misjudge desire so badly.'

'Maybe that's got to do with you,' I say pointedly.

He shrugs like he doesn't understand. Then he says softly, 'I'm sorry they got Mo, but I always told you they would.'

'Yes. I wish it could have been different. Everyone I love gets hurt.'

'Ah, Benjamin.' He sighs.

Hot tears are on my cheeks again. 'I've had enough of crying,' I tell him, defiant. 'I miss you, you fucker, you went and got yourself killed.'

'I love you too, Benjamin. I'm sorry you got hurt the most.'

'That doesn't help.'

'Love is a fire that can never be extinguished.' His face is serious.

Our eyes meet. 'I don't feel that.'

I turn from him and keep my eyes on the moon. I don't get any of it. How can I see and hear my father? But then he's gone, I cannot feel his presence anymore. I go back to bed and I'm almost asleep, drifting, but one word won't go: Phoenix.

This is how it started. I was fifteen and Mo and I were doing well at school, preparing to sit our exams early: maths and the sciences. We kept our heads down and worked hard, but we were also increasingly politically aware. Mo was speaking out about Islamophobia and went on some anti-racist demonstrations. While I was itching to join him, and to protest for climate justice too, Mum said no.

'What do you think the police are doing, Benjamin? They've got cameras clocking up the faces of those attending. They've got spies infiltrating those groups, and at the end of the day they don't make any difference anyway. Those with true power, those few people with economic might, they're not going to change anything. Why do you think the Disciples take the action they do?'

I wanted to defy her. I almost did, but I knew the person she was protecting most was Gil.

'You look like your father. People don't see it because they're not looking for it, but if you start going on those protests – you don't know what facial recognition technology might be triggered or what connection might be made.'

'Gemma, if consciousness is raised things can change.'

'Consciousness? If only it were raised. How many lies do you think people are consuming every time they scroll through their phones? What shit people are happy to believe because it feeds their grievances and prejudice?'

I was mad at her for stopping me. I wanted to feel the high my friends got from being a part of something bigger than themselves. So I decided if I couldn't participate because of Gil, it was time for me to be a part of his world. I was older now. I understood that getting close to him wasn't about mastering a martial art or even participating in the direct action he took. I had other talents. But I didn't know where Gil was or how I could even contact him. Everything went through Mum.

'Gemma, I'd like you to get a message to Gil. I want to see him.'

'Honey, not even I know where he is at the moment.'

It was likely she was lying. 'I'm practically an adult. I want to speak to him. Surely I'm entitled to that – he is my father.'

'Benjamin, I told you, I can't contact him now.'

Maybe she was telling the truth but it wasn't good enough. I searched the Disciples online, using any keyword I thought might throw up something. There had to be a way the Disciples communicated with each other through the internet. Two things repeated. A mass of articles on the eco-terrorists, and a whole lot of stuff about Jesus and his Disciples. I couldn't think of two more diametrically opposed things except my father was playing with symbols: 'Disciples' are loyal and want to spread their truth. Intrigued, I flicked through some Christian websites. I knew very little about religion except for what Mo had told me. He cared about his faith. He didn't drink alcohol and he fasted over Ramadan, although he didn't pray five times a day. I accepted those things as part of him, just as he accepted me, although sometimes I envied him; his world was more ordered than mine.

I scrolled through pages of websites hoping one would let me access my father. But all those promoting the Disciples' views came and went within days. There was no email or contact page – of course not. I was about to give up when one site caught my attention: Joy – Sister of Faith and Solitude. Once, I'd asked Gil why he had such a strange name. He told me it was the Hebrew word for joy.

'Joy?' I said. 'But that's usually a girl's name.'

He laughed. 'No, Gila is the girl's name.'

This Joy's website was old and badly designed. She was a middle-aged woman with a big cross round her neck who wanted to bring peace and healing to the world, and offered her prayers in God's first language: Hebrew.

My breath caught in my throat. This was no ordinary website. I searched the meaning of my name. It was Hebrew too. Benjamin: son of my right hand. Shit. Things were getting freaky. My father lost his left hand just months after I was born. I filled in the query form: *Pray for me, Joy. I've been searching for my father. I think I've found him. I am the son of your right hand. P.S. Do you seriously think this website's secure?* I pressed send.

Three hours later, I got an email from joy@faithandsolitude. org.

ילד חכם

I could hardly hold my phone, guessing that it was Hebrew, and searched its meaning. 'Clever boy'. I wrote back: *I want to see you.* But the email failed; the address wasn't recognised. I couldn't find Joy's website again, but for a few moments I'd made contact – then I lost him.

Four months later, Gil turned up. It was after I'd sat my exams. I was chilling out gaming on my computer when I heard him talking downstairs with Gemma. As usual, he'd turned up without warning. I stayed in my room; I wasn't going to give him the attention he probably wanted. After a while he stood in my doorway. I kept my eyes on the screen but I could see him at the corner of my vision.

'Clever boy,' he said softly.

I stopped playing.

'As it happens,' he said, 'that site proved remarkably secure for some time. Often, people don't see things even when they think they're looking for them.'

I turned to him but didn't reply.

'Shall we talk?' He came closer. Something about the way he held himself kept me on guard. It wasn't so much that I was scared just I didn't know what was coming. I couldn't read him.

'I've had a project in mind for some time,' he said slowly,

'and I've not been able to do anything with it, because I haven't found the right person I can trust.'

Our eyes met. His sparked with mischief. 'What do you say?' He smiled.

'I'll do it,' I said quickly.

'Good. We'll work on it. It'll take time, because it's not for now, but the future.'

This was real. I'd get to see him.

'We'll call it Phoenix.'

CHAPTER 12

Jess

Something's changed with Benjamin. Neither of us has mentioned the night I went to his room, but he's definitely getting better and I don't hate him like I used to. He still doesn't say much when we're eating in the kitchen, but I've caught him glancing at me, and then there's all this other weird stuff going on between us.

Example 1: The bathroom. Since he's been here, I always lock the bathroom door and assumed he did too. But the other day, I'm coming up the stairs after working the breakfasts, and he's shaving with the door open. His bath towel's wrapped around his waist, his chest is bare, and he's staring at the mirror which is half steamed up.

For a few long seconds he stops shaving but his gaze doesn't move from the mirror. He's looking at me, looking at him.

'Be careful you don't cut yourself,' I say as casually as I can, but really, I'm thinking about his bath towel. If it slips down, he'll be standing there completely naked. And suddenly I want it to slip, and for him to try and grab it, but he'll be holding the razor and won't be able to stop it in time. Then what will I do? Laugh, walk away or simply smile? What am I thinking?

Next day, I come out of the bathroom and he's sitting on the bottom stair, waiting.

'Need a pee,' he says, rising, and walks past me. 'Nice smell.'

'Oh.' I'm surprised. 'It's rose and vanilla. You can use some if you like.' But what a stupid thing to say – he'd never use my shower gel.

He smiles, friendly, like he understands, and closes the door behind him.

Example 2: Dancing. On Wednesday Mum and Dad go off to CostCut to do a big shop for the B&B. Greg's in the kitchen making a sourdough starter. I've got the living room to myself and put on some music. I turn up the volume and start dancing, getting wilder with the beat. I'm dancing in a haze of sound and song, my arms and legs moving faster, my body surrendering to the rhythm. After twenty minutes the music slows and I stop. I'm breathing quickly, coming back into myself, and turn slowly to the door. Benjamin's standing there.

'How long have you been there?' I say, my cheeks growing even hotter.

He shrugs.

'Do you often spy on people?' I hate that he was watching. Nobody should see me when I dance like that.

'I don't spy on people,' he says softly. 'I like your dancing.'

I think he means it. 'It's not how I dance in public. Just when … I want to let go.'

'Yeah. You looked free.'

We're quiet and still. 'Maybe you should try it?' I say gently.

'I don't dance.'

'Everybody can dance.'

'Not me.'

Then we're standing opposite each other, neither of us speaking, neither of us moving. But he's smiling gently, and so am I.

We're in the kitchen. Greg and Mum are preparing the evening meal. Benjamin's got his head in the local newspaper and I'm half watching the news on the TV. The sound's switched off but the subtitles are on; I like to test how much I can lip-read. Dad comes in. He's been speaking to Emma in his room. Sometimes I join him chatting over the internet, but tonight he wanted to speak to her alone.

'How's everyone?' I ask, glad for the distraction. The news is boring.

'They're good, and looking forward to your visit.'

Every summer I stay a week or two with my family in France. Mum and Dad are too busy with the B&B to come.

'Apparently, Tommy's so excited he's already making a banner to put above the door when you arrive.'

'Ah.' I'm touched. 'And how's Xav?'

'X-a-v,' Dad says, drawing out his name, 'is driving Emma slightly up the wall. He's got himself a girlfriend and seems to find it impossible to focus on anything else.'

I'm shocked. 'A girlfriend?'

'Julie,' Dad says with a French inflection.

Why didn't he tell me? I've not been paying attention to his social media. Usually, he just posts about his football and group shots with friends. But a girlfriend – that's something he should have told me about, and told me about personally.

'How many weeks till you go?' Greg asks.

'Err, not sure,' I say. 'Decide after the results are out.'

'Xav's only fifteen,' Mum says. 'That's a bit young.'

'Yup,' says Dad. 'He's turning my sister into a worrier. She's thinking about his schoolwork when he goes back.'

Oh, my God. That sounds serious.

He chuckles. 'To be honest, I think it's all pretty innocent, but I let Em get it off her chest. And Xav has promised, Jess, that when you come he'll spend time with you like he always does.'

Somehow, that doesn't make me feel better. Everyone's quiet

for a while, there's just the hiss of onions frying. Benjamin finishes with the paper and pushes it away. I lean over, take it and open it quickly, glad to keep my eyes down. My hand shakes a little. How can I be so upset? He's only my cousin. But we're close … he didn't tell me. I can never forget that Emma and Theo are cousins too (even if Theo was adopted). They got together. It's not that I've ever thought anything would happen with Xav, but … I look up. Nobody else has a clue how I'm feeling, yet Benjamin is gazing at me. I think he can see right through me. Blushing, I turn away.

Later, I'm in the garden. It's good to be outside with the air growing colder. Benjamin comes out and sits near me.

'Hey,' he says.

I shrug. We're quiet, but I don't like the silence. 'Have you got a girlfriend back in London?'

'A girlfriend?' He sounds surprised. 'No.' Then after a pause. 'Which is probably just as well. Given everything.'

'I guess,' I say.

Again, we're quiet.

'Everyone I know has a boyfriend,' I say, avoiding his eyes.

'Really? I doubt that.'

'Well, not everyone.' I probably shouldn't exaggerate. 'But a lot.'

'I wouldn't worry. In my experience, you're probably better off without one,' he says matter-of-factly.

I turn to him. Sometimes he says surprising things. 'Didn't you like having a girlfriend?'

He shrugs, and I don't ask anymore.

I put on my eye make-up carefully. It's Ellie's party tonight. Loads of people will be there, all my friends from school. It's hard to believe we'll be off to uni soon; we'll be in cities all over Scotland. This could be the last time we're all together. Maybe that's why she's asked half the year to come. I'd never have done that but I'm not as friendly as Ellie.

Downstairs, my folks are in the living room. Dad's giving me a lift.

'How do I look?' I swirl round.

Dad smiles. 'Very pretty.' He always says something like that.

'You look lovely,' Mum says proudly.

Greg comes in looking for his reading glasses. 'Good God, Jess. Will you not be cold? You've hardly anything on.'

I chuckle. 'I'm fine.'

Dad goes and gets his car keys and then we leave.

Much later, Ellie's place is heaving. Her parents have gone off for the night and the house is literally shuddering with the beat of the music. In the living room there's a large table with food and drink, although there's not a lot of food left now. I've drunk a bit which is definitely helping me enjoy the party. I'm not worrying about what other people think of me, but I'm very aware that thirty minutes ago Logan arrived. I had no idea he was coming or that Ellie even knew him. He's been chatting in the kitchen, which I've been avoiding, but now I need a glass of water.

He greets me as I enter. 'Hey, Jess.'

'Logan,' I say casually. 'Didn't know you were coming.'

'Well, my sister's known Ellie for years. Gym club.'

'Okay.'

Then he smiles. 'No hard feelings, hey?' The way he smiles, is it possible he likes me?

'Course not,' I say.

'You know you're good, anyway.' His gaze is friendly. 'So, Jess, what's your poison?'

'I've just come in for a glass of water.'

He shakes his head and chuckles. 'That's no way to enjoy a party.' He leans over and picks up a bottle of beer. He flips the top off with his fingers and passes it to me.

Two hours later, Logan and I are sitting on the sofa. We've been talking and flirting, and I've noticed every time his hand's gently touched me. Then he leans over and we're kissing. I'm glad we're both drunk because I've never kissed anyone before and I don't want him to notice. His tongue feels strange in my mouth. The party's thinned so people will notice us. They'll see that Logan, the guy who was always popular at school, who plays bass with Talisman, is choosing to kiss me. Wow. I'm never the one anyone finds attractive, not like that. This is what happens when you talk about music with someone who gets it, who feels as passionately about it as I do, he even likes Falcon Taylor. We're snogging and his hand is on my thigh. I don't mind, it's resting there. I want us to just keep kissing but his hand starts to move slowly up my leg. I'm not so sure now. It goes higher and I push it back down. Then he pulls away from me and leaning back lets out a sigh. I sit up straighter but he doesn't say anything. 'I liked kissing you,' I half whisper, afraid I've upset him.

'Yeah,' he says, but he's looking into the distance.

I don't want to have messed up but I didn't want his hand to go any further. I watch him intently. 'Shall we do it again?' I dare, although my heart is pounding.

He turns and smiles. 'Need a piss,' he says, getting up. I watch him walk out of the room. I hope he won't be gone for long.

'Jess.' The sofa shifts as Fraser plonks himself down beside me. 'How's it going? Good party, hey?'

'Yeah, very good.' I'm never completely comfortable talking to Fraser, mostly because he's going out with Ellie and I'm sure she told him I'd fancied him.

'Yeah,' he agrees. I can see he's quite drunk. 'I told Ellie not to worry, it'd be great. And … see you've been having fun, hanging out with Logan.'

I smile but don't reply.

He pauses like he's trying to think what to say next. 'Just a wee word, okay, but … s'probably best to know,' he says, 'that apparently, he's somewhat involved with Katie Y.' He looks at me then burps.

'Katie Y?' I say, but my voice sounds like a squeak.

He nods. 'Ellie thought you should know. You don't want to get, you know, mixed up in it, do you?'

I can smell the alcohol on his breath and my stomach turns. How does Ellie know what Logan's doing? Suddenly, I've never felt so angry in my life, and with my best friend. What does Fraser mean by 'somewhat involved'? Logan's here alone.

Fraser rises. 'She's just thinking of you,' he says and walks away.

I can see Ellie in the hallway. She's in animated conversation. I haven't seen Katie Y since she left school a year ago but I never liked her. She always behaved as though she was above everybody else just because of her parents' money. But she's pretty, the kind of pretty that's blonde and blue-eyed and nothing like me. Where is Logan? I've been sitting here a while.

I leave the room. The toilet's up the stairs; a few people are lingering near the door but not Logan. I walk into the kitchen and his laughter explodes. He's talking to Jono and Charlie. As I draw closer, he looks across at me, nods and smiles but then continues talking with them. Sport. Football. I don't even try to pretend I'm going to join in.

I walk back into the living room. I'm not enjoying it anymore. Maybe I should be the kind of girl who walks up to Logan and hangs around his arm, smiling like I care about what he's saying? But I'm not. Crisps crunch beneath my feet, the smell of spilt beer is sickening, and Ellie's familiar home no longer feels friendly. Jayden is sprawled out on the floor. If only he had a personality, because in looks, he reminds me of Xav. Xav's got a girlfriend. The world's changing for everyone but me. I want to go home. I get out my phone and text Dad. I'll have to pretend all the way back just how much fun I've had.

CHAPTER 13

Jess

I put the pan of milk on the cooker, turn on the gas and stir in four heaped teaspoons of hot chocolate. I don't care that it's summer, or that it's two in the morning, I just want the hot sweet taste. My mouth's sour from the alcohol and the memory of Logan's kisses. How can you feel so good and so bad in one evening? I remember the touch of his fingers on my thigh. I stopped him because I didn't like it. Was that my mistake? But what if I hadn't? Where were his fingers going? My stomach contracts. He's going out with Katie Y and Ellie knew that.

'Hey.' A soft voice makes me jump. It's Benjamin. He's in sweatpants and a T-shirt. His hair is ruffled like he's been asleep. 'It's hot upstairs.' He goes to the tap to get a glass of water.

I don't respond but look down and keep stirring the milk. I think he's gone but then I hear him. 'You okay?'

I don't have to reply, but what does it matter if I tell the truth?

'Not really,' I mutter. I sense him waiting, behind me. 'Have you ever kissed a girl and then just ignored her?' I ask aggressively.

He doesn't reply. Maybe that's just how guys behave? 'I don't think so,' he says quietly.

My lower lip trembles. I focus very hard on my hot

chocolate but he doesn't go. I get a mug and pour the milk into it but there's enough left for another half cup. 'Want some?' I eventually ask.

He comes forward and nods, but I won't meet his eyes. I pour it out but when I pass it to him I look into his face.

'Please don't cry,' he says very softly, and I hadn't realised I was.

I shrug. 'I mess up. I don't get it. I guess there's something wrong with me.'

'I doubt it,' he says.

Then everything that's happened pours out of me. Logan. Ellie. All of it. 'I can never be like other people. Just ordinary and normal.'

'The guy's an arsehole,' he says.

I look at him through watery eyes. 'You really think so?'

'Yeah, a first-rate arsehole.'

I half laugh. 'Maybe,' I say, feeling some relief.

'And why do you want to be like other people anyway? What's normal?'

His face is calm and his eyes look a bit sleepy.

'I guess it's just … I'd like to have what other people have. You know, a boyfriend, but I can't seem to do it.'

'You'll have them,' he says like it's obvious. 'But if you're hoping they'll make you feel more normal, well, be careful you're not disappointed.'

I like him more than I ever thought I could. We finish our drinks and go to bed.

I'm very aware of Benjamin now. It's like all this time he's been a background noise, but someone's just gone and turned up the volume. I notice the way he holds his knife and fork, his long fingers, and how he sometimes gestures when talking. He's changing. His hair has grown longer and I've no idea when it will be cut. He's eating more and doesn't look so thin. Greg's got him chopping wood and fixing a fence and he seems to enjoy it. I wonder when he'll go; it's not something any of us talk about. Mum and Dad are still strict in not allowing him access to a computer, but he seems to accept that. There's the gun my father has hidden, a notebook and a memory stick too, but it's like they don't exist. Benjamin can't stay with us indefinitely, but when will he go? Perhaps I'll be at uni before it happens.

It's a week since Ellie's party and I want to go to the cinema. I always go with a friend, but right now I'm not in a hurry to see my friends. They think Ellie's party was the greatest success. I can't bear the pictures they've posted. You can see me clearly in the background, on that sofa with Logan. They make me feel sick when all I want to do is forget it. Nobody wants to hear me.

'God, Jess,' Holly said, 'you're so oversensitive. You snogged the guy, what more do you want? At least you've kissed someone.'

Maybe I am oversensitive, but I can't help that, it's who I am. And why do people have to point it out – you're oversensitive. So instead of my friends, what would it be like if Benjamin could come to the cinema, just for one single trip? He must be bored out of his mind spending all his time here. I suggest it to him, and that he could disguise himself a bit. He laughs at the idea, but it's not a happy-sounding laugh.

'I'd love to go to the cinema, but no way.'

'I can ask Dad,' I say, but he just shakes his head.

I decide to stream a recent release and get some popcorn and crisps. I ask Benjamin if he wants to watch it with me. The biggest screen we've got is in the living room and I tell my folks they're welcome to join us, but once I close the curtains and create a dark space there's no entry. As expected, they let me be. Benjamin and I sit on the sofa. He's at one end and I'm at the other. The film's okay but mostly I'm watching him out of the corner of my eye. There's a scene where the main characters make out. He keeps his eyes on the screen, and without looking down he dips his hand into the popcorn and puts a piece in his mouth; one by one he repeats the action. And then I'm throwing a piece of popcorn at him. It lands in his lap. He continues to keep his eyes on the film but picks it up and eats it. He's cool and collected as I throw some more. I aim at his head and the popcorn sticks to his hair. He reaches up, pulls it out and eats it. I burst out laughing and he finally turns to me and smiles.

'I hope you're not going to retaliate,' I say, hoping of course that he does.

He stands, picks up the bowl and comes over. He tips it ever so slightly and a small cascade of popped corn rains down on me.

'Now you've got to eat them,' I say.

'Eat them?' He shakes his head. 'No, they're all yours.'

'Please,' I say, and lie back so that they run off my body, or stick to my top.

Again, he shakes his head but doesn't move. I hold out a piece to him. 'Please,' I say, surprised at how soft my voice is.

He takes it out of my fingers and pops it in his mouth; his fingers touched mine. I pick up another piece. He waits then slowly leans down and places his lips around it; I feel the soft warmth of his mouth. Then he sits beside me and gently offers me some; his fingers taste salty.

I don't know where my parents are or Greg, or how long we'll have our privacy, but I do know what I want to happen. We feed each other a few more pieces, our fingers lingering on each other's lips. Every part of me feels alive. I want him to kiss me. He must know how much I'm willing him to do it. Then his lips touch mine and I'm like a match that's been struck; I'm going up in flames. How is it possible to feel so much? It's frightening, my desire to have his lips against mine and to keep him close. He lies down on the sofa beside me. We're fully clothed and yet I feel naked. He kisses me softly but like someone who knows what they're doing. His arm draws me to him but his hands don't wander anywhere else; I'm glad of that. Then it's over. He stops and sits up. He doesn't move away from me, but he's very quiet. I don't want him to regret it.

'It's okay,' I say. 'It's okay that we did that.'

He nods, but hesitates. 'Jess, I … we just need to stop and think a moment.'

'I like you,' I say, in case he hasn't got that. 'I really like you.'

'Yes, but liking each other isn't the point.'

'Isn't it?'

'Who do you think I am, Jess?' he whispers, serious.

'Benjamin,' I say softly, watching his eyes. 'Who do you want to be?'

Something in his gaze shows me that question's a shock, although maybe not in a bad way.

'Who do you want to be?' I ask again, very gently.

He's still for a long time. 'I've no idea.'

I smile at him. 'That's good. You can be anyone you want.'

He shakes his head again, but not unkindly. We carry on watching the film, sitting closer, our knees touching ever so slightly. I'm only pretending to watch, because mostly I'm completely distracted by him: his body, his breath, the hair that falls around his eyes. The point at which our jeans touch feels hot. Eventually, the agony of watching a film when I'm not actually watching it comes to an end. We both say we're tired and go upstairs. There's a point on the landing outside the bathroom where he has to go one way and me the other. We stop.

I'm racking my brain for something to say. I don't think either of us wants to be alone.

'Perhaps, Jess, it's time to go to bed.'

'Okay,' I say, trying to disguise my disappointment.

'What happened tonight, it's private, yes?'

'Yes.' I smile.

He nods and smiles back. He looks sleepy but happy, and that fills my heart with joy.

CHAPTER 14

Benjamin

The curtains are open. It's dark outside and Jess's body is snuggled into mine. This is becoming a routine. Most nights she comes up to my room. We'll kiss, cuddle and then lie close. We don't take our clothes off because I know we can't go any further. After we've chatted or watched the stars, she'll go back to her room and sleep. I've told her there's no way her folks or Greg can know.

'It's hard to hide it, Jess, when you like someone, but we need to. They wouldn't approve, and there's no way I want to upset them.'

'I don't think you'd upset them, but I can see it's none of their business.'

Now, I'm enjoying the warmth of her body against mine.

'You can't even see the moon tonight,' she says. 'There's too much cloud cover.'

'Yeah, I never knew the night could be so dark until I came here.'

'It can get pitch black, but when the moon's up, like when it's a really bright moon sometimes I go cycling in the dead of night. It's cool, everything looks different.'

'You go on your own?'

'Yeah, it's quite safe. This isn't London. Most times I go

alone but once Mum came with me. Mum loves the moon too. It's got a sacred quality.'

I think about that. 'You're both quite spiritual, aren't you?'

'I guess. Mum's taught me a lot. She doesn't do any kind of ritual stuff, but she knows that there's spirit in every living thing. That's what she's taught me, and even that there's spirit in some things that aren't living.'

'Aren't living?'

'Yes, like when you were in the cottage and you thought you were seeing ghosts, we knew you were in trouble because there are no ghosts there. Mum would definitely have known if there were.'

Gil stood in this room even though he was dead. I change the subject.

'Jess, has Mary … has she never thought about having implants so she can hear? I mean, you sing, surely she'd like to hear you sing?'

'Mum can hear me sing. Just because she's deaf doesn't mean she can't hear me.'

'Doesn't it? Only if she's got some residual hearing, and can pick up on vibrations, but the technology's there if she *really* wants to hear you.'

She turns to face me. 'Benjamin, not everything we hear is through our ears. Just like not everything we see is through our eyes. I know what you're studying, and it's great, what you might achieve, but that doesn't mean you can tell me Mum can't hear me sing.'

I look at her, sceptical.

'Mum's a very sensitive person and like I've been trying to tell you, she picks up on things. She sees things about you you're probably not even aware of. Like … like your fire.'

'Fire?'

'Yes.' She softens. 'When you first arrived, I thought you were all water and mud, but Mum said no, underneath all your misery, there was fire.'

'Is this the sort of thing you usually discuss with your mum?'

'Sometimes.'

'Well, you should be careful, you know, because … other guys, you might just find you freak them out.'

She looks at me a long moment. 'Am I freaking you out?'

'A bit. I mean, nobody likes to know they're being talked about, do they?'

'Oh.' She smiles gently. 'No, I guess not. But we're only talking about you because we care.'

I don't say any more.

It's evening and Jess is sitting at her desk. She's holding the notebook I dared to look inside. 'Can you keep a secret?' she asks.

'I've always kept secrets,' I say, but my heart's beginning to pound.

'Our families are bound together.' She opens the book and takes out the sheet of paper. She unfolds it slowly and passes it over. I stare at the picture of our fathers on that motorbike. I look at it as though seeing it for the first time.

'I don't know if you know what's happening in it,' she says slowly.

'I do.'

'It's your father – and mine.'

'Okay,' I say but my breathing quickens.

'Gil Zimmerman and Dominic Minster.'

'I understand what you're saying, Jess.'

'They went over a cliff together, but how did they survive?' Her eyes search mine.

'I've no idea,' I whisper. 'I've never understood it.'

'No,' she says, 'but I've heard my father say he loved Gil. I keep thinking about that, and if that's what saved them.'

'Love?' I repeat.

'Yes, I don't know how you can survive something like that unless you're driven by the deepest emotion. The water would've been freezing. They must have been terrified. Your father had lost a hand.'

The room almost spins. 'It's difficult for me to talk about,' I mumble.

'I'm sorry.'

I swallow hard. 'Jess, I think … I don't think your father would want me to know that he was once Dominic Minster. He's never told me himself. He wouldn't want me to know.'

'I don't see why not.'

She doesn't get it, in any way. 'Will you do me a favour? Will you please destroy that picture?'

'Destroy it?'

'Yes. Your father has spent years constructing an identity and this one picture – it takes it all away.'

'But anybody can look at it. I got it online.'

'Anybody can look at it, but the fact that you've got it, in this house, in your room, means it's telling a truth about you and your family.'

She looks at me bemused. 'Nobody's going to see it. Nobody *has* seen it, but you.'

'Jess, please, destroy it,' I say loudly. 'It's a security risk. If you don't understand why, that's even more reason to destroy it.'

'Okay,' she says warily.

'I'm sorry, I didn't mean to shout. But that picture upsets me.'

She folds it over and tears it up. 'I'll put it in the bin downstairs.' She leaves the room.

I lie back on the bed, and it's only then I realise I'm crying.

'Benjamin.' It's his voice. I keep my eyes closed; I won't look. I'm afraid if I do I'll find he's changed. That the bullet wounds I didn't see before will have formed on his body, or that death has started to decay him.

'Did you love Dominic, Gil?' I ask softly. Jess's words have stayed with me. 'Is that how you survived?'

He doesn't answer. Even now, he won't tell me.

'I'm more concerned about your survival,' he says. 'It's good the girl likes you. She's clumsy and young but—'

'She'd scare the shit out of you.' I sit up. 'The way she opens her mouth. You wouldn't let her near the Disciples.'

'Of course not. But she's not joining the Disciples. She's just falling in love with you.'

I shake my head.

'And maybe,' he says softly, 'you're falling in love with her. There's nothing wrong with that.'

'Love terrifies me. Getting caught up in other people's emotions.'

'Benjamin, is your heart really that scarred? I don't think so.'

'Why are you here?' I ask. 'Because you run the risk of being found out. Mary picks up on ghosts.'

'She probably does, but …' He shrugs.

We don't speak for a while.

'You just turn up when you want,' I say. 'You don't answer my questions. You don't make anything better. All you want me to do is get the memory stick and those things back. Well, I won't use her.' I flop back on my bed and bury my head in the pillow. I hope he gets the message.

'You won't have to use her,' he says matter-of-factly. 'She'll give you what you want. That's exactly what love's about. And I'm here because you need me.'

Then I feel his hand on my back. It's even warm. He's dead and his hand is warm. I no longer know what is real, what is fantasy.

CHAPTER 15

Jess

We're on my bed. I kiss his cheek and whisper in his ear. 'Benjamin, if you want, I can take my bra off.'

For nights we've kissed and cuddled. Our legs entwine. Our bodies wrap around each other, but we never take our clothes off.

'You can touch my breasts.'

He doesn't reply. I watch his face for some response, then he touches my cheek with his finger. 'If we start with your bra, it won't end there.'

'Does that matter?'

'Probably,' he says very softly.

I don't understand. He's had girlfriends. He must have had sex. But why doesn't he want to go any further with me?

'Don't you find me attractive?' I ask, trying to hold my voice steady.

'Of course I do. I just don't want you to get hurt.'

'Why would I get hurt?'

'Because …' He shrugs. 'It's what happens.'

I gaze into his eyes. They're dark, liquid. 'Happens? You mean like with other girlfriends?'

The slightest nod. 'I think if we get more involved, things will get too intense. I like it the way it is.'

'Okay,' I say, although I'm not sure I am. 'I guess we've both got to feel the same way, haven't we?'

He smiles and then hugs me, but I still don't understand.

Days pass, and suddenly what Benjamin and I are doing – it's no longer enough. I act cool but my heart's on fire. I sit at the table while we eat, but all I want to do is touch him. I watch him painting the fence, and I want to open my window and scream, 'I love you.' When we kiss, it feels like we can't kiss deeply enough. Yet he doesn't want to go any further. But it's not alright to set someone on fire, and then tell them to stay cool. How am I meant to get through the seconds, let alone the hours, and not explode with all I'm feeling? Maybe I hate him? That's possible now. I wish he'd go.

Tonight, the sky is clear and bright with stars. It's almost a full moon. We finish dinner but I don't go to him afterwards. I walk to the shed and get out my bike. I haven't told my folks where I'm going and start pedalling, heading out quickly. The road's deserted and I can travel for miles.

Benjamin

Jess doesn't come to my room. It's a relief because the tension between us has been ratcheting up. This is what happens: I get involved with girls and it turns into a mess. I told her I didn't want to hurt her. I said it for her own good. Closing my eyes, I try to sleep. At least I'm alone.

A sound wakes me. A knock at my door. Adam opens it. 'Did Jess say anything to you?' His face is serious.

I shake my head. *What's going on?*

'She didn't say anything to you about going for a ride?'

Again, I shake my head. 'No. Nothing.'

'Her bike's gone.'

I can see he's worried. 'She said that sometimes when the moon's bright she'll go for a ride.'

'Yeah, but she always tells us when she does that. She's just gone and now it's two in the morning.'

'Shit.' I'm very awake. 'But it's safe? I mean, it's not London.'

'Everywhere's safe, Benjamin, until it's not safe.'

He leaves my room and runs down the stairs. I get up quickly and pull on my jeans and a hoodie. I find them all in the living room.

Mary's staring at her phone. 'Still no response.'

This is serious. But have they checked she's not at a friend's? Surely she's done this before? Yet I already know the answer.

'Right,' Greg says. 'Mary and I will head for the village. Adam, you go to the loch. If we still can't find her then we'll work our way round the surrounding area.'

There's a moment's silence then they head out of the room.

'Adam, I'll come with you,' I say quickly.

He turns to me. He stares as if I'm a stranger, as if he can't quite remember who I am.

Greg says, 'Probably best not to go alone, Adam.'

Adam doesn't respond, but I follow him outside. Greg and Mary get into the pickup truck, and Adam into their car. I jump into the passenger seat and fasten the seat belt. Still, Adam doesn't say anything. He's completely distracted. He revs the engine, puts the car into gear, and we head off quickly. Then it hits me. What if something's *really* wrong? What if Jess is lying in a ditch somewhere, unconscious? A car's hit her. Or somebody grabbed her. They dragged her off her bike … her body in woodland …

It's hard to breathe. The air's being squeezed out of my lungs. I don't say anything because I'm freezing up inside. If something's happened to Jess … I can't take it. Not another death. Another body. Another person I care about.

We keep driving. Adam swings round the narrow roads. If a car passes on the other side, we're not going to make it any-where. But there's no one else about. Of course, Adam knows that. He wouldn't be driving like a maniac if not. I don't really know where we're going, but it's my first time in a car for weeks. In any other circumstance I'd be grateful for the trip. Now, I just don't want to be sick.

Adam slows the car. He turns off the road. The headlights beam across black grass and then glistening darkness. Water. He gets out.

'Jess!' His voice carries. 'Jess!'

In the distance, the slightest glow of light. Probably from a phone. A whimper leaves his lips and then he starts to walk towards it. He disappears into the darkness; I don't know how he can see where he's going. I consider trying to follow but the moonlight's not bright enough for me. I really am a stranger. I followed Adam into the car, but this is a private drama. One I don't belong to.

It's a while before Adam's silhouette emerges through the darkness. He's on his phone – I can hear him speaking to Greg. Jess is okay. She's worked herself up about something, but he's found her and she's safe.

My stomach turns as he comes back into the car. He looks exhausted.

'Maybe,' he says softly, 'you can have a word. Apparently, I'm too old to understand.'

'Sure,' I say as if it's nothing. As if I have no idea what any of this is about.

He lends me a torch. I walk carefully to her and sit down slowly beside her.

'Oh,' she says. 'You decided to come too.'

'You freaked us all out, Jess. Everyone's been worried sick.'

She draws in a deep breath and takes her time. 'I don't think I can go home with you there.'

I can't reply. I just feel panic.

'My heart's on fire most of the time. That's what you've done to me. My mouth feels full of stones.'

Jesus, she's intense. Nobody can accuse her of not being poetic.

'I'm sorry,' I mutter.

She shakes her head. 'I love you,' she whispers.

'Please, Jess. Come back to the car. It's time to go home.'

'Haven't you heard anything?'

'And when we get home,' I continue, trying to hold my voice steady, 'we'll talk.'

'No more talking.'

It's quite clear what's happening. I've played my part but I don't get to leave the stage this time.

I lean towards her and whisper. 'I'll come to your room and make you mine.' Where do those words come from? I don't say things like that.

She turns to me. 'You mean it?'

'Yes.' I nod, serious.

Gradually, she stands. The air is cold, the darkness thick. I shiver. Her warm hand touches mine, our fingers brushing together. Then we walk quietly to the car.

When we get back, Mary and Greg are in the living room. Mary lets rip. She's screaming and signing at her daughter. She's a scary woman but I know she's shouting because she's been afraid for the person she loves most in the world. That's what I see: mother and daughter and the love between them. Jess bursts into tears.

Eventually, we all go to bed. Jess is exhausted. I hug her on the landing outside her room. 'You need to sleep,' I whisper. It's the truth but I don't want her to wake in the morning and start all over again. She needs to know I'm keeping my word. 'Tomorrow, we'll talk about contraception.'

She nods against my chest. I watch her go into her room and shut the door gently.

I go up to the attic but I can't sleep. I stare through the dark. I can't stop what's happening now. I don't think she's on the pill.

I'll insist we use condoms. It will probably be the only thing I have any control over. I try to stop the panic rising in my chest, but it's a long time before I fall asleep.

CHAPTER 16

Jess

My head is on Benjamin's chest and I can hear his heart beating.

'I love you,' I say. Maybe sex wasn't as easy as I thought it would be, but he was kind. I'm glad I've done it with him, that he was my first. 'I'm happy.' I smile.

He strokes my hair with his right hand. 'I'm happy too.'

We don't talk for a while, our bodies warm and close.

'It's probably best if you go to your room if we're going to get any sleep,' he says.

I rise slowly. The single bed is too small for the two of us; still, I'd be happy to stay. I'd hold him all night and forget about sleep. His face is serene. I've not seen him look so peaceful before and kiss his lips then creep back to my room. Lying awake, I just feel too much to sleep. Then I close my eyes and dream.

Benjamin and I are on a motorbike. My arms are wrapped around his waist, my chest against his back. It's a fine day and we're heading out from here. He grips the handlebars, puts his foot down and the speed is exhilarating; I've never been on a bike before. The wind catches his long hair below the line of his helmet. The landscape is open fields and the occasional line of trees. He's my boyfriend now. I have what other people have, even though he'll never meet Ellie or Holly and he's ten times better than Fraser. They'll never know him, but none of that matters.

'I'm not disappointed,' I shout, remembering our earlier conversation. He doesn't reply – I don't think he can hear. After a while we stop. He looks out across the view, pulls off his helmet and shakes out his hair.

'I love you,' I say. My voice rings. 'I love you, I love you, I love you.' I want to cover his cheeks in kisses.

Finally, he turns to me, but the face I see is Gil's.

I wake, shocked. My room is dark. Familiar objects and shadows. Yet he feels very close. Gil. How can that be? My thoughts scramble. I want to find Mum. I want her to reassure me I'm dreaming and there are no spirits in the house, and certainly not Gil's. But I can't go to Mum. I lie back and picture Benjamin's face and count all the ways he's different to Gil. He's younger, much younger, of course. And his features are softer; Gil's were more chiselled. Benjamin's eyelashes are the longest, and his lips are fuller. And yet … I gaze up at the ceiling and think of him sleeping in the room above. I wonder what he dreams of. I hope it's me.

This is what it is to love someone. They walk into a room and your heart fills with joy; it takes a leap in recognition of theirs. Benjamin's very good at not giving anything away. He takes care to keep a distance whenever my folks are around. He acts cool, but I can see the smile that curls the edge of his lips. Sometimes he catches my eye, and it takes everything in me not to grin back.

It's a bright, sunny afternoon. I flop back in a garden chair, close my eyes and let the sun work on my skin. I must have dropped off because I wake with a start. Something touched my nose.

'Brown suits you.'

I squint at Benjamin. He's standing by me with a can of paint in one hand and a brush in the other.

My nose is wet with brown paint.

'I'm working on the outhouse.' He motions with his head down the garden.

'You daubed me,' I say.

'I think you were asking for it.'

'Was I?'

'Yeah, you fell asleep in the sun. Lazybones.' He smiles, teasing me.

I walk to the outside tap, pull off the hose, and fill my hands with water. 'I'm not sure paint comes off with water.' I splash it on my face.

'It's coming off.'

When I'm clean enough, I cup my hands and let the freezing water fill them again, then run at Benjamin and throw the water over him.

He gasps. 'So that's how you want to play.'

He throws some at me but I escape most of it, laughing. Then he switches off the tap and we're still. He puts his finger to his lips. He worries too much about what people think and I glance round. Nobody can see us. I lean into his body and kiss his lips. His wet T-shirt is clinging to his chest, and shows the outline of his chain and pendant – a fire bird, a phoenix.

'You never take your necklace off, do you?' I touch it gently where it lies below his neck.

His head is on the pillow and I'm propped up on my elbows. We're both naked.

'No,' he says.

'It must be special then. Did a … girlfriend give it to you?'

'My mother gave it to me.'

'Oh.' I didn't think a mother would give a son something like that. 'Was it a birthday present?'

'Kind of.'

'Kind of? That's a direct answer,' I tease.

'Kind of,' he repeats.

Not for the first time, I sense how mysterious Benjamin can be. He says things, but you never feel it's everything. I hold the pendant gently. 'Have you always liked the phoenix?'

'Pretty much. I remember Mum reading to me as a kid, and all these brightly coloured pictures.'

'I like the myth too. Each phoenix being born from the ashes of the one before it. Death and rebirth.' I place it carefully back on his skin.

He's quiet.

'I'd love to know what your mum was like,' I say. 'If only you had a phone, at least I could look at some photos.'

'I don't have any of them now,' he says softly. 'Not a single shot of her alone or of us together. But I think you'd have liked her, Jess. If you'd met her. And I think she'd have liked you.'

'Do you? I hope so.'

'She had this cool way of sussing people out – friends or girls who liked me. She'd casually invite them to stay for dinner. She'd just always happen to make enough for three or four, and they'd be sitting there eating and she'd be working them out.' He chuckles.

'She sounds a bit scary.'

'She wasn't scary. Mostly, she liked the people I liked. I promise, she'd have liked you.'

'I so wish you had a photo.'

'And then with my father, the crazy thing about him is, you go online and there are hundreds if not thousands of pictures of Gil, but I don't have, I've *never* had a single shot of him with me. Not one. There's no evidence anywhere we're father and son.'

'That's incredible,' I say, but I don't mean it in a good way. 'I can't imagine not having photos of my family. That would really upset me.'

'Well, it's all I've known. When they were alive it didn't seem to matter, but now …' He pauses. I hope I've not upset him, but he touches the phoenix. 'This is all I have of my mother, and of my father there's just that notebook your dad's locked up. It's full of Gil's handwriting. His messy scrawl that I didn't even get to see growing up. But that's what I have left of him. A single notebook.' He closes his eyes and takes a deep breath.

'There really isn't anything else?' I ask, although I already know the answer. My throat feels tight. 'I'll get it for you,' I whisper.

He opens his eyes, and they're full of sadness. 'No, I don't think so, Jess.' He stretches out his hand to touch my hair. 'Your father was quite clear. You need to leave it where it is. Although, I'd like to think that some time he'll trust me enough to look at it.'

'Benjamin,' I say, keeping my voice low. 'Dad's idea of locking something up is putting it in the cupboard behind the door in his study, which, as it happens, he keeps the key for in the top drawer of his desk.'

He looks at me bemused. 'You're kidding?'

'No. So if you want it, it's really not asking much.'

I sneak into Dad's study. My folks are out and I find Benjamin's notebook quickly; it's hardly hidden. There's a streak of dried blood on it, and that almost stops me, but I'm doing this as a gift for him. My feelings don't count. He'd probably like the whole pouch bag, but that would look too obvious. Dad might realise what I've done. I leave the book on Benjamin's pillow, hoping that he might look at it with me, or even discuss it, but he doesn't. Instead, when he comes down to my room, it's like he loves me even more.

When he's not looking, I take photos of him. Something he said really cut me up: that you might have somebody in your life but have no visual record of them. No matter how much you love them or care about them, there's not a single picture as proof they were in your life. I won't let that happen to me. I take the photos on my phone. He's never said he wants any and I think if I asked him he'd say no, but I don't need to ask his permission. I can photograph the person I love. And the thing is, because he's not posing and there are no big smiles or happy faces, he looks more beautiful to me. I keep them in a private folder, separate from everything else. They're just for me to see.

CHAPTER 17

Benjamin

Jess is out tonight. She got her exam results yesterday, and she's celebrating with friends.

'I've got my place at Glasgow.' She jumped up and down in the kitchen, ecstatic. 'I get to study music. I get to live in halls.'

'Your life really starts now, hey, Jess?' Adam said, smiling.

Now, I'm sitting in my room and the place is quiet without her. The others are downstairs pottering. It's my moment to act. I kneel down, put my hand under the mattress and retrieve my father's notebook. Jess got it for me; it was that simple.

I carefully go to her room, close the door and open her laptop. The screen comes to life and I type in her security PIN – it didn't even cross Jess's mind that she was revealing it to me. My hands shake slightly. It's the first access I've had to the internet since my parents were shot. I switch off every location tracker and then scan the news. A few Disciples' cells have been raided. I read the names of those captured. One person was shot. But not Tom, and I think Cesar, who's in command after Tom, is okay too. Opening my father's notebook, I find web addresses made up of letters and numbers. Sites hidden from public view. I type one in. Nothing comes up. I try another, again nothing. Third time I'm lucky, but it's just a form. You leave your name and message – nothing more. There's a blank section below; I take it that's for a response. Do I trust it? Might somebody have revealed it as a contact point?

'Call yourself Abigail,' Gil had told me. 'Tom and Cesar will know it's you.'

'Tom and Cesar, but nobody else?'

'No. Even two knowing feels too many but if we're ever infiltrated hopefully one will survive.'

'Abigail. I guess it makes sense to use a girl's name. It's not what you'd expect.'

He'd smiled. Later, I looked up its meaning: my father is joy.

I type in the name and my message: *I want to come home.* I press send, then feel light-headed. I've started it now. Events will have their own momentum. I come out of the site, remove it from the search engine's memory and close it all down. I tiptoe back to my room. If Tom's alive, he'll reply on that site, and I'll need to find another opportunity to use Jess's computer. But if he isn't alive … I don't know Cesar like Tom. I'll be dealing with someone new. And if Cesar's gone too …

I look out the window and watch the last light of the setting sun. It's late but I'm not ready to sleep. I go to the kitchen to get a drink and the sweet, homely smell of baking greets me. Mary's icing a cake, piping the word 'Congratulations' across the top.

'Wow,' I say, 'that looks professional.'

She looks up and I repeat it so she can lip-read. She smiles. 'Jess has no idea. I'll hide it until we eat tomorrow evening.'

'She'll love it,' I say, admiring the two layers of what looks like chocolate cake.

She gets out a tin and carefully slips the cake inside. Then she stalls and her eyes meet mine. 'My daughter's very stubborn.'

'Yes?'

'Yes. She's not so different to me when I was her age. If I made up my mind about something or *somebody*, I wouldn't budge.'

I listen but don't answer. I don't think she wants me to answer.

'I think she's made up her mind about you.'

Oh, shit. Mary knows, she really knows.

'When I first met Adam, this may seem hard to believe, but he warned me off him. He told me he wouldn't be good for me. I, of course, was having none of that, and nineteen years later you can see where we are.'

My heart is pounding.

'I know what it is not to listen, and to be determined you know best. And Jess is just the same. So I don't blame you, Benjamin. She made up her mind. But I am going to ask you not to hurt her. Don't burn her badly, because she doesn't deserve that.'

My throat is so tight I can barely speak. 'I don't want to hurt her,' I whisper.

'Adam isn't aware of what's going on. Greg doesn't have a clue. I won't mention it again, and Jess won't know we spoke.'

I nod but can't reply.

'Because I know you've heard me clearly, and I want to trust that, if nothing else, you'll respect me on this. Don't burn her.'

I manage the words, 'No, I won't.'

I go back to my room; I didn't even get the glass of water I wanted. I get under the covers and although it's not cold, I'm shivering.

Jess gets back late. It's almost three in the morning when I hear her on the stairs. I pray she just goes to her room and sleeps. She doesn't; instead, there's the familiar creak of her coming to my room. I lie still but keep my eyes on the closed door. She opens it.

'Benjamin, are you still awake?' she asks too loudly.

'Yes,' I whisper.

'I need to tell you I love you. I'd like to find a way of taking you to Glasgow with me. I realised that tonight. We drove down to the sea and I was standing in the water, and okay, we were a bit drunk, and my feet were freezing, but I realised I've never been so happy, and a lot of that is because of you.'

I can almost smell the sea on her. She sways slightly in the doorway.

'Jess, it's late. Can we talk in the morning?'

'Yes,' she says, 'but only if you tell me you love me.'

Her silhouette seems to dance before my eyes. 'Yes,' I say softly.

'You love me?'

'I love you.'

She smiles and leaves my room.

Jess

I sit cross-legged on my bed. My head is still groggy from the alcohol I drank, but maybe that's the best way to write a song anyway. I play around with chords; I wrote the lyrics a while ago. Last night couldn't have been better. Things were even good with Ellie and Fraser. So if I can just ride this wave of happiness, a kind of creative surfing, I could write my best love song yet. Of course, it's for Benjamin. He's outside with Greg, still, he should be able to hear. Dad told me once it's amazing how much he can hear outside when I play.

I lose track of time but eventually he comes. I've left my door ajar to invite him in. He looks hot and sweaty and probably wants a shower.

'Did you mean what you said last night?' I ask him, smiling.

'Yes.'

'I also meant what I said. That's how much I love you.'

He watches me. 'It's great, Jess, that you got your place at uni. You get to study what you love.'

'Yeah,' I say, and strum another chord.

'It got me thinking. I need to speak to your father soon, about what I'm going to do.'

'Do?'

'Yeah, I can't stay here forever.' He's serious.

I know I can't really take him to Glasgow with me, but I wasn't expecting this. 'You don't have to move on, Benjamin. My folks are fine with you here, and I'll be back in the holidays.'

He's quiet.

'I love you,' I repeat.

'And I you,' he says softly. 'But … we don't own each other.'

'No, of course not.' Yet something about the way he said that feels upsetting. I put down my guitar; any desire to sing has gone.

He's quiet. I don't know what he's thinking.

'Anyway, you're not going anywhere now, are you?' I say.

'No. Not now.'

'So that's all that matters, the present tense, isn't it?'

He nods gently, and almost smiles.

CHAPTER 18

Benjamin

I lie in bed glad to be alone. Jess is tired tonight and I need space to think. Our conversation replays in my thoughts. Maybe I should have said something more honest? But I can't tell the truth. I warned her. I don't mean to hurt people, but it's what happens. The truth comes out and then there's nothing I can do. Mo's face forms in my mind. I see it clear as day. I didn't want to hurt him, but I have. MI5 got him. Gil knew the risk, but I didn't want to hear him.

I was sixteen years old when the lie ran out and I couldn't put it back in its box. The evening it happened, I was sitting in the Qureshis' living room. Mo and I had been studying – we'd got our exams shortly – and I was staying for dinner. I liked being at the Qureshis' because they were everything my parents weren't. Dr Qureshi was a local GP who worked long hours taking care of people. He could be strict with Mo, but I saw that as caring too.

'Family, Benjamin,' he'd told me, 'nothing matters more.' It was at Eid al-Fitr when I'd been invited to their celebration along with lots of their relatives. He'd smiled at me kindly, and I'd felt warm and included.

'You know,' Mo had whispered afterwards, 'Dad's hoping

you'll become a Muslim. He reckons it would be good for you – being part of a community.'

'Well,' I'd said, 'maybe I will.' I half meant it.

Mo's mother ran her own business selling wedding dresses, and whenever I was over she'd pile my plate high with food. Fatima, Mo's older sister, was smart and political and we enjoyed joking with each other. Their lives were secure and ordered compared to mine, and Mo knew exactly what he wanted.

'We'll go to uni, Ben, get first-class degrees and then we'll be able to do anything – the best science jobs will be open to us,' he said one night after revising. 'Yeah, we'll be made.' He'd grinned, satisfied. 'And hopefully, by the end of uni, I'll be married too. That's what I'd like.'

I was studying hard and hoped to get a good job, but beyond that, other conventional family stuff – I didn't know.

'Marriage, Benjamin,' Gil had taught me, 'is a form of oppression. It's always been about property, money, ownership. Even calling somebody *my* girlfriend or *my* boyfriend, what are people actually saying? That they own each other.'

So that evening I was sitting at the Qureshis' after a day of revising, glad I didn't have to go home to eat alone; Mum was working late. Then Fatima said, 'I don't believe they've got him. It's just a government plot.'

'Timmy, what are you on about?' Mo asked disparagingly.

'Gil Zimmerman. There's been some shooting in South London and the rumour is they've got him. But it's just the police putting out some story so nobody's paying attention to that Security and Influence Bill the government want to introduce. They're hiding the real story behind fake news.'

Mo and I had spent the whole day with our heads in textbooks – it was the first I'd heard of it. 'A guy's been shot?' I said as casually as I could. 'And they've identified him as Gil Zimmerman?'

'No. That's exactly what I'm saying. They've shot a guy, but he could be anyone, they're just saying, like on social media, like *maybe* it could be him.'

I felt light-headed. I wasn't quite in my body. We were sitting round a table having an evening meal, but my father might be dead. Shot. Killed. I excused myself to go to the toilet and texted Mum. My hands were shaking. 'What's happening?'

She pinged back. 'Don't know.'

My eyes were fixed on my phone when suddenly I couldn't breathe properly. I was gasping, inhaling quickly or maybe not fast enough, and getting more and more light-headed. My lungs felt blocked, I couldn't get air into them, and there was a horrible tingling sensation in my hands.

Frantic, I opened the bathroom door. 'Dr Qureshi, I can't breathe!'

There were footsteps on the stairs, and then they were all looking at me. I couldn't stop gasping. Fatima watched with wide eyes and Mo looked terrified. I didn't want to die. Dr Qureshi moved quickly and held a paper bag over my mouth. He was telling me to breathe slowly, to calm down, that I was alright.

'You're having a panic attack,' he said firmly. 'Getting far too anxious about those exams, and like I've told Mo, you're two years ahead of everybody. If you don't pass it doesn't matter, you'll sit them again next year.'

I was flooded with shame. A panic attack. Mrs Qureshi and Fatima went quietly back downstairs. Mo looked upset and my head began to clear. Whatever the trick of the paper bag, it was working.

'I'm sorry,' I mumbled.

'Now, take a few moments to calm down.' Dr Qureshi motioned to Mo's bedroom.

'Yes. I'm sorry.'

He tut-tutted like I need say no more. I went into Mo's room. Mostly we studied downstairs but I knew his room well.

I crashed down on his bed, hid my head in the pillow and cried. I didn't even realise Mo was in the room until he spoke. 'I'll come up again in a bit.'

I lay there, desolate. I didn't want to be me. If I had a different father, I'd have a different life. I knew I should try to get home, Mum would be there soon, but I couldn't move. My father did things that could get him killed – how would I live if he was dead?

When I woke, later, Mo was back in the room. He was perched on the edge of the bed, and for a while we didn't speak. He'd never seen me cry before, and I couldn't go through the charade of pretending I got too stressed about the exams. He'd know that was a lie.

'It's okay,' he said very gently. 'He's not dead. I've checked the news and online, and it's not Gil Zimmerman they've shot. Don't stress about it.'

My mouth was dry. I could smell cooking although the meal was over. I turned slowly and gazed at him through the dark.

'I know your secret,' he whispered. 'In some ways, it makes sense. You look quite like him. I just wish you'd have told me. You can trust me.'

What would my father do in this situation? Maybe he'd kill Mo: shoot him or put his hands around his neck and squeeze tightly. I was bewildered. He was my best friend.

'What are you going to do?' I asked.

'Do?' Mo said, surprised. 'Nothing, of course.'

We were quiet for a while.

'Do you want to tell me about him?' he asked.

I shook my head. I couldn't talk about it, I'd kept it all locked inside for so long.

'You can if you want,' he offered.

The silence extended. It might be better to say something rather than nothing. 'It's hard for me to talk about,' I whispered. 'I don't see him. He's a shit father, I just didn't want to think he'd been shot in South London.'

'Okay. That makes sense.'

Again, quiet.

Then he asked carefully, 'You've not been involved in any kind of stuff with him, have you? Like the Disciples?'

'No, Mo. Never. I've nothing to do with the Disciples. I wish *he* didn't.'

He nodded but looked down. I couldn't let Gil come between us; I couldn't let that happen.

Anguished, I said. 'Your family are kind to me, Mo. That matters so much. Gil Zimmerman's irrelevant. Your dad's more of a father to me.'

I waited, then his eyes meet mine. 'Yeah, and you're like a brother, Benjamin. We don't have to talk about it.'

When I next met Gil, I told him what had happened. 'I'm only telling you,' I said, 'because I think you've a right to know, not because I think there's anything to worry about.'

'And when did you become the judge of what's worth worrying about?' He wasn't happy. Maybe I shouldn't have told him.

'What do you want to do?' I asked.

'There's nothing we can do as you've already said. He's your best friend.'

'He won't tell anyone, Gil. I know Mo. He means what he says.'

'Just be aware, Benjamin, that the people we're up against will exploit any weakness they can. Any relationship you have, any person you love, is ripe for exploitation in their eyes. If MI5 ever get hold of him …'

'MI5 are never going to get hold of him,' I said loudly. 'Why would they?' Mo was not going to get hurt because of who I was.

'We don't know that,' Gil said slowly. 'So stop being naïve.'

I close my eyes against the tears welling up. What do the Qureshis think of me now? My family are dead, and they'll know the truth. They'll have seen my picture and listened to the news. But worse, their son's caught up in it. I bet his father was there when he made that appeal, trying to protect him. They were good to me and I deceived them. I hurt them all.

CHAPTER 19

Benjamin

'I've decided not to go to France,' Jess says. 'I've spoken to Xav and he's cool with it – it's more important I prepare for uni.'

'But you were only going for a week,' I say. 'I thought you wanted a holiday.' This is not good. I think she's changed her mind because of me.

'I can see them later in the year. I've got other things to focus on right now, haven't I?' She smiles mischievously.

When Jess is out, it's not difficult to sneak into her room and check the website again. I delay looking at it, afraid of what will follow, but now Tom has left a message. *Your bed is ready and waiting. Just let us know when to expect you. We'll pick you up.* Then his code name: *49*. It's that simple. Let them know a date. They'll tell me where to meet and make it safe. I stare at the screen. But can I do it? Really, any of it? I close my eyes and think of my mother – and I don't know.

We spoke about it once, and only once: my mother's time with the Disciples. It was not long after Gil had dislocated my shoulder, and I was glad I had nothing to do with them. Yet a streak of shame pulsed through me; I knew I'd failed. Then one evening, Gemma and I were in the kitchen making an aubergine coconut curry. We were relaxed and I just said, 'Mum, when did you stop being an active Disciple?'

She stopped cooking and looked across at me. I wasn't sure if she'd answer, but she said softly, 'Not long after you were born.'

Relief. We could talk about it.

'It was because of me then?'

She didn't respond immediately. 'Before you born,' she said in a hushed voice, 'the moments in my life when I'd felt most alive were during active operations with the Disciples. I felt so powerful – partly because of the sheer terror of it, and surviving something you might not survive. It was exhilarating.' She paused, her face serious. 'Then you were born, and Gil almost died. He lost his hand, and something changed inside me. Suddenly, I didn't need that exhilaration anymore. It cost too much. And what I felt for you was the most ferocious love. I wasn't going to let anything come between you and me.'

She was once a different person, somebody else back then. I didn't like that feeling.

'Don't think I don't understand why you've wanted to join them,' she said, 'because I do. But I'm glad he hurt you. I'm glad he stopped you, because I couldn't bear it if somebody else did … the police or MI5.'

I stood there speechless. He did it on purpose. He *hurt me* on purpose. I couldn't reply, but later I realised the shame had gone.

The door to Adam's study is open. He's sitting at his desk and I knock to let him know I'm there.

'I'd like to speak to you.' It's the first time I've approached him like this.

He motions for me to come in and I shut the door. 'Take a seat,' he says, drawing out the stool by his piano.

'I'd like your advice,' I say quietly. 'I'd like to find some way of getting my life back.'

He watches me. 'Okay,' he says softly.

'I was good at what I was doing. I was studying hard. I know if I were able to continue, I'd go somewhere with it.'

'I don't doubt that.'

'But I've no idea how I do that.'

He's thoughtful. 'It's probably good we're having this discussion. There may not be a simple answer.'

'No?'

'No. I think you have to accept,' he says slowly, 'that you can't get your life back. Not without … reinventing yourself. Becoming someone else and living as that person.'

The room has a snug, comfortable feel, which is at odds with the conversation we're having. I need to say it, to take the risk. 'You mean like you did.'

He doesn't reply, but his shoulders tense.

'I know who you are, Adam,' I whisper. 'I know you were with my father when he lost his hand. I know you're brave. I want to understand how I survive like you did.'

'How did you work out who I am?'

'I didn't.' I tell him about the photo Jess showed me. I tell the truth because I know he won't do anything to her; he loves her too much. I also make it clear what I told her. 'And I promise you, I'll never do anything to compromise your safety. I will always keep your secret. No one will ever learn I've been here.'

'No, no one can know that,' he says and I sense his fear.

'I believe you can teach me how to be a different person. How I can accept I'll never be called Benjamin again or tell that truth. How I live with that every day for the rest of my life.'

A silence extends between us.

'You've been honest, Benjamin, so I will be honest back. You face a challenge. Being Adam McKenzie has not been as difficult for me as it might have been. You see I have my sister and cousin. We share the lie. Sometimes, we even speak to each other using our real names. And I married a woman who knows me, *really* knows me. All of those things have helped, but you don't have them.' He pauses. 'I wish I had something comforting to say. I wish I could tell you it will be easy, but you're eighteen and you've already lost both your parents. MI5 killed them so I think you know it won't be easy.'

I can't speak. He's certainly honest. Eventually I say, 'I don't have any brothers or sisters, and I've never found it easy to let people close to me.'

'That's understandable.'

'What you've said is hard to accept.'

'Yes, so take your time. Think it through. There will be practical things we can do. We'll talk again soon.'

I'm sitting with my clothes on and yet I feel naked. *I've never found it easy to let people close to me.* I've said it how it is and now it won't change. I have a future, but I must face it alone. I rise and turn to leave.

'Benjamin,' Adam's voice is soft behind me. 'We've grown to like you. I hope you realise you can stay as long as you need.'

I nod. 'Thank you. You've been very kind to me. Sometimes, I'm not really sure why.'

'Sometimes we act from our hearts more than our heads.'

I nod again, although I'm not sure why, and then go to my room.

I lie on my bed and shut my eyes. I'm so tired.

'Benjamin.' It's his voice again. Gil. 'What are you doing?' He likes to turn up when I feel my worst.

'Trying to figure out how I live the rest of my life.'

'You know where to start. Keep your nerve. Give Tom a date. And let him arrange things for you.'

'What if it's a mistake?' I open my eyes and meet his. 'What if despite everything, and all the plans we made, there's a mistake in it? And then the cost is too high.'

He shakes his head. 'I understand you're afraid. Don't be afraid, or rather, fear is natural, but don't be *too* afraid.'

'Gil, I'm not strong like you.'

'Is that what you're afraid of?'

'Yes.'

'Benjamin, if I didn't know you were strong, I'd never have chosen you to create Phoenix. I'd have done something else.' Then he says slowly, 'Dominic never thought he was strong enough either, but he was.'

There's more I want to say. 'Is it possible that, somewhere out there, I have a brother or sister? You shagged a lot of women.'

'It's possible, but I think if I'd got any other women pregnant they'd have been only too happy to let me know.'

'I'd like to have had a brother or sister.'

'You probably would have. Gemma and I tried. She had a miscarriage.'

I'm shocked. 'I didn't know that.'

'You were very young and she protected you from it – from how upset she was.'

A vague memory. Lifting the toilet seat and seeing blood. 'It's what women do,' she'd said, but I never saw blood like that again. I swallow hard. 'I don't want to be so alone, Gil.'

'You're not, Benjamin. You have the Disciples. I always told you they will provide the protection you need.'

'They barely know me, Gil.'

'Barely know you? You might be their future.'

Then he goes. He vanishes with that last sentence, and I try not to think about what he means.

CHAPTER 20

Jess

Benjamin and I are snuggled together on my bed.

'You were in Dad's study for ages yesterday,' I say, hoping he'll tell me about it. 'You must have had a good chat.'

'Yeah.' He smiles, but he's got that dreamy look he gets when he's not going to say any more. Then he asks softly, 'Jess, did you ever wish you had a brother or sister?'

'Yes and no. It would have been nice to have had somebody to play with and I liked the idea of an older brother, because then I'd meet his friends, but I've also known it would never happen.'

'No? But your parents were young when they had you.'

'Yeah, but Mum almost died when I was born. It was a huge traumatic event so there was no way she was going to have another baby after that.'

'Seriously?'

'Yeah. If it wasn't for Dad, she'd probably be dead. He saved her, but it really affected him too.'

He props himself on his elbows. 'Your mum almost died and your father saved her?'

'That's what I've been told. Not that I know all the details. Mum went into labour, and everything happened so fast there was no way they could drive to hospital in time, and there was no way an ambulance could get here on time, so Dad had to deal with it.'

Benjamin's clearly shocked.

'And when the ambulance did get here, they said Mum was very lucky to be alive. Apparently, there was a lot of blood. And what it's taught me is if I ever want a baby I won't live in the middle of nowhere like here.'

He's silent, staring at me. 'Jess, that's …' He shakes his head.

'I know, heavy duty. You'll never hear them talk about it, but that's why I don't have a brother or sister.' In a way I'm pleased I've had to opportunity to tell him. 'My beginning was dramatic and Mum was only twenty. Dad was even younger.'

He sits up straighter. 'What is it about your father that means he's involved in these near-death experiences? First with Gil and then with your mother.'

I shrug. 'I don't know. I think it's why he lives such a boring life now – too much excitement when he was young.'

We're all in the kitchen eating dinner. I'm half listening to the news, which is the usual boring stuff. Some item about surveillance. Government scientists are about to pilot a new technology: a surface material that when touched picks up a person's DNA. They'll test it on the tubes and buses in London.

Dad's voice explodes. 'When will they stop? When will they stop this bullshit where they think they can own any part of us? They're actually going to monitor us with the sweat from our skin.'

'Yup,' says Greg. 'And insist it's all about cutting down on crime and increasing national security.'

'And you know they're going to get away with it, don't you?' Dad says. 'They'll find a way of pushing it through parliament.'

'Of course they will. I never understand why people don't wake up to what's really going on.'

My family talk like this on occasion, although I don't often join in. But Benjamin's stopped eating. He says, 'Because the system's rigged to ensure everyone believes the same old narrative. So they don't even want to wake up. Ignorance is bliss.' It's the first time he's joined in a political discussion. He turns slowly to me and shrugs. 'It's kind of obvious.'

I don't reply, but Dad's rattled. I can see he's really upset.

Later, I'm in the living room playing my guitar when Dad comes in.

'Jess, have you been in my study?'

'No.' I play a G chord followed by a D.

'Benjamin's notebook is missing.'

I stop. 'Are you sure?'

'Of course I'm sure.'

'What do you think's happened to it?' I ask, uneasy. I don't normally lie to my father.

'I'm going to speak to him.'

I'd been feeling relaxed but now … I didn't even think about what would happen if my father noticed the notebook had gone. I assumed he'd trust it was just there. What made him check it anyway? Benjamin said they'd talked about his future but they couldn't have discussed the notebook. Is this because of the news? Dad's wound up.

Benjamin's footsteps are on the stairs, and then the door to Dad's study closes. At first I hear nothing and try not to worry. But then their voices rise and I creep into the hallway.

'Don't insult my fucking intelligence! I'm not stupid, Benjamin.'

Oh, my God. My father doesn't speak to people like that. He's mild-mannered. When he does blow it, it's not like this.

'Did you not compute for a moment what danger you might be putting me in – or Jess? Or any of my family. Do you know how hard we've had to work to stay hidden, to live a quiet life, to disappear? I, Benjamin, was involved in bringing down a whole fucking department in LifeStar Corporation. Do you think they're the kind of company who'll forgive that with ease? Or the government?'

'Adam, I promise you, the site was legitimate, and I switched off every possible tracker.' Benjamin's voice falters. 'The only person who'll have seen it is Tom. And he doesn't know anything. He doesn't know I'm here. I'll never reveal that to *anyone*.'

'You have no idea what you've done, or what could possibly happen.'

I stand there, frozen. Something's gone wrong, very wrong, and I've played a part in it. The door to the study opens. Dad's eyes look wild.

'I'm sorry,' I say, shaking. 'I'm sorry, Dad. I gave him the notebook because he had nothing else from his father. I didn't think it could do any harm. He was sad and I didn't want him to be sad.'

Dad motions for me to join them. Benjamin looks pale and tense.

'Well,' Dad says, 'he told me he took it, not you. So he's kind enough to lie to protect you, but it still just proves he's a liar.'

I stand near Benjamin and my father looks awful. Old and battered, like a hammer's hit him.

'Jess, you need to realise what a dangerous individual Benjamin is. He manipulated you to get the notebook. He's used it to make contact with the Disciples. It's quite possible that everything he's told us is a lie.'

Bewildered, I turn to Benjamin. 'What? You said you weren't a member of the Disciples.'

His face twitches. 'I'm not.'

'But you made contact with them?'

'Only … only because they're my route to safety.'

I listen, but I don't really know what he's saying.

'Gil Zimmerman was someone I grew to love,' Dad says slowly. 'He saved my life, but that never changed the fact that he was a very dangerous and manipulative man.'

Benjamin grows visibly paler.

'Like father, like son.' Dad's voice is brittle. 'I just didn't want to see it.'

Benjamin shivers. His lower lip trembles. 'I don't know why he sent me here.'

'Because he knew I'd take you in – that was an act of wisdom for you, but possibly the worst mistake for me.'

'Adam, I—'

'Shut up, Benjamin. You think you know the story. You think that photo of the motorbike, and all the footage from that time is the story. It was all about LifeStar and the role my father played as a whistle-blower. The entire world knows that story, but that's not all of it.'

Dad collapses back into his chair. My head swims with questions. There are so many things he's never told me.

'I'd like you both to go now,' he says. 'I need to think this through.'

'I'll leave tonight,' Benjamin says firmly. His face is ashen. 'I'll go pack and then—'

'Oh, no, you won't,' my father spits. 'There's no way you're walking out of here to spread chaos.'

'That's not what I'm going to do.'

'Benjamin, you don't leave here until it's safe. And I don't mean safe for you, but safe for us.' He stares at Benjamin belligerently. 'Have the insight and decency to at least do that.'

Benjamin looks down, he's breathing quickly. 'Okay.'

We leave the room together. I insist he goes up the stairs first as though I need to keep an eye on him. We stop on the landing outside my room.

'You lied,' I say, although my voice doesn't sound right, 'about everything.'

'No, Jess. I didn't.' His eyes are sad and beautiful. I hate him because I can't hate him. There's a question that aches in my throat but I can't get it out.

'When did you join the Disciples?' I ask instead.

'I didn't.'

'What, you've always just been a member?' I don't know how this has happened. How the world has changed in minutes. 'Like father, like son.' I try to sound hard, like my father, but I don't manage it.

He doesn't reply. At least it's better than lying again.

'And you said you love me.' My eyes fill.

'I do,' he says softly.

I shake my head. 'How can I possibly believe you?'

'You can't,' he says. 'That's the worst part about lying, nobody knows when you're telling the truth. I love you but you don't believe me.'

The person I've been so close to is a stranger. I sense his distress but it's nothing compared to mine. Everything's gone wrong – he knows it and I do. We go to our rooms. I only fall asleep when my pillow is wet with tears.

CHAPTER 21

Jess

Dad has a migraine. I heard him throwing up, and given everything that happened last night, I'm not surprised. He'll probably stay in bed today. I help Greg with the breakfasts and try to act normal, but it's taking everything I've got not to cry. The truth's really sinking in.

Mum comes into the kitchen. 'You alright?' she asks.

I nod because I don't want her to worry. She goes and I clean up the breakfast stuff. Greg gets out all the kitchen knives and arranges them on the counter.

'They need sharpening,' he says. 'Could hardly cut the rind off the bacon this morning.'

I sense that he, and I, are delaying getting on with the rest of our day. While I'm with Greg, I can just control my emotions. Without him, I'll start crying and maybe not be able to stop.

Benjamin comes into the kitchen. It's the time he always comes down for breakfast. He's just following the usual rhythm of his day, but surely he knows nothing's normal now. I can't look at him face on. He pours out some cereal and goes to the fridge. He doesn't look at me either, but his hand is shaking as he pours out his soya milk. He eats too quickly; he's nervous. Greg keeps sharpening the knives. None of us speaks. Benjamin finishes his cereal as Mum comes back into the kitchen. The tension in the room is terrible.

Greg stops what he's doing. 'Before you go, Benjamin. Put your hand down here.' He points to a place on the counter just inches away from the knives.

I turn to Mum. *What's going on?*

She signs, 'Say nothing.'

Benjamin doesn't put his hand on the counter. He and Greg just stare at each other.

'Put your hand on the counter,' Greg repeats, but the tone of his voice makes me shiver.

'Why?'

'Why do you think?' He picks up one of the knives.

There's a long pause. My breath quickens.

'You want to cut me,' Benjamin says, barely audible.

'Do you think I want to cut you, or do you know I'm going to cut you?' My grandfather is terrifying. He's not the man I know. This is like some kind of horror movie and I want off the set.

Benjamin stands very still – it's obvious he's afraid. 'I know you're going to cut me.'

'Good, then we understand each other. Put your hand on the counter.'

'Is this to punish me?'

'No, it's just to make myself clear.'

'You're clear,' Benjamin says loudly, trembling slightly. He still won't put his hand on the counter. I don't want him to either. I want to tell Greg to stop, but Mum's expression is ferocious.

'What's clear?' Greg asks.

'That you'll do whatever you need to protect your family,' Benjamin says slowly, deliberately.

'Good. We do understand each other. It goes to show you've been paying attention to the chats we've had.'

He nods.

'So you understand that if I need to, I will kill you,' Greg says matter-of-factly. 'I know exactly where I'll put your body. I've got a gun that's loaded, and I'm not afraid to use a knife – it's messy but it does the trick too.' He pauses. The kitchen is silent, except for Benjamin's breathing. 'I've liked you, Benjamin, but I love my family and you understand I will do whatever is necessary to protect them. You will not contact the Disciples again, and if you even try to, it will be reason enough to kill you.'

Benjamin doesn't move. He's frozen.

'Understand?' Greg says.

'Yes.'

'Now, put your hand on the counter.'

There's a long pause. I'm holding my breath.

Benjamin says, shaky, 'You still want to cut me?'

'Not in a way that will hurt you.'

Benjamin winces. He looks pale and sweaty. I can smell his fear and want to tell Greg to stop but I can't speak.

'You've got to trust me now,' Greg says.

Benjamin hesitantly puts his hand on the counter. Greg picks up the small paring knife and very carefully draws it down the back of Benjamin's hand. It's the lightest cut, probably not much more than a paper cut, but his blood beads on the surface of his skin.

'That's so that you remember how serious I am.'

Benjamin slowly draws his hand back.

'Now go upstairs,' Greg says, 'put a plaster over that, and then get outside. There's work for you to do.'

Benjamin leaves quickly. Greg still looks terrifying. I didn't know someone so old could be so scary, but he's strong. He turns to Mum and they exchange a knowing look. She nods, satisfied. Then he turns to me.

'Come here, Jess,' he says, softening. He opens his arms to hug me. I embrace him and try not to cry but don't succeed.

Dad surfaces in the evening. We eat together while Greg takes food up to Benjamin. We can't face him at the moment, and he's staying out of the way. We need to adjust to what's happened. The one thing I'm thankful for is that none of them realise that Benjamin and I have been sleeping together.

'I'm sorry,' Dad says as he finishes. 'I made a wrong call. And I realise now we should have destroyed his stuff. When we agreed to let him stay here we should have burnt the notebook, buried the gun, and smashed the memory stick.'

Greg clears his throat. 'Instead, we did the decent thing. They were obviously important to him. We just didn't imagine he'd be so stupid as to actually use them here.'

Dad shakes his head.

I want all of this to be different. 'Is it possible that he's not a bad person?' I ask. 'I mean that he doesn't *want* to be a bad person, just …' My words slip away.

Dad says, 'His father was Gil Zimmerman, and like you said, Greg, Gil would always have used him. If I try to think the best, perhaps he's somebody who's had little choice. And the truth is I don't think he's had much *real* experience of the Disciples, because getting that notebook and not anticipating that I might notice, not putting it back, was just incompetent. It's the sort of stupid mistake …' He pauses. 'That I might have made at his age.'

We're all quiet. Surely that means it was alright that I loved him. I didn't know any better. I couldn't have known.

'The problem with Benjamin,' Mum says slowly, 'is that he's like a wounded animal. I sense it in myself, a part of me that might want to look after him. In a way he's never had a real father – he's Gil's son. But wounded animals can be very dangerous.'

Yes, that's it. That's why I can't hate him. Even now, when I should.

'Aye, wounded animals can be very dangerous,' Greg says bluntly, 'and on occasion, I shoot them.'

Dad laughs. It breaks the tension. 'I'll speak to him tomorrow,' he says. 'When I feel calmer. When I can think straight.'

I lie in bed and gaze at the ceiling. Benjamin will be in bed too. I strain to hear him but there's nothing. No creak of a floorboard. No sigh. I stare through the dark until I'm sleeping.

A noise wakes me. At first, I'm not sure what it is. Then I hear someone talking. It's muffled but I try to tune in. It's Benjamin's voice but who's he talking to? It's four in the morning. I open my bedroom door and listen.

'Everything's messed up now … don't tell me you can help … I tried but I was never as good as you …'

I start up the stairs. He'll hear me coming.

'Benjamin,' I whisper, my ear at his door. He's quiet now. I turn the handle and very slowly open it. The curtains are open and he's standing at the window; the moon is shining in behind him. He turns to me slowly.

'You look like you've seen a ghost,' I say, shocked at his appearance.

'Maybe I have.' There is nothing aggressive about him, he just looks afraid.

'You should get into bed. It's cold now.'

He does as I say, as though he's a small child that needs instruction. Every instinct in me tells me he needs to be hugged – he's so alone. I pull up the covers around his neck and snuggle him in. His eyes are wide and glassy. 'Sleep,' I say, then go back to my room.

CHAPTER 22

Benjamin

Adam calls me into his study and shuts the door. I feel like I'm sitting in the headmaster's office, only I never sat in the headmaster's office. I was too good a student.

'I want to clear everything up,' he says. He's calmer today, but I sense his determination. 'What's on the memory stick?'

'I don't know.'

'That's a lie. Now tell me the truth.'

I try to appear calm, controlling my breath. What do I do?

'My intention is to destroy it,' he says matter-of-factly, and he opens his hand. It's sitting on his palm. 'Unless you can give me a good reason not to.'

Oh, God, no. My thoughts spin. 'I-I'd like to ask you not to do that.' My mouth is dry. I sound breathy. 'It would be going against Gil's wishes, and … while I don't fully understand your relationship with him, I think you might want to respect his final wish.' Have I done enough to save it?

He leans forward and whispers, 'I might, Benjamin, but I want you to tell me what's on it.'

I look into his blue eyes. Who is Adam, *really*?

'Tell me,' he whispers, 'and I won't destroy it.' He turns the memory stick over and back with his fingers, playing with it, or more likely me.

'It's an operation,' I say slowly. 'We worked on it for some time. A significant amount of time. It's different to the others. And now it matters even more. Now he's dead.'

'How many people does it involve?'

'Mostly, probably, just me.'

'What about guns, bombs or incendiary devices?'

'None. Nothing like that.'

'There's no violence?'

'No. I told you, it's different.'

'But you're very good with computers, digital technology and I suspect much more.'

'So you understand,' I say softly.

'Where do the Disciples come into it?'

'I'd need somebody, somewhere to hide – in the event. They provide security, false papers, things you understand. They got you your new identity.'

'But the Disciples have been infiltrated, Benjamin.'

I freeze. I wasn't expecting that.

'Or don't you realise that?' he asks gently.

'My father always said that … if he died, and it wasn't during an operation, I should take it that he'd been betrayed.'

'What if it's Tom?'

Did I mention Tom? I don't remember ever mentioning Tom but I must have.

'No,' I say with difficulty. 'No way.' Yet I can see he really thinks it could be Tom.

'They killed my mother, Adam. Tom loved her, okay. He was there throughout my childhood. He loved her. There's no way he'd have betrayed them.'

His eyes hold mine; they pin me down. 'He put your father on trial when I knew him.'

'No.' I shake my head. 'Bullshit. Watch what you're saying. Tom's a loyal person. One of the best.' I don't want to lose it with him, but I might. He's pushing me too far.

'Benjamin, listen to me. You need to hear me,' he says firmly. 'I'm not going to destroy the memory stick, but I am going to ask you to give it up. To recognise that you cannot carry out any such operation without it almost certainly resulting in your capture, if not your death.'

'You don't know that,'

'Let it go, Benjamin. I lost my father at your age. I sought revenge, and it almost killed me and it almost killed Gil. And that was with the Disciples' support. Whereas you cannot rely on them. They've been infiltrated, and you don't know where the traitor is.'

I'm not quite in my body. This is worse than the other day. 'You're just saying that because you want to destroy the final link there is to Gil. You're taking my father away from me even after death!'

'Benjamin. He's gone. I can't take him away from you – he's already dead. Dead. But you want to live. And I want to ensure you live too.'

A wave of nausea crashes over me, but I won't allow myself to be sick.

'He's gone, Benjamin. I have to get it through to you.'

I try to slow my breathing, but I don't manage it and there are tears on my cheeks.

Then Adam's hand is on my shoulder. His touch is firm and warm. Neither of us speaks until I'm calmer.

'I know how painful the truth is,' he says, softer. 'But you must accept it. Your life depends on it, and my safety.'

It's evening, and they call me down to eat with them. I've planned what to say. I'll show contrition because whatever else I do or don't do, they need to trust me again.

I walk into the kitchen and they're all sitting there.

'I'm sorry,' I say, although my tongue feels numb. 'I'm sorry that I caused you to fear for your safety, and that I acted without speaking to you, Adam, or even recognising that I should have. And I'm sorry, Jess, that I let you bring the notebook to me. I don't believe I was manipulating you, but I understand that it may feel like that.' I should say something to Mary and Greg, but I can't address them directly after the incident with the knife.

'Have you learnt your lesson?' Greg asks softly.

I nod. 'I hope … I hope you don't hate me.'

'Do you think I hate you?' he asks, but not aggressively.

'You're angry with me. I get that.'

'Indeed. I want you to learn your lesson but I don't hate you.'

Our eyes meet, and then I turn to Mary. 'You've only shown me kindness, I hope I can make things up in some way.'

Mary's the hardest to deal with; I'm sure she can see all the holes in me.

'I'll give you the benefit of the doubt,' she says, then motions for me to sit at the table. Food is served. I listen as they chat, and let out a private sigh of relief. Somehow the situation is saved.

I sit in the dark and quiet of the shed. For days now, Jess has been getting ready for university. They're all helping her to load up the car – instruments, duvet, books, and tins of food. It's a family thing; they won't miss me. Adam and Mary leave early tomorrow with Jess. They should be in Glasgow by lunchtime then they'll see Jess settled into halls. They'll spend the night away, now that there are fewer guests.

'Make the most of it,' Greg said. 'Benjamin and I will hold the fort.'

'Of course,' I said obligingly.

I sit in the shed and try not to think. There's the smell of the wood, and the old cushions that go with the garden furniture. It's all so ordinary. Nothing exceptional. Yet I have a choice to make. 'Sometimes we act from our hearts more than our heads.' Adam's words have stayed with me.

Someone is coming down the garden.

'Benjamin.' Jess opens the door. 'What are you doing in here?'

'Chilling,' I say. 'Did you get everything into the car?'

'Yeah, easily. Do you … do you want to go for a walk? It won't be dark for another hour and my folks don't mind.'

'Sure.' It's her last night here and maybe we'll find a way to say goodbye.

We head out the back. I glance briefly behind at their cottage; it's already beginning to stand out against the darkening sky.

'You excited?' I ask as we walk along.

'Yeah, really excited now. And maybe a bit nervous too.'

'Well, that's only natural.'

'Did you feel nervous when you started uni?'

'Hm, not really, but it was different. At first I wasn't staying in halls, and then when I was, it wasn't far from home. I got to take my dirty washing back and have a meal with Mum.' I shrug and smile.

'Well, it'll be too long a trip for me and my dirty washing.' She chuckles.

We walk for a while in silence.

'I'll miss you,' she says.

'No, you won't, or if you do, you'll be making a mistake.'

She doesn't respond to that. She's going to have a great time.

'I think, really, I've been lucky with what happened between us,' she says.

'Yes? Why's that?'

'Just because I'll be starting uni, and I won't be as awkward and gawky as I might have been if you'd not come along.

Instead, I think I can get a boyfriend now. I can be cool enough for a guy to like me.'

'Okay. So maybe I have been good for you.'

'You have, Benjamin.' She turns to me, her eyes bright. 'And despite everything, a part of me will always love you.'

It takes me a moment to respond. 'Thank you, Jess. I …' I want to get something right. 'You've been a friend. A very special friend. I've not had that before. A *big* part of me will always love you.'

Her eyes grow glassy with tears. We might both cry, but that won't help anything. Instead, we keep walking. Jess points to the setting sun, and how beautiful the sky is tonight.

CHAPTER 23

Benjamin

They leave early. I'm in bed pretending to sleep when they drive away, then I get up and help Greg with the breakfasts. We've found a way to get on again. After some chores, he suggests I take a couple of hours off in the afternoon. 'I've lived with Jess every day of her life,' he says, and I sense he wants to be alone.

I leave him in the kitchen trying to fix some old electric gadget and go upstairs. I creep into Jess's room. She spent days packing but there's still stuff on her desk and the floor; she obviously couldn't be bothered to put it back. I search her desk and wardrobe, then find what I want in a drawer under her bed. An old tablet – I knew she'd have one. It's ancient but I don't care and take it and a charger up to my room. After I turn it on, it connects with the internet and I go to the website where I type in my one-word message: *Tomorrow*. Then I hide the tablet under my pillow, lie back and think through the rest of the plan: how I'll get to where they tell me to go. It hits me. I'm in the middle of nowhere here, and wherever they suggest, it could take hours to get to. Returning to the website, I send another one-word message. *Late*. Shit, am I already messing up? I feel slightly sick. I need to keep contact to the minimum. A reply comes through in an hour. *Golden Fleece Services. M6. Midnight.* It's happening. It's real. Tomorrow I'll see Tom. We'll meet at a motorway service station. It will be dark and I'll be back in England.

Next, I focus on Gregory.

'D'you ever play chess?' I ask him over our evening meal.

'Chess?'

'Yeah. Fancy a game?'

He looks at me, surprised.

'It's so quiet without them. I …' I let my voice trail off.

'You mean the place is particularly quiet without Jess.'

'Yeah, it's really noticeable.'

'You miss her,' he says softly. 'Well, we're all going to have to get used to it. If it makes you feel better, we can play chess.' He perks up a bit.

Neither of us are particularly good players. There's no way I can drag it out so I prepare for what comes next. I can't get it wrong.

'I'm going to make myself a hot drink,' I say. 'What can I get you?'

He shakes his head but I can't have him refuse.

'Mint tea,' I say. 'I'll make us both a fresh mint tea.'

He mutters something and I pretend not to hear. In the kitchen, I boil the kettle and set out two mugs. The fresh mint's on the side and I cut us both a long stalk. Then I pull a couple of sleeping tablets out of my pocket. Dr Lee prescribed them ages ago when he stitched my arm. I didn't use them but I didn't throw them away. Crumbling them into Greg's mug, I make the tea and put it down by him. He shows no interest but we keep playing chess. Eventually, almost absent-mindedly, he picks up his tea and takes a sip. I keep the game going, willing him to keep drinking. An hour later he's drunk three quarters of his tea and that's hopefully enough. He yawns and says he's tired, and we both go to bed. I lie still until I guess he's asleep. Now it's a race against time. I pack my rucksack and tiptoe downstairs. Greg's snoring loudly; he must be out cold.

In Adam's study, I'm surprised to find my notebook in his desk drawer – it's not even locked, but then the damage is already done: I made contact. I don't actually need it now but put it in my rucksack. Looking around the room, I wonder where to search next. Even though it's futile, I check the cupboard behind the door and I'm stunned. The leather pouch is still there. The gun, the money and the memory stick are all just as they were when I arrived. I don't understand. How could Adam have left them there? It doesn't make sense. Surely he didn't trust me? He'd have been a fool to trust me. Icy cold fear slips down my spine. Is he MI5? Somebody who's allowing me to incriminate myself? Have they got him too?

I fall back into his desk chair and close my eyes; I need to think. What do I do now? This was meant to be the easy part. Fuck. I sit there, silent, almost paralysed.

'Benjamin, get on with it.' It's Gil's voice.

'What's going on?' I don't open my eyes, afraid that if I do he'll go.

'Who do you think Adam McKenzie is?'

'I've no idea any more,' I say, breathy.

'Dominic Minster was a Disciple,' he says pointedly.

I open my eyes. Gil is standing still, his expression questioning me.

'Are you saying he wanted me to find them?' I ask, incredulous.

'I'm saying he's a complex person. He was then and he still is.'

I let that sink in. I underestimated Adam.

'Now, get on with it,' Gil says.

I put the pouch in my rucksack then go to the shelf by the front door where they keep the keys to the pickup truck. I take them carefully but Greg's bedroom is too close, so I creep through the house and leave by the side door. Gravel crunches loudly beneath my feet and I pray Greg won't wake up. I sit behind the wheel and remember when Mum told me she'd teach me how to drive.

'To drive?' I'd exclaimed. 'To add to the toxic pollution around us?'

'It's a skill you must have. I don't expect you to ever own a car. That's not the point.' Then after a pause she'd said, 'Gil insists on it.'

Now, I understand why.

I drive off slowly, afraid Greg will charge out and place himself in front of the vehicle, but that doesn't happen. I'm quickly weaving down dark country lanes. It's the worst conditions: a moonless night, almost pitch black, and I barely know what I'm doing. My only consolation is there isn't another car about. But I get into my stride and within an hour I'm on the motorway. There's more traffic but I shift up to fourth gear, put my foot down and feel a rush of exhilaration as the truck speeds ahead.

Jess

I lie back in the unfamiliar bed. This is my home now. This small room with a desk and wardrobe. I've only unpacked a few of my belongings but I'll have loads of time tomorrow. Some of the others I'm sharing the flat with have arrived. We'll all use the same kitchen, and share bathroom facilities. The other people seem nice, but it will take a while to get to know them.

I'm glad Mum and Dad took me out tonight. We hardly ever do that and I think they enjoyed it too. I love sweet and sour chicken and crispy chilli beef. In a way it's a shame Greg missed out. I think of Benjamin in his room. Will he miss me? What will it be like when I eventually go home, and I'll have experienced a whole new world but nothing will have changed for him? I turn onto my side and fall asleep.

'You look like you've heard bad news,' I say. I'm in the foyer of Mum and Dad's hotel.

Dad makes an effort to smile. 'No, we're fine.'

They're not very good at hiding their emotions. Then I realise maybe they feel sad. They're going shortly and I'm staying. 'I'll still be coming home,' I say. 'I'm only at uni. It's not like I'm gone forever.'

'You'll still be coming home, Jess.' Dad's smile is genuine.

'I'm up for going to the art gallery with you,' I say. They suggested it yesterday, enjoying a bit of culture before heading back.

'No, we'll just hit the road,' Dad says softly. 'We'll go another time.'

I thought they'd want to spend the morning with me. We won't be seeing each other for weeks.

'Is something wrong?' I turn to Mum. Something must be wrong.

'We got a text from Greg,' she says slowly, 'he slipped yesterday. He's fine, but hobbling about a bit. It's best we get back.'

'Greg. You're sure he's okay?'

'Of course.' She half smiles. 'Don't worry.' Yet neither of them look like people who aren't worrying.

'He's got Benjamin to help him,' I say. 'If nothing else he can take care of him until you get back.'

They both nod. I kiss them before they get in the car, then watch them drive away. I walk back to the halls of residence. Now I start the rest of my life.

CHAPTER 24

Benjamin

I cross the border into England and stop in a small market town. When the shops open, I pull my baseball cap down low and buy something to eat and some stationery. Sipping coffee in the truck, I try to ignore how tired I am. I glance at my watch. Greg will be up now. He'll understand what I've done and what a liar I am. He's probably told Adam and Mary. Maybe even Jess knows too, but maybe not. Mary will protect her. She won't want me spreading any more hurt than I already have. 'Please be happy, Jess,' I whisper.

I write them a letter telling Greg where I'll be leaving the pickup truck. They can't exactly call the police to say their car's been nicked. I thank them for everything, and promise Adam I'll keep him safe. I enclose a gift for Jess, that's important too. They'll get it in a few days and by then, I'll be another person. A member of the Disciples. Everything Gil wanted of his son.

Golden Fleece Services. There are a few cars about and I park at a distance from them. Alert, I glance alternately ahead and then in the rear-view mirror. I open a can of Coke. Just before midnight I go inside to have a slash and as I walk back a motorbike drives over. The rider raises the visor on the helmet. It's Tom. Without saying a word, he motions to the pannier where

I find another helmet; I put it on and then straddle the bike. I hold him tight, aware we could be driving for hours.

Much later, we arrive at a small country cottage. There are fields on either side; I'm still in the middle of nowhere. We go in and take off our helmets. He looks older, strained, but he's still Tom; his grey-blond hair and beard have grown longer. His blue eyes hold mine.

He speaks first. 'This place is an old Disciples hideout. We haven't used it for years so it should be safe.'

'You've no idea how glad I am you're still alive.' My voice is too loud, my emotions too big.

He comes to me. We hug and I'm crying. 'They killed them, Tom. Those fucking, evil bastards. I was there. They just put fucking bullets in both their backs. They didn't have a chance.'

He withdraws from me a little, his cheeks streaked with tears too. 'I know.' He nods. We stand there a while, aching with our mutual hurt and anger.

'I think he was betrayed,' I say boldly.

'No doubt about it,' he says through clenched teeth. 'Things are toxic at the moment. They've hit us hard, Benjamin. There's a lot of tension and paranoia. Cesar and I don't spend more than two nights in any one location. We need to find the traitor and put a bullet through his head.'

Suddenly, I feel exhausted. 'Tom, if it's safe, I need to get some sleep. I've been up for days.'

'Yeah,' he says. 'Let's eat something first, have a drink, and then we'll get some sleep.'

I follow him into a small kitchen. He puts the kettle on and finds a packet of porridge. He makes it and I'm silent. The place is freezing.

'You look well, Benjamin,' he says softly. 'Wherever you've been, they've been looking after you.'

I don't respond. I won't talk about the McKenzies, not even with Tom.

'Were they current or ex-Disciples?' he asks, which doesn't seem the smartest question.

'I haven't been with anybody,' I say.

He nods and smiles. I eat my porridge in silence then he takes me upstairs and shows me a room with a bed. There's a musty smell and the bedclothes don't look clean, but I don't care. Exhausted, I flop down on the bed. Tom stands at the door, watching me.

'Sometimes,' I say very quietly, 'Gemma would do that. You look like a concerned parent.'

'We're practically family, Benjamin, yes?'

I nod. It's some comfort.

'Get some rest now. I'll be in the room next door. We'll talk later. I promise you revenge will be sweet.'

I want to tell him I care less about revenge than staying alive. He goes and finally I sleep.

When I wake light is streaming into the room. It must be late morning, maybe even early afternoon – I've been out for hours. I rise slowly and go downstairs. In the kitchen, two things strike me at once. Tom is sitting at the table, and on the table are my notebook, the gun, and the memory stick.

'You went through my things.' I'm surprised.

He shrugs. 'Of course. I wouldn't be your father's second in command if I didn't check your stuff.' I must look bemused because he says, 'Much as I love you, Benjamin, anything's possible.'

He's serious. 'You really think I might be a traitor?' I'm shocked. 'That I'd actually conspire in the death of my own parents.' I shake my head. Maybe I don't know him anymore. 'You really are paranoid.' Events have obviously affected him.

'Things have been difficult,' he murmurs.

'Well, I'm putting that stuff back, now you've checked it.' I get my rucksack.

'We'll need this.' He holds on to the memory stick.

I nod.

'I think it's possible,' he says slowly, 'that this is the only copy.'

'Let's hope so, given what you've told me.'

'And you're the only one with the password.' He smiles. 'I'll get my laptop.'

'We have to plan its implementation,' I say firmly. 'I'm not going to act until we know it's safe.'

'Of course,' he says.

We sit side by side at the table, the laptop open before us. I pick up the memory stick and insert it in the USB port.

'You're nervous,' Tom says gently.

Is it that obvious? 'I'm not like you. I'm not experienced at these things.'

'You're not bringing the network down today,' he says.

No, I think, unsure why my heart is pounding.

The screen asks for my password. I put it in and press return. Password incorrect. I swallow. I type it in more slowly; I can't make another mistake. Password incorrect.

'Shit.' I'm sweating.

'Take your time.' Tom's eyes feel like they're burning my skin.

'If it fails to recognise it a third time, we'll be permanently locked out.' I stare at the screen. I don't understand. The password's engraved in my memory.

'Take it out,' Tom says carefully. 'Relax, and then start again.'

I take it out, turn it over in my hand and inhale deeply. I'm looking at it, silently begging it to behave, when I notice the small print: 128GB. It's meant to be 1TB. It's not the stick my father gave me. Terror and confusion collide in my mind. Tom keeps watching; I sense he's wary.

'I need to go to the bathroom,' I say.

'Yeah. Take a few minutes. Splash some water on your face.'

I close the door behind me and lock it. I need to calm down but I can't. Now I see it. Adam let me get my things back – because he's got the memory stick. Who is Adam McKenzie? Some kindly middle-aged dad spending his days running a B&B – or a cold-blooded Disciple? Or a traitor? But a traitor would never have cared for me like he did; he'd have handed me in sooner. Some middle-aged dad wouldn't want me to fuck up. A cold-blooded Disciple would do whatever was needed. He knows there's a traitor. He won't risk me giving Phoenix away.

I go back into the kitchen. 'It's not the right memory stick.'

'What?'

'I need to go for a while,' I say. 'I'll be back again, but I need to go and get it.'

'Benjamin, are you out of your fucking mind?'

'No, I just need to get it. I should have checked it when I left but I just assumed it would be okay.'

'Who's got it?' Tom asks firmly.

'It doesn't matter. I'm going to get it.'

'No, Benjamin. I'm going to get it. I'm sorry but I can't leave you to make any more mistakes.'

'I can't tell you who it's with. I made a promise.'

'Benjamin, stop the fucking bullshit. This isn't the school playground. Who's got it?'

'I can't tell you,' I say, louder. 'You know how it works. You said yourself you're not spending more than two nights in any one location. The only way cells survive is by not knowing each other.'

He hits me hard across the face. I'm stunned.

'You either tell me who's got it,' he says, 'or I'll assume you're the traitor and treat you likewise.'

I am no longer entirely in my body. Some part of me is looking down from above, and Adam's words repeat in my head. 'What if it's Tom?'

I run for it. Out of the kitchen, and towards the front door.

But it's locked. There's no key. He hits me from behind and I'm on the floor. He wrenches my arms back and I feel cold metal handcuffs around my wrists.

'Stop struggling.' He sits on my back, grabs my hair and hits my head on the stone floor. I shriek but stop struggling. Fear grips me. I'm in trouble. I'm only just beginning to realise what that means.

CHAPTER 25

Benjamin

My arms are bound and I'm strapped to a wooden chair. Tom kicks it over and I go crashing down. Stone floors are the worst. My right eye is barely open, swollen from one of his punches. Tom's made it clear he'll kill me.

'They want to know who's been hiding you, Benjamin, and they want the memory stick. You've already given me the password, clever boy – you didn't think to hide that, did you?'

'I was stupid enough to trust you,' I mumble.

'And now you can tell me what else I need to know, because although they prefer you alive, they'll accept you dead, if that's what it takes.'

Given the pain I'm in, I know he's already broken some of my ribs, and I try not to think about internal bleeding. He punched my stomach too many times; it made me vomit.

'Like father, like son,' he'd said brutally as he hit my left hand hard with a rolling pin, then pulled on it until I screamed as the handcuff ripped my flesh. It's probably broken too.

I'm winded, aware my body's gone into shock; I can't stop shivering. But he's tired too.

He brings my chair upright. 'We'll take a little rest, shall we?' he says, breathy. 'So you can consider your future, and just how painful it's going to get. I'm not afraid to gouge your eyes out.'

When I asked him why he did it, how he could have loved my mother and then betrayed her, he just punched me. He has no conscience. He's sold his soul and that's what terrifies me most. If I lose my eyes … just thinking of what I studied … I throw up again but it's only bile.

He drinks from a glass of water then brings it to me. I fear he'll smash it into my mouth, but instead he gently lets me drink.

'This is actually the hardest part, Benjamin,' he says softly. 'This rest we're having. It's when your mind can adjust to what's happening. When you realise that maybe holding back that name, all the loyalty you're showing, just isn't worth it because in the end everyone cracks.'

He sits comfortably in a chair opposite me. 'They've known who you are, Benjamin, for some time. Of course, they understand you're a smart kid, very smart, and essentially a good kid. And your friend Mo and your professor, Atholl, both testified on your behalf.'

I cry again. Hearing Mo's name in this situation cuts into me.

'Poor Benjamin,' Tom says as if he's kind. 'You just want to go back to your life, and that's possible. You only need to tell me who you've been with. You don't need to face them. They need never know you told us. We'll get the memory stick back, and you can get on with your studies again and doing all those things a young man your age wants to do.' He smiles as if it's easy. 'Think about it.'

He goes to a shelf where I hadn't even noticed there were books and picks one up on playing golf. 'I'm just going to read a while.' The bastard's never played golf.

'Why did you do it?' I ask softly. I don't have the strength to speak any louder.

He watches me. 'You'll really start to feel how much I've hurt you,' he says. 'Your adrenaline will subside, you'll feel exhausted, and realise the pain you're in.'

'Why did you do it?'

'Your father never understood that power should be shared. Despite everything he preached, everything he said he stood for, he never managed to do that. I realised I'd had enough and I met someone. I have two children with her. It's time for me to lead a different kind of life.'

'How much have they paid you? I bet you were cheap to bribe.'

'Because I'm holding this book, and taking a rest, I'm not going to hit you for that. Not just yet.'

He opens the book and pretends to read. But he's right, the pain's intensifying; he knows exactly what he's doing. After a while he says gently, 'It may look like I've betrayed everyone, but I haven't. I only gave them the names of a few cells – enough to make a good news report. Enough for it to look convincing. So my conscience is actually quite clear.' He smiles at me.

A single spark of relief. Adam and Tom knew each other, but Tom's not betrayed him. I will remain silent no matter what.

'And just so you know how I'm going to proceed,' he says, 'I won't gouge your eyes out immediately, I'll cut your ears off first. They've given me twelve hours with you. No bugs. No wire. Just the two of us. I promised them I'd deliver, and I will.' He turns back to the book.

I want to scream. My voice is howling inside, terrified. I'm not going to be able to hold out. I'm not brave enough.

Outside, the rumble of a motorbike. Tom looks up, pulls a gun from his jacket and stands by the door. The bike comes to a halt; a key turns in the door, then it swings open. Someone in bike leathers walks in and Tom puts his gun away.

'Cesar, I wasn't expecting you today.'

Cesar takes off his helmet and his dark eyes meet mine. 'What's going on?' His gaze darts between us.

'Benjamin's the traitor,' Tom says. 'I picked him up as we agreed, but when I brought him here, he attacked me. I'm trying to ascertain just what he's done, and how deep the damage goes.' He turns to me. 'He was fool enough to pull a gun on me and imagine that was it. He'd got me. I kicked it out of his hand.' He turns back to Cesar. 'We knew his relationship with Gil was difficult, that goes back a long way, but not even I could have envisaged just how much he hated his father. It proves what the statistics show – most murders happen within the family.'

'He's lying,' I shout. It takes all my strength. I don't know why Cesar's here or how close he is to Tom, but he's my only hope. 'Tom betrayed my father and he's about to betray you.'

'Your problem, Benjamin,' Tom says coming forward, 'is that Cesar and I know each other, we've lived together, fought together, we're Disciples. Whereas you've always been on the outside. You're an unknown entity. Somebody who's never actually proved himself, until, of course, this unfortunate moment.'

'Cesar, you cannot believe him. I would never betray my father. They killed my mother. Tom's the traitor.'

Cesar stands very still and I sense he's not sure what's going on. He withdraws a pistol from his jacket and focuses on me.

'Please, Cesar. I haven't done anything wrong.'

'How long has this been going on?' He walks towards me.

'Perhaps an hour or so,' Tom says without emotion. 'Like all good traitors he's a coward underneath. He was about to speak and spill the beans, but you arrived. I wish you'd told me you were coming early because clearly, now, he thinks he's got an opportunity to retract.'

Cesar draws a chair up close and sits opposite me. He stares into my face; it feels like a belligerent act. Tom stands watching from behind as Cesar leans across and rips open my T-shirt. He'll see the wounds Tom's inflicted, and I flinch, afraid he'll add to them.

'Please, Cesar,' I murmur. 'Believe me. He's the traitor.'

Cesar touches one of the bruises on my chest. I wince,

trying not to cry out, but he presses into it harder. I cry out and still he presses harder again. Tom is smiling behind him. My life is over as Cesar slowly raises his gun and holds it near my head.

'Where did you put his wire?' he asks Tom.

'Wire?' Tom says. 'He wasn't wired.'

It happens in seconds. Cesar turns, pulls the trigger and the bullet hits Tom in the neck. Tom's eyes widen in shock and horror as his blood spurts out, his hand clutching desperately to stop it. Our eyes meet as death invades him. It's the most terrible moment but I can't turn away, transfixed by the horror of what's happening. Then Tom is a dead man in a pool of blood.

I hear whimpering. It's Cesar. The gun slips out of his hand and he's shaking. It feels like ages before he turns to me but I can't speak. I'd loved Tom. He's dead. He was the traitor. I'm afraid I'll never forget his dying eyes. Cesar releases my hands from the cuffs but then I can't get out of the chair.

'I'm sorry,' I whisper. 'I can't move.'

He helps me up and drags me outside. Somehow, he gets me on his bike and I hear his voice telling me I need to hold on, he's going to go fast. I'm drifting away but the smell of petrol is thick in my nose. I have to stay awake, and as we head off the air rushes by and I'm reviving. I'm alive. *I'm still alive.* I don't know what decided it for Cesar. How he made the right choice – or maybe he just figured a traitor would wear a wire. I need to ask him, but then I realise I probably never will.

CHAPTER 26

Jess

It's been a week now, and I think it's reasonable that when I phone Dad I ask after Benjamin. It shouldn't arouse any suspicion; he knows we got on well enough, and I'd like to hear his voice.

So far, I've made a big effort not to phone home. I don't want to be one of those people who can't stop phoning their mother and who seems to need constant support. I want to appear cool, like I'm only having the best time so whatever I feel, I'm not going to call it homesickness. I've been texting Mum, but no more than that. Greg's okay now, and everything with them is carrying on as usual.

I sit in my room and ring Dad. I'll never tell anyone how glad I am to hear his voice and after chatting for a while I'm relaxed.

'How's Benjamin?' I ask casually.

There's a pause. 'Yeah, you know, Greg's keeping him busy.'

'Can you put him on? I'd really like to have a word.'

This time there's a longer pause, much longer. 'He's busy right now.' Dad's voice is flat.

'What's wrong?' I ask, because I realise something *is* wrong. 'Tell me.'

'He's gone, Jess.'

I hold the phone but I can't speak. I don't understand. Benjamin's meant to be there. I need to know he's there, it helps me feel okay.

'Jess?' Dad asks softly.

'I'm shocked,' I say, afraid I'm going to cry on the phone.

'Yeah, and so were we.'

'When did he go?' My lower lip trembles.

'The night we were in Glasgow.'

'He's been gone a week!' I shriek. 'Why didn't you tell me?'

'Mum didn't want anything to interfere with your first week away. We wanted you to enjoy yourself. She was worried … you'd worry if you knew.'

'Is that why you went back early? I couldn't understand why you left so early.'

'Yeah. Greg hadn't slipped but we think Benjamin drugged him.'

'Drugged him?'

'He slept through everything. Benjamin stole the pickup truck and Greg doesn't sleep through things like that.'

This is going from bad to worse.

'But it's okay,' Dad says quickly. 'We've got the truck back. He wrote us a letter to tell us where it was.'

My throat feels tight. How can all of this have happened and he's only telling me now?

'And he thanked us for all we'd done for him, which felt kind of ironic.'

'Nothing else?' I ask.

'Nothing else really. Although … he enclosed something. Mary says that it'll be for you.'

'Yes,' I mumble. My heart is pounding.

'A necklace. There's a phoenix on it.'

Any effort to hide my emotions disintegrates. I burst into tears.

'Oh, Jess.' Dad sighs. Then he says very gently. 'We're okay – I think we're okay.'

I understand he's talking about our safety. I know how much he feared Benjamin just walking off, but I never doubted that he'd keep us safe. Benjamin would never tell on us. That's not what I fear.

'Is he going to die, Dad?'

'Oh, God, Jess. I hope not.' Even Dad's struggling. 'I've done what I can to minimise the risk.'

But I can't hear anymore and end the call. Shaking, I weep. I only understand how much I love him now he's gone. How did I fail to realise that? I love Benjamin Turner. I don't think it will ever stop yet I'll never see him again.

I cry myself to sleep. At some point I wake and put my hand to my throat, feeling for the phoenix, but I don't have it yet. The phoenix he never took off; the phoenix his mother gave him. I start crying again. I think he knew he was going to die.

My fingers fumble as I turn on my phone and search for the headline I saw a few days ago. It was about the Disciples but I didn't bother reading it because I didn't think it relevant; Benjamin was at home. Now I read what I can. There was some kind of shoot-out – a body found in a cottage. They're linking the incident to the eco-terrorists and the police confirm it's a sign of the pressure they're exerting; the Disciples may be turning on themselves. Benjamin's name isn't there. Surely if they'd killed him they'd have said so? I turn off my phone but feel little relief. From now on, every time I see the Disciples' name, I'll hold my breath. I'll look for his name and one day … I'll find it. I cry until my chest feels heavy and my eyes cloud with sleep.

Benjamin

The room is dark and claustrophobic. I'm lying on the floor on an air mattress. My left hand is in a splint, breathing is painful and my face is swollen. Pain is everywhere. I try to sleep but when I close my eyes I see Tom's face – his eyes as he knew he was dying. I'm afraid I'll never stop seeing him.

Fran comes in periodically to check on me. I know I'm lucky. Cesar was afraid, given the level of Tom's betrayal, that there was nowhere safe for me to go. Except for his sister Francesca, who he trusts implicitly; she's not a Disciple. I'm also lucky because Fran's girlfriend is a paramedic and she's patched me up. I take painkillers that make my mind fuzz and my thoughts space out. Every day I tell myself I'm lucky, but what I feel is … I'd be better dead. If Cesar had made the wrong call, if he'd shot me instead, I wouldn't be in pain now. I wouldn't see Tom when I close my eyes or face a future I can't begin to imagine.

Sometimes, to sleep, I take my mind back to the attic in Scotland. The sloping ceiling, and the window looking out at the moon. I think of Jess – her smell, her touch, the softness of her skin, and it provides a moment of relief.

I don't cry. That surprises me, but it's too much effort. Instead, when he comes, Gil cries for me. He sits in the corner of the room, his back against the wall, with his knees bent to his chest and I watch the tears streak his cheeks. He doesn't speak. What is there to say? We both know it now. Tom was his friend, his second in command, Mum's lover, and the cause of their deaths. Betrayal is cruel and bitter. There is nothing left to believe in.

Jess

A voice wakes me. 'Jessica.' Nobody calls me Jessica, not since I was six and insisted I was Jess.

I open my eyes. The room is dark and I was dreaming. Then I see a figure standing in shadow. I shake my head, but they don't go. Strangely, I'm not as afraid as I should be.

'What are you doing here?' I ask slowly. 'You're dead.'

He smiles but doesn't answer. I think of Dad's description. 'A very dangerous and manipulative man.' Gil Zimmerman. Has he manipulated death?

'My son's in trouble,' he says softly, and I'm surprised at the sound of his voice.

'Yes,' I acknowledge. 'And it's all your doing.'

'I think you can help him,' he says, ignoring my accusation.

'How? I've no idea where he is.'

'He's hurt, badly. Physically and mentally.'

I listen but don't respond. What am I meant to say?

'The physical wounds will heal but …' He pauses.

His eyes hold mine. A dead man's eyes that somehow glisten.

'You know how to make him feel better,' he says.

'No. He's gone. I didn't want him to go but he left. You're to blame for what he's done, not me. So I can't help him.'

'Thirty-seven Curzon Road.'

'What?'

'That's where you'll find him. Flat two. East London.'

I shake my head. This is mad. I'm listening to a ghost.

He smiles again. 'But you believe in ghosts, Jess. It's not mad at all.'

'What? You can hear my thoughts, can you?'

'Let's just say we're both attuned to Benjamin right now. He wants you, you want him, but somebody's got to bridge the gap.'

'I don't want him,' I say, even though I know it's a lie, but I'm not having Gil tell me what to do. 'He betrayed my family.'

Gil shakes his head. 'He wouldn't be so hurt if he'd done that. He didn't betray your family.'

'No? Then what do you call drugging Greg, nicking our pickup truck, and going without a word?'

'A minor inconvenience.'

'Huh, well, it's pretty major to me.'

'A minor inconvenience.'

We stare at each other. He's fading. Good, he's going. I don't want him here. Then he's gone. I lie back in my bed and look at my bedside clock. It's four thirty in the morning. I hope nobody heard me; they'll think I'm mad. Maybe I am. It's the craziest thing that's ever happened to me. Then I wonder – why did my mind conjure up a ghost? Or is it some strange extrasensory perception thing? Is Benjamin lying somewhere thinking of me, or maybe his father, or seeing a ghost too?

I should ask Mum. Mum would definitely have a view on it. But if I give her any details she'll know how much I'm thinking of Benjamin, and then she'll wonder why. Thirty-seven Curzon Road. I'll check it on a web map tomorrow. No, this is bullshit – I've got a class tomorrow. I need to figure out the library and I've loads to do.

CHAPTER 27

Jess

I'm sitting on the train to London. I told my flatmates I'm going to see an old friend of the family, and it would be a boring trip. I can't tell the truth: thirty-seven Curzon Road.

I get through most days without thinking about Benjamin. I've plenty to do, making new friends and enjoying my classes. But at night, I can't control my thoughts and replay moments we spent together; my skin aches for his. We got too close. I couldn't see it at the time, but now I live with the consequence. I can't fancy any other guy. Mum sent me Benjamin's necklace and I wear it every day, but it's not really mine; I'm just looking after it until I can give it back.

Curzon Road doesn't look friendly – a long line of terraced houses, most of which need repairing or decorating. There's a car with its windscreen smashed and in lots of the front gardens there's a clutter of stuff: rubbish, broken bricks or old bicycles. Number thirty-seven has two doorbells. One reads Ground Floor Flat while the other is smudged black ink. I can't make it out, and the longer I look the more I panic. What am I doing? This is mad. I'm standing here because of a ghost.

When I'm calmer, I press the second bell. There's no response and I press it again. Eventually, I hear footsteps on stairs and the door opens. I'm staring at someone in uniform; I wasn't expecting that. They work for the ambulance service.

'Yes?' she says.

'I-I'm looking for Benjamin.' Is that right? Should I have said that? But it's the only name I have for him.

'Nobody's here of that name.' She shuts the door quickly.

My hand shakes slightly as I try the Ground Floor Flat. Nobody answers and I ring it several times but still nothing. I ring the other bell again. My heart is pounding but I keep ringing until the woman appears, only this time she's in casual wear.

'What's your problem? I've just finished work, I'm trying to get some sleep.'

'If you could tell him it's Jess. I think he'll want to see me.'

She slams the door in my face. What else can I do? I sit on the low wall of the front garden and wait for something to change. People walk by and ignore me. A dog sniffs my leg until its owner pulls it away. I hate this place.

The door opens behind me and this time I'm looking at another woman. Short hair, jeans and a bulky hoodie. She nods at me and I follow her up the rickety stairs and into her flat. She doesn't stop to introduce herself but leads me down a corridor and then motions to a room at the end. The door is ajar and I push it open. There's a packed bookshelf, boxes with household stuff, and then Benjamin sitting on a mattress. I gasp. His face is black and yellow with bruising. His left hand is bandaged, and the way he sits, it's obvious he's uncomfortable.

'It's okay,' he says, 'it was worse. This is me getting better.'

I draw closer and slowly sit on the mattress beside him but can't speak.

'How did you find me?'

I decide to tell the truth. 'Your father told me where you were. He said you were hurt, and I should come.'

'My father?' he whispers.

I nod. 'He … I wasn't sure if I was dreaming or maybe hallucinating, but he was in my room. And now I'm here.'

He's quiet.

'You're shocked?' I say.

'No. Not really. Sometimes I see him too.'

'Your father? As a ghost?'

'If that's what you want to call him. Yes.'

We both lean back against the wall. I need the support.

'Are you glad to see me?' I ask because I'm not sure.

'Yes, Jess. Very. I just … haven't spoken to anyone properly for a long time, so it's an effort. I need to get used to it.' His eyes meet mine. 'But I'm very glad to see you.'

Even if I wanted to hug him, I can't. His body seems too hurt.

'You just left,' I say softly. 'You lied to my parents, drugged Greg, took the truck. I would like to know the truth. For once.'

'I'd like to tell it to you.' He puts his head back and closes his eyes. He pales, despite the black and yellow bruising. 'I'd like to tell you it all, if you can bear to hear it.'

Later, we lie side by side. Our clothes are still on but it feels good to be close.

'So you see, Jess, I kept my promise to your father. I was never going to reveal where I'd been. But it kills me inside that it was Tom. He was brutal.'

I'm shivering. It's a reaction to what he's told me, but I understand him better now. 'You went through something terrible,' I say. 'Nobody should ever treat another person like that. It's torture.'

'It's what happens,' he says matter-of-factly.

'And I can't believe my father changed the memory stick.'

'He's a cunning man. A real …' He stops.

'A real what?'

'Nothing.'

'A real Disciple?' I whisper.

He nods, but thinking about my father like that is too much.

'I can't imagine having a childhood like yours,' I say. 'Going into your mother's room and finding Tom in bed with her rather than your father. That would do my head in.'

'That part was okay. When you're a kid it's natural to love the people who look after you – you just don't expect them to destroy you later.'

'No. How can someone switch from love to hate like that?'

'He said he'd got his own kids, and now they don't have a father either.'

We're quiet for a while.

'Benjamin, what will you do now?'

'I've no idea, Jess. When I think of the future there's nothing there. It's blank.' He doesn't even sound sad, just tired. 'I wish I could sleep, that I could close my eyes and really sleep.'

It's getting dark, and I go out to get us some pizzas. By the time I'm back they're almost cold, but we still enjoy them. Benjamin asks about uni and we chat. At some point he even smiles.

'So,' he says, as we finish eating, 'I like the sound of your friends.'

'Yeah. I'm lucky the way it's worked out. There's this girl on my course, and she's really not getting on with the people in her flat.'

'And guys?' he asks, leaning back and closing his eyes.

'None,' I say as casually as I can.

'You didn't shag someone in Freshers' Week?'

'No, you know I'm not like that.'

'Probably just as well. I shagged someone in Freshers' Week, but I didn't really enjoy it.'

Why are we talking like this?

'I still love you,' I say, serious.

He opens his eyes and his gaze meets mine. 'Yes,' he says very softly.

I feel his necklace round my neck. 'I need to give you this

back.' I open the catch, take it off and place it on the floor in front of him.

'It's yours, Jess.'

'No. It's actually about you. It's private – between you and your mother.'

'It's all I have to give. Please accept it.'

I shake my head. 'I don't want your necklace, I want …' My lower lip trembles.

'Jess,' he whispers.

I shake my head.

'Please don't cry.'

I look down into my lap trying to hide the tears on my cheeks. 'Can't you just say you love me?'

He's quiet but his breathing quickens. 'I'm so glad you're here, Jess. So happy to see you, but …' His voice wavers. 'If I tell you I love you I don't think it will help.'

I glance over. His face is a mask of anguish. 'Somebody I loved beat the shit out of me. I watched them die. They almost killed me. And I'm fucking terrified, Jess, I can't feel normal feelings again. I've been pushed too far. I can't get it back. I don't even know what love is anymore.'

Tears track his cheeks. I'm crying too, relieved he doesn't say any more. Then I hug him. I hold him as we cry. I kiss the curls on his head. I hear a voice comforting, 'I love you, I love you,' but don't realise at first it's mine. I hug him until the feeling in my arms alters and I no longer know what is my body, what is his.

Eventually, he gently disentangles himself from me. 'You know we're connected, Jess, on some deep level. I don't really understand it, but we are.'

'Yes,' I say, but there's no point trying to name it.

'I'm so tired,' he says. 'You'll stay, won't you?'

'Yes.'

He lies back and is instantly asleep. I watch him for a while then reach over, pick up the necklace and put it back on. Exhausted, I lie down too. His body warms mine and I fall asleep.

CHAPTER 28

Benjamin

I wake and Jess's body is curled into mine. Light seeps in from behind the curtains and suffuses the room. I feel calm. At last, the terror and panic I've felt for weeks has gone. I gently spell *I love you* on Jess's back and lie there quietly. My head clears and my thoughts sharpen. It's imperative I get a new identity. I have to become someone else.

'Hey,' Jess says, turning to me, her voice sleepy. 'You look serious.'

'Just thinking,' I say softly. 'My head's less fuzzy. There are things I have to think about.'

'At least you look better than yesterday.'

'Well, you're here.' I smile and touch her cheek with my hand.

'What are we going to do today?' she asks lazily.

'Do? I don't know. What would you like to do?'

'I'm not sure. I've got classes tomorrow, so I'll probably have to go back later, but I could stay and miss them.'

'No, you definitely can't do that. I won't let you cut a single class for me.'

'Well, do you want to go outside – like for a walk?'

'I should probably try that, although I don't know how far we'll get.'

We're quiet for a bit. Then she gently places her lips on mine.

'Does it hurt if I do that?' she asks softly. She glances at my bruises.

'Not if you do that.'

We kiss and I draw her to me. The day disappears and we don't really do anything at all.

Jess needs to leave if she's going to make her train back to Glasgow. Neither of us wants to part, but we must.

'When will I see you again?' she asks.

'I don't know, Jess. I'll write to you, okay?'

'Write to me? You mean like pen on paper?'

'Yeah. I won't risk any kind of digital communication.'

'Okay,' she says, but sounds disappointed. 'I'll miss you.'

'Yes.' I nod and smile.

She picks up her backpack.

I don't want her to go just yet. 'Jess, thank you,' I say quickly. 'Thank you for coming. You're sweet and kind, and I'm not sure I've ever been that back.'

Her face brightens with a wide smile. 'Sometimes you are, Benjamin.'

But I know that's not true. 'Your family, they've every right to hate me. Please don't tell them you've seen me again.'

'Okay,' she says, 'I hadn't really thought about it.'

It's getting late. We hug and then I hear her feet on the stairs, the front door open and close, and from the window I watch her walk away. There are only a few people about, walking in the drizzling rain.

Night time. I flick through my father's notebook, and remember Olivia's summer house, and my blood trickling onto the last page. I was a different person then. I read each name again trying to judge who could be of any help; it's not easy when you don't know who they all are. One entry almost makes me laugh, it's so out of place: Best World Wholefoods. It's a London address, and the word Baz is written below it in brackets. Didn't my father mention that name, a long time ago? I may have found a place to start … go into the shop, keep a low profile, check it out. The bruising on my face is still too obvious so I'll need to wait a while, but my strength is returning.

Cesar and I are alone in the flat's small kitchen. Fran and her girlfriend are out. 'What will you do now?' he asks slowly. 'You can't stay here indefinitely.'

'No, of course not.' Have I stayed too long? 'I need to acquire a new identity.'

'I'm not sure who we can trust to do that.'

'No. Don't worry. I think I have a contact. Nobody you know.'

He fidgets and I sense his discomfort.

'I'll go as soon as I can,' I say, placating him. 'As soon as it's safe.'

'I don't know how we go on now – the Disciples.'

I'm quiet. I know where this conversation is leading, and I don't want it.

'What are your thoughts?' He's blunt.

'I don't have Phoenix anymore,' I say carefully. 'I may never be able to get hold of it. So my thoughts are, for the time being, we need to lie low. I think … Tom's done the worst he could. It's possible they've arrested all those they're going to. For now, focus on staying safe.'

'For the time being we need to lie low,' he repeats and shrugs. 'Then what?'

'I've no idea, Cesar.'

'Don't you want to step up?' he asks, and it sounds like he thinks I should.

'If you're asking if I want to lead the Disciples, then my answer is no.'

'Gil believed in you. He told me he thought you could do it.'

I've no idea when such a conversation took place.

'You should think about it,' he says firmly. 'Consider what's happened and the part you play now.'

I don't answer immediately. 'Okay.'

'If I were you, if I'd lost what you have, I'd want revenge. I'd want to kill the fuckers behind it.'

I nod, but don't say any more.

I wake. The room is dark and I'm breathing fast. Fear grips me. I was dreaming; I was being chased. Then something Tom said hits me. 'They've known who you are, Benjamin, for some time.'

Why have I only just remembered that? Because he started talking about Mo and Atholl and I couldn't think straight, but now … he was telling me they've been watching me. How? Where? It doesn't make sense. I've only been a schoolboy and student, which has meant nothing to anybody but my teachers. I didn't go on protests. I never said anything controversial. I haven't done a single thing to attract attention to myself. Yet, somehow, they've known who I am. I think of Mo. I've got to see him.

I apply Fran's concealer to my face and smudge it in. The bruises hardly show. I pull my baseball cap down low and walk outside. It's easy to lose myself in the rush-hour throng. Still, I decide not to take the Tube (with its CCTV cameras) and walk the long distance to college instead. I sit in a café window and wait to see him; some nights Mo stays late in the library. Is he still living at home now or in some student house? After I've drunk two long coffees, at eight o'clock, Mo walks through the university's gates and heads in the direction of the Tube. I quickly follow. The streets aren't crowded but I don't approach him until he's walking through an empty square.

'I need to speak to you,' I say in a hushed voice. My heart is pounding – I've no idea what he thinks of me now. Will he want to call the police or run?

Without even glancing at me, he steps away and walks faster. He must think I'm some bloke accosting him. I catch up and gently hold his arm. 'Mo, I need to speak to you.'

He stops and turns. His eyes widen, shocked.

'Mo, I'm sorry,' I say quickly. 'I know they got you.' I keep my voice calm – I don't want him to run.

He shakes his head. 'What are you doing here?'

'I need to speak to you. Please, don't be afraid.'

But he is afraid. 'Are you armed?'

'No. Of course not.'

'They told me if I ever see you, I have to report you. If I don't report you, then I'm complicit. I could face a jail sentence.'

'They're full of shit, Mo. They're not going to know we met. They're not going to know anything.'

'You're full of shit. You lied to me. You're a Disciple.'

'No. They've lied to you. That's not true.'

'After I saw the news, I kept ringing your home. Over and over, I was so worried. But nothing. And then they came and picked me up in the middle of class. Agents walked right into the lecture theatre and took me out. The whole fucking world could see!'

'They're fuckers, Mo. And you couldn't reach me because I had to run. They shot Gemma. My mother, at home, point-blank range. They fucking killed both my parents.'

He takes that in. 'Shit.'

'They didn't report her death because how could they? They shot an innocent woman.'

I feel very sick and I'm breathing hard. Mo's silent.

'Let's find somewhere to talk,' he says, calmer.

CHAPTER 29

Benjamin

We sit under a large oak tree, hidden beneath its branches. No one's about anyway.

'They scared the shit out of me,' Mo says quietly. 'Not at first – at first they were reasonable.'

I listen carefully.

'They were sympathetic and said I must be shocked, you'd been a close friend, and I should start at the beginning and tell them everything I knew about you. So I went back to when we first met at school, and how we became friends and the way we hung out and studied together. I said sometimes you'd stay for meals and my family knew and liked you. They were recording everything and somebody was taking notes, and at first it felt okay. Then suddenly, without even changing the tone of their voice, they asked, "How long was he a member of the Disciples for?" And I was shocked, you know. I said you weren't.

'"Do you really expect us to believe that you didn't know what he was up to?"

'I said I didn't. You had nothing to do with the Disciples. And that's when they told me to think very carefully because withholding information was a criminal offence. And I thought, shit, am I in trouble too? "I'm telling you everything I know," I insisted. But I was getting scared and sweating and afraid they could pick up on the fact I was lying.

'Then they started asking about the science projects we worked on, and I went through what we'd been studying, and how you'd got a project from Atholl and I was doing one for Professor Gupta, but they said that wasn't what they meant – they wanted to know about the projects we were working on together for the Disciples.

'I kept telling them there weren't any and I had nothing to do with the Disciples.

'"Ah," they said. "So you're admitting he did have something to do with them?"

'And that's when I realised it didn't matter what I said, they were going to twist it. I began to feel physically sick.

'"Why are you protecting him?" they asked.

'"I'm not," I said. "I'm telling the truth. Neither of us had anything to do with the Disciples."

'There was a pause, and they went and got me a cup of tea. It was like they'd gone into "good cop" mode and I sat there praying they'd let me go home. But they came back, and something in the way they looked at me, I knew things were about to get a whole lot worse. So they started talking about interviewing my parents given the amount of time you spent at our home.

'I begged them not to do that. My folks had nothing to do with it. But they just smiled. "We'll be the judge of that."

'Then I was shouting, "Leave them out of it. They're upset – they feel Benjamin used them. There's nothing to be gained from going to them."

'And this female agent said, "Are you special to them, Mo? I bet you are." She went on about how I was their only son, and how much that must mean to them, my folks being honourable people and how would they deal with the shame of me being linked to terrorism.

'And I hated them, Benjamin. Like it was just so easy for them to come out with all that stuff as if they knew what my family was about, as if I'm some fucking Asian cliché when they were talking about real people. *My* family and *my* friend.

'"Why are you doing this to me?" I asked.

'"We want you to tell the truth, Mo, and right now you're not." I looked into this guy's eyes, and I could see he wasn't going to stop. If he'd had thumbscrews, I swear, he'd have used them. He turned to his colleague. "Raymond, can you go and pick up Dr Qureshi and the sister, Fatima."'

Mo pauses. His lower lip trembles. 'That's when I lost it,' he whispers. 'All I could think of was how it would affect Dad. My father, who'd always done the right thing. And Timmy had just got engaged, and if the guy broke it off … it would all be my fault. All my fucking fault for having known you. So I told them everything.

'How I'd figured out you were Gil Zimmerman's son, but nobody else had. And that you didn't see him and even part of why my father tried to look after you was because you were a boy without a father. And maybe I should have told Dad when I learnt your truth, and he'd have probably got me to tell the police, because he never did anything wrong. They must never blame him. I knew your secret. I was the one guilty of keeping it to myself.'

I look down and close my eyes. Nothing I do will ever make anything better for Dr Qureshi or help his sense of betrayal. 'I'm sorry, Mo. None of it should have happened. I'm sorry.'

After a while he says, 'I swore I didn't believe you'd ever done anything wrong, and if I'd ever imagined it possible, I'd have grassed on you. You were a good person.

'"Aren't you naïve, Mo?" they said, and that's when they told me I had to do that appeal, asking you to come back, and if I ever saw you I had to report you immediately. Anything else and I'd be complicit. I'd be charged with second-degree terrorism. It was only because they could see how naïve I was that they weren't charging me then.'

As calmly as I can, I say, 'So when I've gone, you need to phone them and tell them what happened. Tell them I put a gun to your head. You couldn't contact them any earlier because I had a gun at your head.'

He's still. 'I might not.'

'You must, Mo. You know that, for your own safety.'

'They said at some point you'd come – you'd seek me out.'

'Did they?'

'Yeah, and they interviewed Atholl. He was really upset about you and … that was another thing they kept going back to ask me – about our science projects. Did we ever discuss the fact that the sponsor of our projects was LifeStar Corporation?

'I said we didn't and anyway LifeStar Corporation wasn't the name on the research proposal. It was Sensory Science Tech, and I once looked them up and they were part of Research for Health International.

'"Which is part of LifeStar Corporation," they said.

'I really couldn't see what they were on about and why did it even matter?

'They wouldn't answer that. But when I spoke to Atholl he said they were right and they were probably asking because historically, a long time ago, the Disciples attacked LifeStar Corporation. Did you know that?'

'I know a bit about the Disciples in the past, but I didn't know Research for Health International was a subsidiary of LifeStar.' I can't take in all the implications of what he's saying, not now.

'The worst thing about what's happened,' Mo says in a hushed voice, 'is that despite everything – I've missed you. How fucking stupid is that?'

'You're my best friend, Mo. I've missed you too. I've hated knowing they'd get you. I never wanted to hurt you.'

He's quiet. I need to go but I'm struggling to find the energy.

'What will you do now?' he asks.

'I don't know. I really don't know.' It's the truth, but it's also what I need him to report back to them.

'And if they get you?'

'They'll probably kill me.'

He shifts where he sits. I sense he wants to say something but he stalls.

'Thank you for being my friend, Mo. Whatever you hear or read in the future, please know that my friendship with you has always been real. They'll tell you brown is black, but it's always been real. And now you need to stay safe. You must tell them we met. I put a gun to your head.'

He turns to me, his eyes glistening. 'I have to tell you something else Atholl said,' he whispers, urgent. 'He said, "Benjamin's the kind of guy who'd be an asset to both sides." I didn't think about it at the time, I was just too upset, but now … maybe that's important.'

'Atholl said that?'

He nods.

Then, because I know I will never see him again, and because my mind's in utter confusion, I draw him to me in a hug. He hesitates a moment then hugs me back. We've been like brothers, but now it's goodbye. We get up and go our separate ways into the night.

CHAPTER 30

Jess

'I'm thinking, Dad, that maybe I won't come home for reading week.'

'You won't come home?' He sounds upset. They must be missing me.

'Well,' I say, 'maybe I could for a few days, but I wasn't thinking of coming for the whole week.'

Benjamin and I have been corresponding. I know exactly where I want to be reading week.

'Well, of course it's up to you, Jess.' A slight pause. 'I'm sure there's plenty going on in Glasgow. I can understand, there's nothing for you to do up here.'

'Not really,' I say apologetically. 'But I'll be home for Christmas, I promise.'

'Too right you will. Em and Theo have booked their flights. Tommy's practically packed his bags.'

'Will Xav be coming?'

'Of course.'

I wonder how I'll find Xav. Maybe I'll be able to speak to him about Benjamin? We can swear each other to secrecy.

After our call, I feel bad for lying to Dad, but I'm very glad of the truth. I've booked a room in a cheap hotel in London;

it's in my name but Benjamin will be paying for it. I can't wait
to see him again.

Benjamin comes out of the bathroom with a towel wrapped
round his waist. He looks at me lying on the bed and throws
it aside.

'You have the most beautiful body,' I say. 'No naked man
could be more beautiful.' I grin.

'And is that your biased or unbiased opinion?'

'Unbiased.'

'And just how many naked men have you seen?'

'Hundreds.' I laugh.

He lies on the bed beside me, beads of water still on his chest.
He seems thoughtful. 'Jess, will you help me with something?'

'Of course,' I say, and listen.

This is the plan. I'm to go into Best World Wholefoods.
He describes the interior; he's checked it out. I should look
around until any customers have gone, and the owner should
be hovering by the cash register. He's a middle-aged black guy
with short dreadlocks. 'It's possible the guy knew your father
too. I'm pretty sure he did. He was called Baz back then.'

'Are you saying he's a Disciple?' I ask slowly.

'No, he's not. Not now. But he was once.'

I didn't realise he'd be asking me to get involved in something like this.

'If you're not comfortable with it,' he says, 'then you mustn't
do it, Jess. Tell me now – we need to be truthful with each
other.'

'Why do you want to contact him?'

'I think he may know people who can help me get a new
identity.'

'You mean like a passport?'

He nods. 'And a National Insurance number, and maybe

even a new birth certificate. I'll need them if I've any hope of rebuilding my life.'

'Then of course I want to help you.'

I enter the shop close to the end of the trading day. A customer is paying and the owner is just as described. I hover near the massage oils. A younger woman is stacking shelves and banters with the owner. I'm worried she's in the way; I can't speak to him while she's there, but then she disappears into the back. I pick up a sensual oil and walk to the counter.

'Great choice,' he says, and smiles at me.

I nod, nervous. 'I think you know a friend of mine.' The words feel like cotton wool on my tongue.

'Yes?' he says casually.

'You knew his father and he'd like to meet you.' I'm breathing quickly. I feel I'm getting it all wrong.

He grows still. Our eyes meet.

'What's his name?' he asks slowly.

'He's the younger brother of Joseph, in the Bible.' Benjamin said he should understand. The Disciples sometimes communicate like that – using stuff from the Bible.

His eyes don't move from mine. 'And you are?' he asks carefully.

I panic. 'I haven't got an answer to that.' I sound like an idiot. Why didn't Benjamin prepare me for that question?

He looks at me bemused, then calls out. 'Bry, can you come mind the shop?'

The girl I saw earlier reappears. Baz steps out from behind the counter and she takes over. He motions for me to follow him and we walk through the stockroom into a tiny kitchen. I tell myself that all of this is good; Benjamin suggested it could happen. We stand opposite each other.

'What do you think you're doing coming into my shop like

this?' His words are sharp but his voice is quiet. 'It's a considerable risk.'

'I'm sorry,' I mutter.

'Joseph's younger brother was Benjamin. There are a lot of Benjamins in the world.'

'But only one is Gil's son,' I whisper.

He's silent. Maybe even shocked. 'I can't get involved in this.'

'Please,' I beg. 'There's nobody else he can turn to.'

'He's obviously turned to you. What are you, his girlfriend?'

I nod. 'He needs new papers. He doesn't want anything else. He said you might know somebody he could go to. He just needs a contact.'

'It's not as simple as that. He sounds as naïve as you.'

My head is swimming. I can't even get him over the first hurdle.

Then Baz asks, 'What kind of state is he in?'

'State?'

'Yes, is he hurt?'

'No. I mean he was, but he's not now.'

'And does anybody else know you're here?'

I shake my head.

He's thoughtful. 'I don't get it. He doesn't need me. Tell him to go to Tom.'

'Tom's dead,' I say, but my stomach churns.

'Dead?' His face pales. 'Who the fuck are you to come in here and spout that bullshit?'

I shrink back. He's about to throw me out but I'm telling the truth.

'Tom was the traitor. Tom hurt him badly. He could've killed him.' Somehow I get the words out.

His face alters with shock. He slumps back onto the table and puts his head in his hands. 'Fuck.' He's shaking. 'Jesus fucking Christ. What happened?' Then softer, mumbling, 'Tom was a good guy, really good.'

I don't reply because I can see how upset he is and there's nothing to make that better.

'Please will you help Benjamin?' I ask.

He lowers his hands to look at me and seems older now. 'Who are you?'

'J-Jess,' I stutter.

'Where is Benjamin?'

I give him the address of the hotel.

'Room number?' he asks.

'Twenty-four.'

He nods. 'I'll see him at eight o'clock.'

I feel the most intense relief; I've done it. 'Thank you, Baz.'

'Nobody's called me that for years.' His eyes are sad.

I thank him again and leave.

CHAPTER 31

Benjamin

It's eight o'clock and there's a knock on the door. I take a deep breath and open it. Despite his casual dress I can tell he's on edge.

'Benjamin.'

'Baz.'

Although he's in my hotel room, he nods at the bed, indicating I should sit. He takes the chair by the desk.

'Where's the girl?' he asks.

'She's out. She won't be back for a while.'

'I want you to tell me about Tom,' he says bluntly. 'Before we discuss anything else, I want to know what happened.'

I give him every detail because it helps me feel better, but I can see he's distressed. They must have been close.

'If it's any help,' I say, 'I've wept about it since. Maybe you remember Tom as a loyal Disciple, a brother in arms, but I remember him as almost a second father.'

We don't speak for a while. I want to discuss what I need but I wait on him.

He says, hushed, 'Benjamin, I left the Disciples ten years ago. I've got myself a different life now. I'm not going to let anyone screw that up for me.'

'No. I don't want to get anyone into trouble. I just need a new identity.'

He stares at the ceiling a moment and shakes his head. 'You're an innocent kid. A new identity involves the criminal underworld.'

'But the Disciples managed it, they did it often.'

'Often? Where do you get your facts from? No. Not often. Once or twice.'

I feel my heart skip a beat. 'So you can't help me?'

'I'd like to, Benjamin, but I can't. It's too dangerous. We're not talking about a single document. This isn't about getting some half-baked driving licence or a dodgy passport. You've got to get stuff that registers through the whole system. And they'd want a lot of money, more money than you're going to have, and if you don't have the money then you risk owing a debt to the kind of people you never want to be in debt to.'

Yet Adam got a new identity and his sister and cousin. 'I've got money,' I say, although I don't know if it will be enough. 'I thought it would be easier than you've said.' I'm angry it's not.

He shrugs and shakes his head then gets up to go.

'Wait,' I say, because I'm not ready to give up hope. 'Would you stay a bit? I'd really like it if you could possibly talk about my father. You knew him. I think you knew him well.'

He pauses and sits back down. I don't think he's keen to stay but I sense he's kind.

'Okay, Benjamin. But it depends what you'd like me to tell you.'

'I'd like to know how he managed to survive. You know sometimes it seems like he was a cat with nine lives.'

'I guess,' he says softly, 'he was a powerful man, and lucky and brave.'

'Yes, he was very brave. I've watched that footage, you know, that stuff online when he went over that cliff and into the sea. Did you know him then?'

He nods.

'Then how did he survive that? It's like he survived something you can't actually survive.'

'That's dramatic footage, of course. But there were two of them on that bike. Dominic didn't survive, so …'

He's keeping the secret too. I shouldn't push it; I can ask him other things. Anything he says will help me know my father better.

'The thing about Gil,' he says, 'is that he had this unquenchable belief, this optimism that he could achieve what he wanted, what was needed in the world. And he swept us up in that, he helped us believe with him, and to do things that we never imagined we could do. There were times when things got difficult, and people were feeling low, there was even a group despondency, and he'd walk into the room and the energy would alter. He'd change it. He'd literally light it up.'

Baz seems happier just talking about Gil, and I remember my mother, her eyes bright and smiling because Gil had shown up. The world always felt better when he came around. I can even believe that somewhere out there his flame still burns.

'I'll help you.'

'What?' I say, coming back to the present moment.

'I'll help you,' Baz says softly.

'You will? Thank you. I—'

He puts a finger to his lips and gets up. 'How long are you staying here?'

'How long do you think it will take?'

'A good few weeks, maybe more.'

'I'll be here,' I say and move to open the door. 'I don't know if it's possible but … I like the name Joshua.'

'I'm not making any promises. We'll see,' he says and leaves.

Jess and I spend the following days doing the kinds of things I could never have imagined months ago when going anywhere in public felt dangerous. We go to the zoo and walk in the park. The bruises on my face have gone but I'm always aware of where cameras are watching; I pull my cap down low and the collar up on my jacket.

'It's like we're a regular boyfriend and girlfriend,' Jess says smiling. 'We're normal.'

'Normal?' I tease. 'What's normal?'

She shrugs. 'Just standing in front of the gorillas and having a kiss.'

'The gorillas weren't impressed.'

We're walking through the park and I slip my arm around her.

'I think the gorillas were impressed.' She giggles.

'They were just thinking about their next meal, kind of like I am at the moment.'

'You're hungry again?'

'Of course.'

'Let's find you something to eat.'

Later, when we go to bed, she comments, 'You're not as super-skinny as you were.'

'Oh.'

'Yeah, you were too thin. When you were in that hideout, that flat.'

'Well, I feel better than I did then, obviously.'

'I think you're a bit eating disordered,' she says with assurance.

'Eating disordered? No. I get stressed when somebody tries to kill me, and then I don't want to eat. But that's not disordered, it's just a natural response.'

'I guess,' she says. 'But, anyway, you're more normal now.' Then she looks down my torso, thoughtful. 'I sometimes wonder, if when a guy gains or loses weight, does his penis too?'

Our eyes meet; she's completely serious and we both burst out laughing.

I lie awake and stare through the dark, Jess's body nestled into mine. I can't sleep with my thoughts turning. Why does

Jess always want to be normal? There's no such thing and cert-ainly not with us. I'm paying a fortune to get a new identity and I've almost been killed twice. My best friend's expected to report to MI5. But she doesn't see it. 'We're like a regular boyfriend and girlfriend.'

I remember something Gil said: 'People see what they want to.' At the time he was talking about politics. 'People look for supposed facts, and evidence that supports their point of view, but really, always, they see what they want to. They can't help it – that's why it's so hard to change people's minds.'

'Then why do you bother?' I'd asked him.

'Because I hold on to hope – that there's some chink in people's consciousness that wants to know the truth.'

We were talking about politics but perhaps it goes beyond that. Jess sees what she wants to. I don't blame her. She loves me and I love her – we prove it each day – but she's not seeing the other stuff, and none of that is going to go away.

CHAPTER 32

Jess

I pack my rucksack and sit on the edge of the bed. 'Okay, the train doesn't go until three, so we've still got six hours together.'

'Jess, I think maybe we should have a chat.'

'Isn't that what we've been doing all week?'

'Yes, but this is different.'

'You sound very serious.'

He sits on the bed beside me then says in a hushed voice, 'What do you think is going to happen once I get my new identity?'

'I don't know. I haven't really thought about it, except that you'll feel safer.'

'Okay, we haven't talked about it, but I think we should.'

I feel alright, relaxed, but I'm not sure that will last.

'I'm going to have to go abroad,' he says slowly. 'Probably America. I've thought about Europe, but I don't speak any European language well enough. In America, they speak English. There's a large and varied scientific community, a lot of colleges and universities, and it's possible I can find my way there. I can be the person I want to be.'

I'm very still. I hadn't expected any of this. 'That's quite far away,' I say softly.

'At least a seven- or eight-hour flight.'

I grip the handle of my rucksack, my nails digging into it.

'I just think it's important you know,' he says.

'Because it doesn't include me?' I whisper.

He doesn't respond.

'But I love you,' I say, and my voice shakes slightly. 'I thought you loved me.'

'I do,' he says softly. 'And I'm only telling you what might happen so we can start to get used to it, both of us. So you don't keep thinking we're a normal girlfriend and boyfriend because we're not.'

'Is this because of what I said yesterday?' He didn't like it, but haven't we felt great together?

'No,' he says, but I don't think that's true. All the happiness of the last week, such deep and wide happiness, suddenly seems in jeopardy.

'Have you bought a ticket to go?' I ask, unsure.

'No. You know I haven't even got my papers yet.'

'So why are we talking about it? It's ages away.'

'I just feel we're in deep with each other, Jess, and somehow we're going to have to find our way out of that.'

My breath is heavy in my chest. Did I do something wrong? I don't understand. We're in deep together, and yet it feels like we're sitting on opposite sides of the room. Is this him breaking up with me?

'Will I see you again after I leave here?' I ask, but my lower lip trembles.

'Yes, Jess. I'd like that.'

'Because I'm going home for Christmas. My aunt and uncle are coming over and I haven't seen Xav and Tommy for ages.'

'You're going home for Christmas.' He nods.

'So then when will I see you?'

'We don't need to decide that yet.'

I wipe my cheeks – I hadn't realised I was crying. I go to the bathroom, lock the door and stay in there a while. A pit is opening in my stomach and I'm shivering – I need to leave. There'll be an earlier train. I can't walk around with Benjamin now pretending nothing has happened. When I go back into the room he's standing by the window.

'I'm going to go now,' I say, but the words taste like mud in my mouth. 'You make me very sad. I've been happy with you. I thought you were too, but now you just make me very sad.'

He swallows. I think that hurt him; I think those words pierce.

I pick up my rucksack and leave the room. My tears start again as I reach the street. I don't understand. Why couldn't we just be happy? The future's far away. I keep walking, waiting for him to charge after me – to beg me to come back, to hug me and insist we spend the next six hours together … but he doesn't even follow.

I tap the mike. 'Testing, testing.'

Zoe giggles. 'God, Jess. I didn't think people actually did that.'

'Of course, how else can you check the balance?'

Half my flat are in the pub with me. It's open-mike night, and as I'm taking it seriously, I asked the guy in charge if I could check the sound before it started. I get a drink and a group of us sit together. The people performing don't have a lot to offer and there are yawns and a few heckles. The place fills up – I'm going to have a large audience. Some third-year comic leaves the stage to a weak round of applause. It's my turn and, as confidently as I can, I walk to the mike and adjust my guitar strap.

'Hi everybody. I'm Jess and this is a song I wrote myself – "Cool Blue Night".' I strum the first three chords then start to sing. Somehow, performing in front of people, all the sadness I've been feeling goes. My energy flows and I don't doubt myself. The song is about Benjamin, but it's not his now, it's for everyone in the audience who's lived through a Cool Blue Night. When I'm finished my flatmates help whip it up: Zoe and Lacey cheer, Amir whistles. Other people are applauding too, and one guy catches my eye. He's clapping and smiling and when I sit down, he keeps looking across at me. I go to buy us a round, and then he's at the counter too.

'Great song,' he says, 'I really liked your song.' He's got a posh English accent.

'Thanks.' He's the antithesis of Benjamin. Blondish hair and blue eyes, taller and built like he plays rugby.

We stand near each other, an awkward silence between us. The barman presents me with four pints.

'Oh.' There's no way I can carry them all back in one go.

'Let me help you,' he offers, and I do.

Later, back at the flat, everyone's got an opinion.

'Oliver,' says Amir, doing his best to impersonate an English accent, 'definitely likes you.'

'Likes her?' Zoe says. 'That's an understatement.'

'I don't get you, Jess,' says Lacey. 'You write all these love songs and say you want a boyfriend, but you won't even go clubbing with the guy.'

'I didn't say I wouldn't go clubbing with him. I just didn't want to go tonight.'

'I think you're going to have to make more of an effort.' Lacey shrugs. 'I'd have gone out with him.'

'Me too,' says Amir. 'He's cute.'

'I reckon you're still hung up on that guy in London,' Zoe says slyly, 'the one you insist *nothing* happened with.'

'I'm not,' I say, but feel myself blush. 'And I'll text Ollie tomorrow.'

I'm lying next to Ollie trying not to move. He's sleeping. The bed is so small, I can barely breathe without disturbing him.

Don't the people who design these rooms ever give consideration to what students actually do? I stare at the ceiling. We've only been on two dates and I thought tonight might be a big mistake; I stubbed my toe and then tripped on my jeans, but it turned out okay. I can't say I love him, but maybe in time I'll fall in love. I always thought love should come before sex, but that was before Benjamin. I've slept with somebody else now. Would Benjamin even care? We got in too deep and this is me finding my way out.

CHAPTER 33

Benjamin

It's late. I'm on the top deck of a bus with a cheap mobile in my pocket. I've worked this much out: sitting on a moving bus will make it harder for them to trace my call, and I should have at least three minutes undetected. I'll only use the SIM card once. Gazing out the window, I watch the streets below. The Christmas shoppers have gone but the storefronts are lit with festive decorations. Even when Mum was alive, I didn't like Christmas. It only highlighted the family I didn't have, and Gil described it as a capitalist trick. I rest my head against the cold glass and grip the phone. Soon I'll take the biggest risk, but it wasn't meant to be like this. I thought I'd have Jess on my side.

She sent the letter to the hotel. My name wasn't on it, only the room number. I read it calmly, hearing her voice as it told me she'd made a decision: she didn't want to see me again and I shouldn't try to contact her. She'd felt very sad after our last meeting, but she was also grateful for what I'd given her. She was seeing somebody else. Her last words: *I wish you all the best.*

I put the letter back in the envelope and hid it in a drawer. I've kept it like it's something worth keeping when every sentence is a shard in my heart. But it's teaching me a lesson. The price you pay: I pushed her away. Why did I do that?

Two nights later, it all felt worse. I dreamt I was in a hotel room while Jess and her anonymous boyfriend made love on the bed in front of me. There was a lot of sighing and they changed position. And I just sat there with a flame of sheer white pain burning through me. My mind yelled, 'What did you expect? You pushed her away.'

I drafted four possible letters. So what if she didn't want to hear from me, I was entitled to a last word. None of them were sent. Only when Baz gave me my documents did I post her the briefest note.

Glad you're well. Benjamin Turner is past tense. I'm Joshua Gresham. Take care. We knew love.

She didn't send anything back.

Now, the world goes by in a Christmas haze. Thinking about Jess never makes me feel good and I get off the bus at the next stop. I don't make the call. I can't tonight when my head's in the wrong place.

'Benjamin.'

I don't open my eyes, pretending to sleep. It's Gil, and if he's here, it's a sign that I should be handling things better.

'I'm Joshua now,' I say softly.

'Funny, that. Joshua was our second choice of name after Benjamin.'

I sit up on the bed. 'Yes, Mum told me. If you hadn't got a thing about second names I'd have been Benjamin Joshua.'

He looks calm and relaxed in the chair by the desk. 'Let's talk about what you're doing, shall we?'

I'm not sure I'm going to like this conversation.

'You messed up with the girl. Jess provided you with some kind of happiness. She was also your ticket back to Adam. He's still got Phoenix.'

I wait a long moment before responding. 'I'm not sure it's relevant now.'

'It's relevant, Benjamin. It's the best revenge you can take. It's my life after death. The Disciples' resurrection.'

'But what about my life?' I whisper.

'You've done the right thing, you've got a new identity. That's part of it.'

'I want to talk about Atholl,' I say bluntly, because it's important. 'I think he knew who I was. I don't understand it all, I can't join all the dots, but it's eating me up. He knew I was your son.'

'Go on,' he says slowly.

'Tom said "They've known who you are for some time," but how did they know? Mo didn't tell them about me until he was interrogated, however, Atholl … he's the only other person I've been close to. He's been a mentor. He pushed me on, he gave me a break, but now … I'm not sure what any of that was about.'

Gil sits still, watching me.

'The project I was working on, that I was so proud of, I've discovered it was being sponsored by LifeStar Corporation.' I watch his face; he should be shocked.

'So?' He doesn't seem bothered.

'I think it was a test.' He needs to understand. 'Somehow, they figured out who I was and then they gave me a test – a project sponsored by LifeStar Corporation. They'll have wanted to see if I would try to get into their system, or sabotage it or something like that. They wanted to see if I was linked to you. If you were directing me.'

'LifeStar's a company with many subsidiaries, and it will sponsor a lot of projects. So it wasn't necessarily a test. They just gave you a project because you're good.'

'Don't you care? I thought you'd care.'

'This isn't news, Benjamin. When you told me you were doing research for Sensory Science Tech I knew what that meant.'

'Why didn't you say anything? You hate LifeStar. You've done everything you can to bring them down. I don't understand.'

'Don't understand what? My son was working on a project to help restore people's sight.'

'Gil, I could have done something. I could have got into their network. I had to upload every result I got directly onto their system. I had a password and could have infiltrated it.'

'And how long do you think it would have taken them to trace such activity back to you? Minutes? Hours?' He raises his eyebrows. 'And then what?'

I pause. 'They'd have locked me up.'

'That's if you were lucky. They'd have destroyed you. Completely.'

Shit, he's right. I'm not thinking straight. 'Then it wasn't a test.'

'Be careful what questions you ask, Benjamin,' he says firmly. 'There may be answers you can't bear to hear.'

I close my eyes, exhausted. He doesn't say any more, because he's gone.

Tonight, I'm the only one on the top deck of the bus. A camera is watching me, but it's just for the driver to check what's going on. If MI5 watch it later, I don't care – I'll be gone. I dial his home number. I phoned the department secretary, made up some story and got it off her. It's past one in the morning so he should be asleep and that's good; I don't want him to have too much time to process what's going on. It takes a while for him to pick up.

'Hello.' His voice is deep; he sounds groggy.

'Professor Atholl, it's Benjamin,' I say slowly, clearly.

'Benjamin?' There's a pause, a muffled sound as though he's dropped something, then, 'Benjamin.' His voice is clearer. He's awake now.

'I saw Mo,' I say, trying to keep my voice slow and steady.

'He told me you said I'm the kind of guy who'd be an asset to both sides.'

I let the silence expand between us.

'Yes,' he eventually says. 'We should talk.'

'I think they want to kill me. I can't know they won't.'

Another pause. 'They would much rather you were alive. They do want to negotiate.'

I glance at my watch. It's been almost a minute. 'I'll think about it,' I say, and hang up.

The bus pulls in at the next stop. I walk down the stairs but my legs feel like jelly. I step out into the cold December night, shivering. I had to know what he was thinking and what he knew. Atholl was my favourite teacher. I'd sit in his room for tutorials, and he always gave me time. Yet he didn't say anything that showed the smallest degree of care or affection. Nothing like, 'I'm so glad you're alive,' or 'Thank God you're okay.' Not a single word. Instead, he sounded cold, like they'd already got to him, like he might even be an agent. 'They would much rather you were alive.' My heart is pounding. Is that what he's been all along?

I miss Adam. Really miss him. I keep my head down as I walk past Euston and King's Cross station but all I want to do is go inside, buy a ticket and head north. Words from our conversations repeat in my head. 'I wish I could tell you it will be easy, but I think you know it won't be easy.'

I want to sit in his study and tell him how much it hurts, and what I've got wrong and not been able to see. And I'm glad he's got Phoenix. The memory stick. It would only complicate things if I had it. I'm discovering the truth except I don't know where it leads. Did Adam ever experience that?

Yet I can't go to Adam. It's too dangerous, and I won't betray him like others have betrayed me. I also hurt his daughter, although she's handling what happened much better than me.

The worst thing now, though, is I can't hear Gil anymore. He turned up when I didn't want him, and now he's disappeared when I do. Adam was right again. 'He's gone. I can't take him away from you – he's already dead.'

It's dark and cold and I'm standing in a park. They've closed all the gates; everyone's gone but I'm still inside.

'You fucking bastard,' I shout at the air. 'Where are you now? Hey? Atholl's an agent, I've worked that out. You're meant to show up and help me.' I glance to my right, my left: nothing. 'Gil, you're an arsehole. You only care about you – not me.'

The moon stares down impassive, and suddenly I see what it sees. I'm a man in a park, raving.

CHAPTER 34

Jess

Oliver is sitting beside me on my bed as I scroll through the photos on my phone. There's shot after shot of us playing in the snow, and Rufus our fantastic snowman.

'Rufus looks better in my scarf than I do,' he says.

'A bit.' I smile.

The pictures have come out well. Great selfies of us together. Given snow is so rare now in Glasgow we had to make the most of it; I even skipped a class.

'That one I don't like,' he says, because his hat's askew, 'but that one I do.' I scroll on. 'I think we look good together, don't you?'

I nod. We snuggle into each other, and his body helps to warm me up. Our lips meet and his mouth tastes slightly of the biscuits we've eaten. We kiss for a while and then go back to looking at photos.

'So this is my dad and mum.' I bring up a few pictures and he stares at them a while.

'Can I say something?'

'Of course.'

'You don't look anything like them.'

'Really? Most people think I look like Mum.'

'Well, maybe a bit, but you're much prettier.'

'Yeah, but she's thirty-seven, so how pretty do you expect her to be?'

'I like your dad's distinguished beard. I think my father should grow a beard. He shaves very badly so he should definitely grow one. It would look a lot better.'

I scroll through another couple of shots. It feels strange showing Ollie my parents. A part of me wants to keep them private.

'I can't wait to meet them.'

'You will,' I say shyly.

'I will?'

'Ollie, most people want to avoid their girlfriend's parents, not meet them.'

'Do they? Well, I'm different. I'm intrigued by people.'

'You can't meet them this Christmas, not properly. Only when they pick me up. We've got a very full house. Lots of relatives staying.'

'Christmas break is four weeks. Would you like to come down to London? My folks would be happy to put you up. We've got a big house near the Thames. Honestly, you'd like it.'

I look away and don't answer. Something about Ollie feels very intense and I don't know what to say. Instead, I tell him I'll think about it, and pop to the bathroom. I stay in there longer than I need to and when I go back he's looking at my phone.

'Ah ha,' he says, 'I've found your mystery man. The one you never name.' He sounds cheerful but blushes slightly like he knows he shouldn't be doing this.

I sit back down beside him. He's found the folder with my pictures of Benjamin.

'I guess from a girl's point of view he's what you'd call alright. If nothing else you have good taste in men.' He smiles, but I'm not relaxed.

'I meant to delete them. I'd completely forgotten they were there.'

'I don't mind them, although I do find it kind of weird you never mention his name. That's like he's still got some hold over you.'

'It was Josh,' I say firmly. 'Okay. Joshua. He's irrelevant now.'

'I believe you,' he says softly. He looks at a few more photos but I'm very uncomfortable. 'You know who he reminds me of?' he says. 'That guy we were discussing in my politics class – what's his name? Oh, yeah, Gil Zimmerman. The guy they shot. The leader of the Disciples.'

'Josh hated the Disciples,' I say, but my voice is too loud. 'He was very political, and he loathed them. He'd hate it if he heard anyone say that.'

'So I know how to wind him up then, if I ever met him.' Ollie smiles again and shrugs. I tell myself he means no harm. I have to stay calm.

'Pass it over.' He gives me my phone and I delete the folder and all the photos in it.

Ollie watches. 'Jess, you didn't have to do that. I was just teasing.'

'Actually I did. Like I've told you, he was somebody I should never have got involved with. I don't need him on my phone.'

It's two in the morning when Ollie goes back to his room. Alone, I cry, soundlessly. But it's ridiculous, Benjamin and I are finished. I'm going out with Ollie and I didn't need to delete the photos; Ollie didn't even mind them. Yet I couldn't risk him thinking about them anymore or making some other connection with his politics class. They were my only pictures of Benjamin; I always thought I might show them to Xav. How can I be this upset? My feelings don't make sense. Things are good with Ollie; maybe I don't love him yet but things, mostly, are good. And with Benjamin ... I loved him. Even when I hated him, I loved him. What am I on about? *Even when I hated him, I loved him.* That's mad. Well, I am a bit mad about Benjamin but maybe that's alright. I comfort myself with that, and finally fall asleep.

Dad slams the car boot shut – everything I need is safely on board. He gets in the driver's seat. 'Your mum drove down so I'll drive back.'

I'm pleased because that means she can read my lips and we can talk. 'What did you think of Oliver?' I ask her.

'He seems nice.'

'And?'

'I only met him for ten minutes, Jess.'

'Mum, you've usually got more of an opinion than that.'

'He likes you,' she says.

'I like him too.'

'It's only your first term.'

I sit back and look out the window. I don't think she likes him. I hope she's not going to be like this with everyone I go out with. 'The thing is, Mum,' I say drawing closer, 'you only ever went out with Dad. It's not like you ever experienced anything else. The world's not like that now.'

'I'm not sure the world was like that then,' Dad says jovially. He glances at me briefly.

'No,' I say, 'you were just a couple of freaks.'

I stare at the landscape as we head out of Glasgow. We'll be driving for hours and I already feel bored at the prospect of going home. At least Aunt Em and Theo arrive in a week, then I can chat with Xav and play with Tommy. I wonder what I'll say to Xav, how much I'll tell him.

After a while I ask Dad carefully, 'Did you ever hear anything again from Benjamin?'

'Benjamin? No, although I take that as a good sign.'

I watch his reflection in the rear-view mirror. Will I ever tell him that I know he's got the memory stick? Probably not. I'd have to confess that I saw Benjamin after he left.

'You think of him?' Dad asks.
'Yeah. Sometimes. I hope he's okay.'
'Sometimes,' Mum says, reading Dad's lips, 'I think of him.'
I bend over the back of her seat to give her a hug.
'Hey?' She turns to me and smiles.
'I missed you,' I say. 'I'm glad to be going home for a while.'

CHAPTER 35

Benjamin

I'm standing outside the university gates. It's late afternoon, cold and dark. Light shines out from the windows and there's a distant silhouette in Atholl's office. I'm surprised he's there – his wife and kids are probably at home. Perhaps he wants a break from them. The kids screaming and fighting over toys. Is there a turkey in the fridge? Is somebody wrapping presents for him? Does he ever think about what he's done to me?

It's quiet. There aren't many students about, just those from overseas and those who don't want to go home for Christmas. I pull up my coat collar and wear my woollen hat low, almost covering my eyes. Entering the building, I walk down the familiar corridors and the place is deserted; nobody pays me any attention. I reach his door and listen. Silence, except for a burst of laughter far away. I knock twice and place my hand in my pocket, wrapping my fingers round the gun.

'Hello?' He sounds tired.

I walk in and raise the gun. 'Put your hands up,' I say as quietly and as controlled as I can. 'I'm not going to hurt you, but I need to feel safe. So you'll put your hands up, walk away from the desk, and sit with me.' I motion to the chairs we use for seminars. There's a small table in the middle.

He raises his arms and comes forward. I push a couple of

chairs back from the table, creating space between us. If he leaps at me, I'll have enough time to shoot first. He sits.

'I trusted and admired you,' I say.

I wait for him to answer but he must think it better not to say anything. It's possible he's afraid.

'My parents are dead. Both of them. My life has been destroyed, and I think you've played a part in that. I want you to tell me how you knew.'

'Knew?' he asks.

'Yes. I've figured out enough to realise you've known all along who I am. I don't get that. You couldn't possibly have known from my A-Level results, or my application form, or the quality of my work that I was Gil Zimmerman's son. But somewhere along the way you figured it out, *they* figured it out. Then decisions were made and a plot to kill my father was hatched. You said they want to negotiate but I need to understand how they knew first.'

'Benjamin,' he says, his voice surprisingly gentle; he's not afraid. 'You can put the gun down. This room isn't bugged. I've got no emergency alarm. I *am* a university professor.'

I think he's trying to unnerve me. His gaze is kind. 'Yes, but that's not all you are.'

'Benjamin, I don't understand how you *don't* know.'

I shake my head, bemused. 'People say I look like him, but lots of people look like somebody else.'

He says slowly, 'How do you think the security services recruit people?'

I answer carefully, considering it. 'Like every other government agency. They advertise. You fill in a job application form and if they like you, you get an interview. And I don't doubt there's the usual backdoor corruption. They'll home in on particular people they like because they've got the right kind of accent, colour of skin, politics.'

'They'll home in on particular people because they've got

the right kind of talent,' he says pointedly. 'Sometimes they recruit directly from universities. Oxford and Cambridge traditionally. But places like here too. Some of Porton Down's staff were recruited directly from Imperial.'

I think of Porton Down and its scientific work into chemical weapons, poisons and disease.

'Okay, but that doesn't answer my question.'

'You're a bright student. The kind of person that interests them. Of course they check people out before they approach them. They started looking into you and the background checks didn't add up, so they looked a little deeper.'

'A little deeper?'

He nods.

'Just how deep? Did they have informants in the Disciples? Was Tom involved?'

'Tom?'

'You know who Tom is.'

He shakes his head. 'No. What happened was I found a photo of you with your father.'

'What?' I stare at him. 'No.' I grip the gun. 'No such picture exists.'

'It does. I found it in your mother's bedside table.'

I look at him and hear his words, but something's not adding up. He's speaking English, I should be able to understand, but …

'What the fuck are you saying?' I ask, strained. 'Why would you ever be near my mother's bedroom?'

'Why do you think?' he asks very softly.

My hand is shaking; I need to hold the gun tight. 'Are you telling me you slept with my mother?'

He doesn't answer.

'She's dead,' I say loudly. 'They killed her. And you're saying you slept with her.'

'She wasn't meant to die. It got out of hand.'

'No.' I'm trembling. 'No. I heard it. It was a decision they made.' I feel sick, almost giddy. None of this is making sense. 'How did you ever get near her?'

'We met at the Science Festival Fundraiser. I thought you'd remember.'

'You spoke to each other for a few moments, that's all.'

'It was a little longer than that and we met a few times afterwards.'

I'm breathing too quickly. I don't want to believe this. 'You're a married man.'

'No. I don't know whatever made you think that.'

'My mother … she'd never have gone with you. You're lying.'

'Am I? As it happened, she initially approached me. It's possible your father encouraged it – she certainly asked a lot of questions, in the nicest possible way of course. We spent a couple of very pleasurable afternoons together, but I appreciate she didn't tell you. Indeed, we agreed that would be best – we didn't want you worrying about any kind of favouritism. You should be judged on your work alone.'

'Shut the fuck up!' I yell. 'You're playing with my head.' I stand up and point the gun at him. I should shoot him, kill him now. We're not having a conversation. He's laying a trap.

He shifts where he sits. I think he's afraid now. He says softly, 'There's a folder in the top drawer of that filing cabinet marked "Potential".' He motions with his head. 'If you bring it to me, I can show you.'

I keep the gun pointed at him but move to the filing cabinet. Riffling through its contents, I barely take my eyes off him. I find the folder, place it on the low table, and shake out its contents. Papers scatter and then a photo slides into view. I pick it up. It's real, printed on shiny paper. A small image taken years ago, the colours slightly faded.

I am three or four years old and sitting on a sofa. To the right is my mother and on the left is Gil. Both of them are smiling. They're leaning towards each other like people in love, like parents sheltering the child sitting between them. What I see is a family. Once. A long time ago. I had no idea my mother had such a picture.

We're silent. Atholl's watching me. I wonder if he can see it – my heart splitting into two, three, four …

Somewhere in the room he continues. 'I'm sorry, Benjamin. I'm sorry it ended as it did. Please, save yourself now. Negotiate.'

But I am not in my body. I'm not even sure I'm there. I'm a lost soul whose world has shattered.

CHAPTER 36

Jess

We pull off the road near the loch. I'm in the car with Dad, Xav and Aunt Emma while Mum's got Theo and Tommy in the pickup truck. Greg refused to come. 'I'm not going swimming in water just above freezing – you're off your rockers.'

We walk to the water in our down jackets, hats, gloves and scarves. The snow has partially melted and scrunches beneath our feet; our breath clouds in the air. There's not another vehicle or person to be seen. We huddle closer. Not for the first time since they arrived, I feel a sudden intense happiness, like a big warm hug. I love being with them all. We're a family, coming together and even sharing secrets.

I went with Dad to collect them from the airport. Given everything that had happened with Benjamin, and me starting uni, I was worried I might not be able to relate to them like before. But when we all squeezed into the car, Tommy plonked himself on my lap and talked a hundred and one words to a minute. He had us all laughing and I knew then everything would be okay.

Since then we've settled into a chilled holiday routine. Walks together and hanging out. Streaming films and playing computer games, and one evening Xav and I had a freak-out dance session. Most nights, everyone goes to bed before midnight then Xav and I will sit up chatting into the early hours.

One afternoon, I walked into the kitchen and Dad and Emma were alone, chatting.

'Don't blame yourself,' she said. 'You did your best.'

'You wouldn't have been so naïve.'

I glanced across at them. 'What you talking about?'

Both of them fell silent. I understood. 'Benjamin.' I was glad in a way they were talking about him. 'What do you think, Aunt Em?'

'I think I'd have made the same decision as your father,' she said softly. 'I'd have found it difficult to turn him away. Although I wouldn't have trusted him. And I'm sorry he behaved as he did.'

'You mean drugging Greg and stealing the pickup truck? It wasn't good, that's for sure, but it wasn't *bad* bad, either, was it?'

'Possibly not,' she said. Then after a pause, 'Did he become a friend?'

I blushed. 'A bit. I mean he was around a lot, and it's easier to be friendly than not.'

'So you're also caring like your father.' She smiled.

Somehow, their discussion gave me permission to talk about Benjamin too and I told Xav about him. I didn't say anything about us sleeping together, just that I'd grown to like him as a friend.

'The Disciples are such a secret between our families,' I said.

'Yeah, but when one of them has stayed with you for weeks, I guess you've got to talk about it.'

I realised though he didn't care that much. He was into his girlfriend Julie, although that didn't sound serious to me, not like I'd experienced with Benjamin.

Now, at the loch side, the landscape looks beautiful and the water calm. Dad unzips his jacket and starts to take his clothes off.

'Dad, you're not really going in, are you? It's freezing.'

'I said I was, and so I am.'

He's down to his underwear in seconds.

'You're not seriously taking everything off?' I say, shocked as he removes them too.

Theo chuckles. 'Look away, Jess.'

I turn to Mum but she just shrugs.

My father, pale and naked, walks quickly into the water. The scar on his left shoulder, a childhood wound, looks particularly pronounced. He whoops and shivers and then dives down, submerging himself completely.

Tommy is jumping about, excited. 'Come on, Dad, let's do it too.'

Theo hesitates and then unzips his jacket. My uncle isn't as slim as Dad so I'm kind of amazed that he too just strips off. He's got even more tattoos than I'd realised. 'I'll leave my underwear on, promise.' He smiles at me. Tommy takes his lead from Theo and then both of them, naked but for their briefs, run into the water. Their shrieks will be heard for miles.

Xav turns to me. 'Shall we?'

'No way,' I say quickly.

'Theo,' Aunt Emma calls out. 'Two minutes only. It's far too cold.'

My father finally emerges. He's so far out into the loch; I don't know how he does it. I wave for him to come back. Theo and Tommy splash about near the edge, and Mum turns and goes to the pickup truck.

'I'm getting towels and blankets – they're going to need them!' I can't tell if she's annoyed or amused.

'Jesus, it's freezing.' Theo wades out of the water. His teeth are chattering. 'I've no idea what made me think that would be a good idea.' Mum comes back and opens a large towel, and then a blanket for him.

'You didn't think, sweetheart,' Emma says gently. 'Too busy imagining you're still a kid with your cousin.' She turns her attention back to the water. 'Tommy, come here and out now.'

'I'm going to Uncle Adam.' Tommy's swimming quickly further out into the loch.

'Tommy, come back!' Emma shouts.

Then I have this powerful feeling that I know what's going to happen. Something's about to go wrong. The afternoon will stop being the safe fun we were having. Mum must feel it too because we both scream.

'Tommy!'

He disappears below the surface.

'Dad, Tommy's gone under!' I yell. His small body has gone.

But Dad's seen it too. He races back across the water, swimming faster than I thought possible, and dives under. Aunt Emma throws off her coat and wades out with her clothes on. She goes under too. Every second's interminable. How long can Tommy hold his breath? And in such freezing water? How will Dad and Emma get to him in time?

Theo stands on the water's edge, shaking. Xav's eyes are wide with horror and I stop breathing. One second, two, three … ten, eleven. Dad's not come up yet and neither has Tommy. What if he can't find him? The water ripples; Emma's reached them. I count more seconds. I don't understand what's happened.

All three of them burst through the water's surface. Tommy is coughing, crying. 'Mummy, Mummy.' He holds on to Aunt Emma, pulling at her hair. They swim back quickly, holding his head above water.

Theo and Mum coddle them in towels and blankets while Tommy's crying. 'Mummy, I breathed underwater. I could feel it in my chest. I thought I was going to die.'

Silent tears track Xav's cheeks and I'm crying too. When we're a bit calmer, and it's clear that everyone's alright, we head back to the cars. Emma won't let go of Tommy. She gets in the pickup truck with Mum and Xav; they drive off quickly.

I get into the car with Dad and Theo. Dad starts the engine but doesn't move. I think it's hitting him, just how crazy it was to do that. To even let Tommy consider it. He turns to speak to Theo, but what he says surprises me completely.

'I didn't think it could be hereditary. I never thought that.'

'Let's not talk about it now,' Theo says firmly. 'It's too much, okay? We need to get back.'

We head home in silence. I catch Dad's eye every now and then in the rear-view mirror, aware that later, we have to talk.

CHAPTER 37

Benjamin

Atholl speaks in a low voice. 'They know you've not been involved in any act of violence. There's nothing you've done that means you can't go back to the life you want. You can finish your studies. You can live as a free man.'

Exhausted, I sit down but keep the gun pointed at him. 'Are you telling me they don't consider me a criminal?'

'You just need to give them Phoenix.' His eyes hold mine.

'They've already got that,' I say softly. 'You may not know Tom, but they do. And when they found him, and his laptop and the memory stick – they had Phoenix. Only I can't access it any more than they can because the stick's corrupted. So they want something that even if I wanted to, I can't give them.'

He's still. I don't know how much he believes me.

'Benjamin, you may not be able to provide every detail but you know the structure of the plan. You can take them through your thinking.'

'And in return I get my freedom? Except they'll monitor everything I do. They'll listen in to every conversation I have and put a tracking device beneath my skin. They'll have me in a cage only I'll be able to walk down the street and attend one of your lectures, and they'll pretend that's freedom.'

'You'll be able to earn their trust – and all those things,

202

which will seem necessary at first, will eventually go. You'll be free to live your life as you want. You can have a career, a home, friends, family.'

I look at him and wonder if he's rehearsed this. What in the world makes him think he knows what I want?

'They killed my family,' I say bluntly. I consider shooting him, watching the light fade in his eyes and letting him know just what I think.

'Benjamin,' he says, his voice firm, 'I'd like to suggest that you don't really know what your father was doing with Phoenix.'

'I know exactly what he was doing. And if that stick hadn't been corrupted, it would have ensured the Disciples would never be forgotten.'

'That is only one of two scenarios,' he says pointedly. 'The other is that it's a tool of negotiation. I appreciate it never crossed your mind that MI5 recruit directly from Imperial, but I'm sure it crossed your father's.'

He pauses. I tighten my fingers on the gun and shake my head.

'You really think he didn't know?' he asks.

'Why would he?'

'He led the Disciples. He'd have made it his business to know such things. It would be basic homework, especially as he'd have to consider if new members were genuine or agents.'

I want to tell him to shut up, I don't want to hear this, but …
'Okay, let's say you're correct. What does that have to do with me?'

'Your father would have known your attendance here was a potential risk to him.'

'No. He'd have stopped me.'

'Would he? Only you can answer that. As I've said, I suspect your mother approached me to try and suss the situation out. Who knows?' He shrugs. 'But it's surely fair to say he always knew at some point he might be caught or killed. And then, depending on *your* situation, Phoenix would allow you to negotiate with us.'

A clanging sound starts in my head. The room doesn't look right. 'My father would never want me to give you Phoenix. He fought his whole life. Never.'

'In normal circumstances, no. But he's dead. Your mother's dead. I think he'd want you to survive, don't you?'

The sound in my head is getting louder, piercing my thoughts. I stand and point the gun at him. 'You're fucking with my head.'

He stays very cool. 'I'm helping you see something.'

I need to get out. My thoughts are like a whirlwind, and I can't be in his room when they start adding up into something that makes sense. I stagger towards the door, feeling like I've been punched in the stomach; I'm winded. I look down the corridor but it seems to go on forever.

'Think about it, Benjamin.' Atholl's voice is clear behind me. 'I'm here for you to contact me again.'

I find my strength and run, heading out into the cold night. He'll phone them now and they'll try to find me, but I won't let them. I run down streets, slink down lanes, and eventually find an empty derelict warehouse. Somewhere to hide for a while and make sense of what I remember.

The last time I saw my father, before the night he was shot, was on a clear spring day. We'd had no contact for months, but had agreed to meet then. The trees were budding and although it wasn't warm the sun was high in the sky. Mostly, when we'd met up, it had been to work on Phoenix. It had developed in stops and starts, proving the longest project because it went beyond anything the Disciples had done before. But now it was complete, and this meeting with Dad would be different. It was just about us: father and son. I took a train out of London and joined him with my bike. We rode through the countryside and although I was the better cyclist, I didn't push ahead. I wouldn't let him out of my sight; it just felt good that we were together. We stopped under a tree for a picnic, and we didn't talk a lot but that also felt good; we were at peace with each other. Then I offered him a slice of cake.

'Hmm, it's good. Carrot cake?'

'Yeah. I don't think you've tasted my baking before so I made it for you.'

'Well, it's good.' He smiled gently.

There was a pause, and his mood altered. He said slowly, 'Benjamin, I know I've not always been a good father to you.'

I listened, surprised.

'I sense sometimes how much you want my approval, so I want you to know that you've turned into a young man I like and admire … and that's because of who you are. It's *despite* the fact you've had me as a father.'

'Okay,' I said, aware it felt an important moment.

'There's one thing all fathers want for their children.' He paused again. I had no idea what was coming but he was very serious. 'There's one thing more than anything – a deep biological and psychological drive – they want their children to survive.'

I didn't answer; he hadn't finished.

'I want you to survive, Benjamin, whatever happens to me and your mother.'

I shivered. 'Why are you saying this, Gil?'

'Because I'm the leader of the Disciples.'

I watched him, concerned. 'Is this your way of telling me you're going to disappear again?'

'That's always possible but it's not why I'm saying it.'

'Because … mostly, I thought, parents come out with stuff like "I want you to be happy and to do what you want with your life", not just "I want you to survive." But clearly, that doesn't count with me.'

'I want those things for you too, Benjamin – that's why I've allowed you to make the choices you have. I haven't interfered. But surviving, I demand of you.'

'You demand?' I said, perplexed.

'Yes.'

A flash of rage. I was so angry, incandescent, in a way I couldn't explain. 'Why is it, Gil, that even when you try to say something good about me, you leave me feeling like shit?' I stood up, my lower lip trembling. He was going to piss off again and I wouldn't see him for months, years. I knew what was happening. And who did he think he was – he hadn't interfered with the choices I'd made?

'You're leader of the Disciples, but you're not my fucking commanding officer. You're my fucking father!' I stormed off towards a tree in the distance. I stood under it, my back to him. Why was I crying? Why did I feel so angry?

After a while I heard his footsteps behind me.

'May I?' he said very softly, and he put his arms around me, hugging me from behind. This was our relationship. He hadn't hugged me for so long he felt he had to ask permission.

'Forgive me, Benjamin,' he whispered.

He enveloped me in his arms and kissed the back of my head.

'Please, Benjamin, forgive me for everything.'

CHAPTER 38

Jess

When we get home, Aunt Emma, Theo, Xav and Tommy retreat to the B&B where they're staying. Dad goes to take a warm shower, and I have a strong sense that we all need to be alone. My aunt is furious with Dad; I've never seen her look at him like she did today, like she was screaming at him without a word leaving her lips, like her eyes were daggers.

I find Mum in the kitchen and give her a hug. She embraces me back, warm and comforting.

'I don't want us to be fighting with each other,' I say as we release.

'Everyone's just in shock. It'll be alright.'

'It's Christmas tomorrow and I couldn't bear it if there's tension between us.'

'There won't be, Jess. Your dad and Emma have a bond between them that's very deep. She's upset, and your father should have thought about it more, but they'll get over it.'

'I don't understand what happened. Why did Tommy go down and … why did he say he was breathing underwater?'

'When Adam comes out of the shower he'll speak to you, okay?'

I nod but don't feel any better.

She puts her hands through my hair, drawing it out. 'Your

hair's got so long, Jess. I should give it a trim before you go back.'

She's trying to change the subject to cheer me up.

'No way, Mum. I might be a student but I'm not that skint.'

I go up to my room and lie down, exhausted.

A knock on my door wakes me. I must have fallen asleep. 'Yes.'

Dad comes in. His hair's still damp but he looks warm and snug now; he's in clean jeans and a sweatshirt. 'Hey, we need to talk.'

I sit up on my bed and he sits on the edge of my comfy chair.

'I need to explain something to you, and before you say anything just hear me through.'

'Okay.'

He takes his time. Whatever he's going to say I think it's difficult for him. 'So you've always understood that Emma, Theo and I were caught up with the Disciples and MI5 when my father whistle-blew on LifeStar Corporation. You've read it online and watched the footage. Perhaps you've wondered about my father, and what it meant that he was a geneticist, but perhaps not.' He pauses.

'No, not really,' I say, 'only that LifeStar were working on a genetic weapon of mass destruction.' The words sound strange in my room; they don't feel real. 'I've wondered more about how you and Gil survived going over that cliff.'

A long moment's silence.

'It's all linked,' he says.

My heart is pounding. I almost wish Benjamin was here so I wouldn't be listening to this alone.

'What's in the public domain was never the whole story,' he says, his voice low. 'Grandpa Minster did something to Emma and me, to our genes, he … he did things he never should have, but as a result, Emma and I can breathe underwater.'

I sit very still. 'That's impossible, Dad.'

'Not as impossible as you think. Why else can I dive down and swim so far out in the sea, or in that loch today?'

I remember the times he's done that. Never when we're around other people, but when we're on our own as a family.

'You're saying that was you breathing underwater?'

He nods.

'Dad, you're beginning to freak me out.'

'I've never told you about it before because I've never thought it relevant. But today – with Tommy – I think you have a right to know.'

'Tommy didn't breathe underwater,' I say abruptly.

'He did.'

Now he's stressing me. I remember what he said to Theo. 'What are you saying, Dad, that you think I might be able to too?'

'I don't know, but maybe it's possible.'

'Bullshit … bullshit!'

He stays still and calm.

I'm shaking I'm so upset. 'How dare you tell me this? How dare you? It's got nothing to do with me.'

'I understand you might feel afraid.'

'Afraid?'

'Yes. MI5 wanted us back then. They wanted to understand our genes and, while I don't think they'd be half as interested now, it's one reason I was so concerned about Benjamin revealing he'd been here.'

I stare at him. Everything he's saying is only making things worse. 'So you're saying my genes might be like yours.'

He nods.

'What? I'll go and stick my head in a sink full of water then, shall I? To see if I'm like you. Will that make you happy?'

He flinches, and when he speaks his voice is very low. 'No, Jess. It won't, and you're not going to do any such thing. If you can't breathe underwater you'll drown. I'm telling you about it because I don't want to lie to you. I can't pretend what happened today didn't happen.'

'What did happen to Tommy?'

'The cold got too much for him. I think he even passed out. He went under and when we got to him he was breathing, deep down in the water.'

'So he could have died if he'd not been able to do that.'

Dad grits his teeth and shifts uncomfortably. I've never been so angry with him. If he'd not gone into the water we wouldn't be having this conversation.

'And how did you find out *you* could breathe underwater?' I ask aggressively.

He doesn't answer.

'How, Dad?'

He shakes his head. 'It doesn't matter.'

'It does to me.'

Still, he won't answer. There are other questions though. 'So that's how you and Gil survived going over that cliff into the sea?'

'Yes. I saved him.'

'Because Benjamin couldn't understand it either.'

'You spoke to him about it?'

'Once. He said Gil wouldn't give anything away.'

'No. Gil would have kept it secret too.'

'Is there anything else I should know? Are there any other secrets that might affect my life?'

'No, and Emma's speaking to Xav and Tommy.'

'Because it's a shock. It's Christmas tomorrow and I don't want to be feeling shocked. I don't actually want to know any of this.'

'No. I understand that.'

'You're an adult, Dad. Tommy's a kid. You should never have let that happen.'

'So it's a big moment, Jess.' His eyes hold mine, serious and sad. 'You understand now, adults too, your father, can mess up.'

'Yes, you messed up,' I say.

'And my father messed up, in what he did to Emma and me. It's why we had to run. But I've always worked, and managed, to keep you safe. I've always done the best I can for you, Jess.'

He's upset, close to tears. Then I imagine him at my age, and how much he went through.

'I'm here for you, Jess, even if I sometimes mess up. And my father wasn't there for me.'

My throat feels tight. 'Okay.'

He gets up to go then pauses. For a moment I think he's got more to say, some other revelation, but to my relief he just says softly, 'I love you.'

I nod but can't reply. He knows anyway, I love him too.

Much later, Xav and I are in my attic room. We're trying to play chess but neither of us is very good.

'Are you sure it's the bishops who move diagonally and the rooks horizontally?' I ask.

He checks the rule book. 'Yeah. Definitely.'

We make a couple of moves each then he says, 'We're a family of freaks.' He doesn't sound happy.

'Yeah.' I sigh. 'But there's not a lot we can do about it. The one good thing is, at least Tommy's okay.'

'I don't see why your dad had to strip off and go into the water in the first place.'

'No. Unfortunately, I fear he's a big kid.'

'Mum said it's because it makes him feel free.'

'Really?' Does that mean that Dad feels trapped the rest of the time?

'She should have stopped him. You know they speak through their thoughts anyway, so even when he was underwater she could have called him back. What's the point of being a twin if you don't use it?'

What is Xav on about? I'm not listening to any more bull-shit tonight.

He takes one of my rooks. If I don't start paying attention, I'm going to lose.

CHAPTER 39

Benjamin

I wake. What day is it? Christmas Day or Boxing Day? No idea. There are shrieks of laughter in the hotel corridor. Doors open and bang shut, and somewhere a drunken voice is singing. My mouth is dry. I should probably try and eat; I haven't for days, but I don't want to eat.

Atholl's got to me. It's what they'll want, it's success for MI5. How did I ever imagine when I walked into his room that I was in charge? Because I held a gun and thought it would protect me. Wrong. I can't forget a word he said. Atholl slept with my mother. If only it were a lie, but Gemma loved Gil enough that if he'd wanted her to check him out she would have.

I think of the home we shared, Mum and I. I want to go back in time and put my key in the door. I'll call out her name as I open it and find her alive. No bloodstains in the hallway. No floorboards ripped up in my room. We'll hug and the softness of her body will comfort me. And then I'll tell her never to do anything for Gil when he's leader of the Disciples. I'll promise her I'm okay, and I don't want to study or go to Imperial. None of that matters. She just needs to always be there so that I can come home, and we can share a meal; I know she's there for me.

'Be careful what questions you ask, Benjamin. There may be answers you can't bear to hear.' Gil knew. I didn't listen because

I couldn't stop. I had to know, and now I do. I killed my mother, and probably my father too. Tom played his part, but I was the chief culprit. I was innocent and ambitious so they checked me out. They stole the one picture she had of us – my family.

Tom. I see it again, the life drain out of his eyes and his blood on the floor. I feel no satisfaction. He'd have given them the exact time and place; he knew Gil's movements, but MI5 were always going to get them. I sealed their fate long before. Maybe they just waited until Phoenix was complete. They shot my mother and I was hiding under the bed. Coward.

Noise in the corridor. Voices. Two women are making up the rooms. I put the 'Do Not Disturb' sign on the door so they won't bother me. I consider the possibility: I might never leave. I close my eyes and beg the world to be different.

I dream. I'm six years old again and walking down a hallway, the longest hallway, towards a front door. Gil's jacket is hanging up at the side and I put my hands in his pockets. The gun is hard and heavy.

'Benjamin, what are you doing?' Gemma is suddenly behind me.

I turn around and point the gun at her like it's a joke. I pull the trigger.

Who's that in the mirror? I'm looking at a reflection but don't see me, just my father. He says, 'I've allowed you to make the choices you have. I haven't interfered.' Is he real or a figment of my imagination? Does it even matter?

It's another evening, and to my surprise Baz is sitting on the chair by the desk. I thought he left weeks ago. Perhaps I'm dreaming.

He's still talking about my father. 'Gil would walk into the room and the energy would alter. He'd change it. He'd literally light it up.'

I don't say anything back, although I want to be on my own. Then the bathroom door opens and Gil walks out. He looks alive and well.

'Baz!' He walks towards him and they embrace. I'm his son but he doesn't see me.

'God, it's good to see you,' Baz says. 'I've missed you.'

Gil smiles. 'Of course you have. I'm a man people miss.'

'And I thought they'd killed you.' Baz shakes his head, incredulous. 'Man, how do you do it?'

'I'm like a cat with nine lives. Remember, I drove off a cliff into the sea. I didn't drown. I just keep coming back.'

Baz glances furtively at me, and then away. He whispers to Gil, 'Benjamin's here.' He motions with his head.

Gil doesn't turn to me. Instead, he sighs. 'What can you do? They don't make Disciples like they used to.'

I wake; my body is drenched in sweat. I can't bear another moment in bed. I've got to get out. Breathe some air. Touch reality. I find a bookshop and there's a big 'Sales' sign up in the window. Christmas must be over; that's a relief. I wander around. A sales assistant asks, 'Are you looking for anything in particular?' He smiles brightly. I think he's glad I'm not buying books online, I'm actually in a shop.

I want to tell him I'm looking for me, but the words won't come. I don't buy anything. I can't find the answer in a book.

I sit on a park bench in a square nearby. No one else is about. The temperature's freezing but the one good thing about the cold is that you feel it – it pinches your skin until you go numb. I stay there a while until the day starts shrinking towards night. When I look up, the sun is sitting in the trees. The trees are naked, without leaves, but despite that they're strong enough to hold the sun. An orb of fire. Then I see it, glowing. A nest. What nest is made of fire? Of course, I get it: a phoenix's nest. I keep looking till the sun burns my eyes. It's there, a phoenix, only it's so small it must be a baby. It's hiding from everyone but me. I go back to my hotel room and sleep.

I wake again. My mouth is parched and my eyes feel like there's sand in them. I haven't showered in days and can smell my own stink. I realise I'm probably losing it. I understand: I can't lose it. In the bathroom I avoid looking in the mirror. Turning on the shower, I feel the warm water; that's a good start. Then dried and dressed, I sit at the desk and take long deep breaths. I need to think. Somewhere, I have a future. There are options, choices.

I imagine killing Atholl. It'll be a moment of sublime satisfaction. I'll have taken revenge, I'll have found relief. But I've never shot anyone; I can't start now. Enough people have died. I try to imagine negotiating with him – but my imagination stops.

The papers for my new identity mean I have other possibilities. Joshua Gresham can apply for courses in America. He can win a scholarship to pay his way. Joshua can succeed … only Imperial had me tagged so what's to say other places won't too? It doesn't matter if I'm called Benjamin or Joshua. The more I excel, the more that strips away my safety.

There's the option I've tried to avoid: I take on my father's name, and as Benjamin Zimmerman I step up as leader of the Disciples. I get the memory stick back and reunite with Cesar. I take over where Gil left off. But … who am I kidding? I can't fire a gun and I had no idea what Atholl was up to. I don't think like my father.

At last, I realise I've run out of options. None of them add up.

I throw the gun in the Thames where it can corrode in the filthy water. It didn't help me with Tom, and I couldn't pull the trigger on Atholl. The gun's irrelevant now.

Back at the hotel, I continue to accept reality. I get out my father's notebook. I've exhausted its contents and used up all the help it contained. I tear out the pages, shredding them by hand, and rip the back cover from the spine. Something catches my eye, hidden within the folds of the cover, and I pull it out slowly. A small photo. I'm three or four years old and sitting on a sofa. To the right is my mother and on the left is Gil. Both of them are smiling.

My father had a copy too.

I can no longer feel my body. I am no longer there.

I put Joshua Gresham's documents in my rucksack and go outside; it's raining. I see the rain but I can't feel it. I start walking – it doesn't matter where. There are too many people. And shops and signs: Sale; Best Discounts; Final Countdown. Who gives a fuck? I gaze at the windows all dressed up as if what they're selling matters. Then I see him. A stationary figure among the crowd. Gil.

Dad.

Like he is in the photo. A young man who has a strange, messed-up family. His gaze is kind. He's smiling. And I need to get to him before he goes. Gil always goes. But I can travel through time and space. I can get back to then, and undo all that went wrong.

'Benjamin,' he calls me. 'Benjamin.'

I run to my father.

Run.

Somewhere a scream. I'm flying. Falling through the air. Too late … there is tarmac beneath me. Pain … darkness … voices fade …

CHAPTER 40

Jess

It's been a good day. We went shopping. I stood in the changing room trying on some skinny jeans and for the first time I thought of Ollie. Maybe he'll find me sexy in these? Yeah, I definitely think he will. Two pairs of jeans, three tops, a new coat and some knee-high boots later and I realised I'd done pretty well. The sales this year were good.

Now, I'm looking forward to Mum's best mac and cheese. It's a week's worth of dairy in one hit (normally she keeps our dairy intake down), and I love it. She stands proud at the top of the table brandishing a large serving spoon.

'Mary, I thought you said you'd rustle up something light,' Theo says. Aunt Em's been teasing him about his weight.

'It's light-ish.' Mum dishes it out to Xav and Tommy first.

'Mac and cheese is not light-ish, Mum,' I say.

'Just one spoon for you, Theo?' She turns to him.

'Well, given all the effort you've gone to, perhaps two spoons.'

Dad chuckles. 'At least two spoons for me.'

'Three please, Mary,' Greg says. 'I don't know what's wrong with all you youngsters, you've lost your appetite.'

'We had burger and chips for lunch,' Xav says.

'I didn't,' I remind him.

'No, Jess had the bean burger with salad. The *vegan* option. Yuck.'

'Mum, can't you make this sometimes?' Tommy asks Emma.

'Don't eat too quickly, love, or you'll burn your mouth.'

The phone rings. It's the business line in Dad's study. No one uses it socially.

'Ignore it,' Mum says.

It carries on for eight rings and then cuts out. We continue eating but the phone rings again.

'I thought I'd put it on answerphone,' Greg says.

Dad gets up. 'I'll check.'

'Adam, leave it. It's the holidays. It can't be important,' Mum says.

'Won't be a moment.' Dad leaves the room, shutting the door behind him. We hear him pick up and then there's just the distant murmur of his voice.

I push my fork up a couple of pieces of macaroni and eat them slowly. It's creamy.

Dad comes back into the room and the look on his face shocks me. We all stop.

'That was St Barts Hospital in London,' he says slowly. 'Apparently, a Joshua Gresham has had an accident. Quite a bad one, and when they asked him if there was anyone he wanted to contact, he told them Adam McKenzie and the name of our B&B. He didn't have our number but they checked it online.'

For a few seconds everyone looks serious and bemused; they don't understand.

'Oh, no.' My voice shakes. 'Oh, God, no.' Then everything I'd been keeping secret, everything I thought Dad and Mum would never know, comes tumbling out of me.

They all listen, silent. Dad's face gets paler as he learns each new thing. I was sleeping with Benjamin. I went to him in London. He was betrayed and beaten up by someone called Tom.

'Jesus,' Theo mutters. 'That fucking bastard.'

I helped him get new documents from a bloke called Baz. And then, the last time I saw him was the happiest we'd been but he went and screwed it up.

'But I don't want him to be hurt, Dad,' I say, tearful because it's hitting home, what's really happened. 'He was horrible to me, but I don't want him to be hurt.'

'Of course not,' Emma says gently.

Dad is more upset than I think I've ever seen him. 'I need to have a few moments on my own.' He gets up and leaves the room.

I turn to Mum. 'I'm sorry.'

She's close to tears herself. 'It's alright. I knew, Jess. I knew you were sleeping with him.'

'You did, but you never said anything.'

'No. Not to you. But I spoke to him.'

'He never told me that.'

'No, we agreed he wouldn't.'

Xav and Tommy are fidgeting. I can see they don't know what to do or say. Uncle Theo's clearly thinking about the Disciples and Aunt Emma watches me kindly. I can't stop crying now.

'You still love him,' she says. It's obvious.

Greg finally speaks. 'One of us will have to go to him. And it should probably be me.'

Dad won't come out of his room. He's been in there for ages. Dinner finished a while ago and all the washing up is done.

'I'll go to him,' Mum says.

'He's angry with me,' I say. 'What if he doesn't forgive me? I wasn't meaning to lie – I just didn't tell the whole truth.'

'Of course he'll forgive you, Jess. But he's upset. Tom and Baz are people he knew, so it's distressing. That call came out of nowhere.'

She knocks gently on the door to his study and disappears inside. I decide to find Greg. He's digging out an old suitcase in his room.

'You really are going to him, aren't you?' I say, but not like I'm unhappy about it.

He nods.

'Should I come too?' I ask, although I'm not sure how I'd handle it.

'No. The best and safest option is that I go alone.'

He opens the suitcase and it smells musty. 'Can't remember when I last used this.' He opens a drawer and counts out five pairs of underwear.

'Will you stay with him then, for a while?'

'I think I should prepare for that, don't you?'

His eyes meet mine. Then he says gently, 'Sometimes, we feel responsible for people even when they don't deserve it.'

'Yes. He doesn't deserve it but if you go it will help him. He liked you. I don't think he ever really had anyone like a grandfather.'

'Just as well, considering he drugged me and took the truck.'

'But you forgive him, Greg, because you're kind.'

'Is that what I am, Jess?'

I nod and feel my lower lip tremble.

Greg changes the subject. 'And you say he was staying in a hotel?'

'Yes,' and I tell him where it is.

'I might have to go and get his stuff.'

'I guess. If he's broken bones he could take weeks to recover.'

'Aye.'

'But you won't be away for weeks, will you?'

'Hope not,' says Greg. 'No.'

I try not to think about what happens next or how bad Benjamin is. I just feel exhausted. I leave Greg, go to my room and collapse on my bed.

Greg's and Dad's voices break through my slumber – they're outside. I realise Greg's going. I hear the boot of the car slam shut. Jumping out of bed, I throw on my dressing gown and rush downstairs.

'Wait.' I'm crunching across the gravel in my slippers.

Greg puts the window down on the driver's side.

'I've got something for him,' I say, and my breath plumes in the air.

CHAPTER 41

Benjamin

My sleep is full of muffled pain, and an awareness that I can't move properly. My right leg's been pinned and rendered immobile. The fracture in my right arm is less serious; still, it's in plaster. My ribs and chest ache but there's nothing they can do for that but give me painkillers; the bones will heal in time. I'm told I'm a lucky man. They feared I had a brain injury – but the scan came back normal.

The painkillers they give me are strong. The room spins and I have to close my eyes. Sound swirls: the voices of other patients, snoring, and the occasional moan. A woman is visiting the man in the bed next to me. I hear her voice but I don't look. I sleep again, aware of pain.

'Joshua.' A soft voice in the fog of my mind. 'Joshua.' I know it. I need to open my eyes. I have to push through the fog, then I see him sitting there.

'Greg?'

'Aye.' His gaze is full of concern. 'Did nobody teach you how to cross the road?'

I wish I could laugh. Instead, I watch him watching me. He looks tired and he must have been driving for hours. They got the call and he came.

'Thank you.' There are things I need to say but my mouth's

too dry. I close my eyes because crying is only going to make me hurt more. My chest aches and my throat is tight.

He touches my hand; his fingers are warm. 'It's okay,' he says very softly.

There are tears on my cheeks and my fingers curl around his.

When I wake up the next day he's sitting there again. He glances over the top of a paper and twiddles a pencil in his hand. 'This is what I've been reduced to – crosswords.'

I give my best attempt at a smile.

'I'd like to say you look a fraction better than yesterday.'

The lunch trolley comes in. A tray is brought over to me and placed on the table that can be rolled across my bed. Greg looks at what I've got.

'How are you meant to eat this in your state?' He picks up the knife and fork.

'I've no idea.'

He helps raise my upper body, then cuts up the food.

'I'm not really hungry,' I say.

'I don't care. You're going to eat.'

I take small mouthfuls. I can't eat a lot but he seems satisfied that at least I've eaten something. Everything I do feels exhausting. My mind fogs, clears, then fogs again.

'Greg, I'm sorry I lied to you.'

'What?' he says, drawing closer and keeping his voice low. 'Because you drugged me and stole my pickup truck?'

'Yes, you trusted me and …' I stop. 'I'm sorry.'

He whispers. 'I don't know how much I ever trusted you, Joshua.'

'No?'

'No, but I did always like you.'

My throat feels choked. 'Okay.'

We're quiet for a while.

'Is Jess alright?' I ask.

'She's good.'

'I'm sorry I hurt her.'

'No point saying that to me. You'll have to speak to her about it.'

'If she'll speak to me.'

'Depends on how foolish she's feeling, doesn't it?'

'I guess,' I say. I close my eyes and sleep some more.

For the next few days he comes in and cuts up my food, makes sure I eat, and sits quietly while I sleep. There aren't any words to describe how glad I am he's there. At some point the nurse has a chat with him about my progress.

'You're likely to be here another week or so,' he says. 'Then, obviously, once you're discharged it will take time to recover. They'll give you crutches, and Jess said you've been staying in a hotel.'

I consider the stairs there. The small, tight shower and the friendless room. How will I move around on crutches? 'Yes,' I say, trying to hide the panic I feel at the thought of going back there.

'Is it a suitable place for you?'

'Not really, no.'

There's a long pause. 'So we'll need to think about what you're going to do.'

I nod but lie back. I feel sick.

'What if I were to suggest taking you home with me?'

I swallow and nod again. I can't speak; my throat feels swollen.

'I haven't spoken to Adam or Mary yet.'

'Okay,' I mumble.

'But I will,' he says. 'Jess will be back at uni, and if need be you'll keep out of her way.'

I shut my eyes because I don't want him to see me cry again.

But what if I can go back to somewhere I was happy? The attic room. The pain in my body lessens a little and my mind calms. I was happy there.

Two days later, Greg tells me he's going back to Scotland. 'I'm out of clothes and underwear.'

I grow hot and sweaty. 'You're going?' I say, trying to hide my distress. I'll be alone. I don't have anybody else.

'I am,' he says softly. 'But then I'll come back. Not immediately, but before you're discharged.'

'Okay.' I'm grateful.

'Joshua, there's something important I have to discuss with you.' He sounds very serious. 'Before they let you go, you'll see a psychiatrist. The concern is … you walked in front of that car. It was a deliberate act.'

My heart quickens. 'That's not how I remember it.'

'How do you remember it?'

'I was upset,' I whisper.

'What were you upset about?'

I take a few deep breaths – I'm not feeling good. Greg stands and draws the curtain round the bed to increase our privacy.

His face is very near mine and I don't have to speak loudly. I realise I have to say it, but it takes such effort.

'I killed my mother. They paid the price for my actions. My mother and father.'

He's very still. 'Bullshit.'

He needs to understand. 'They knew who I was, Greg. I became a pawn in their game. But if I'd not gone to Imperial, if I hadn't been so ambitious, if I'd cared less about my studies …' I'm breathing too quickly.

'If you'd cared less, what? You imagine they wouldn't have killed them?'

I nod.

'No, Joshua. You've been spending too much time on your own. Driving yourself crazy over a situation you could not control, and you're wrong to ever imagine you could.' He moves to whisper in my ear. 'MI5 killed your parents. They pulled the trigger. They made that choice. You could never have prevented it.' He sits back slowly.

'Sometimes,' I whisper. 'I see my father, and *he* knew.'

Greg watches me carefully.

'I ran across the road because I saw him. I wanted to make what happened different, to reach him and then make it different.'

He's shocked. I can see it in his face. I shouldn't have told him because he'll tell the psychiatrist now. I've got to get out of this hospital.

He says slowly, 'It's grief, Joshua.'

'What?'

'You've got to find your way back from the dead.' He pauses. 'I'm going to tell you something I've never shared with anyone. I lost my wife when she was young. Mary was at home then, at school. I had responsibilities, so I never told anyone how bad it got for me. But there were moments when all I wanted to do was join her.' He stops. I'm listening.

'It's a dangerous moment,' he says, 'when you feel like that. When you feel the dead calling you into their world. You've got to get yourself back from it.'

I don't move or speak. He's always been honest, but this feels raw.

'I've got something for you.' He removes an envelope from his pocket. 'Open your hand.'

He places it on my palm. My silver chain and pendant. 'Jess wanted you to have it.'

I look at the phoenix my mother gave me.

'It's powerful,' he says, 'the phoenix. A mythic creature. Symbol of rebirth and renewal.'

I can't speak. I have it again. She kept it safe for me.

'Do you know what myth is, Joshua?'

At first I don't hear him, but then I mutter, 'Stories.'

'No. Visions.'

I turn to him. He says, 'There are two kinds of vision, Joshua. There's the world you look at with your eyes – all the material and physical things around you. Then there's the world you look at with your inner eye – that's what we see with our soul. That's where myth comes from.'

He watches me. 'You were studying eyes from what Jess has told me. You wanted to help people see. But now you need to see for yourself, to use your inner eye, and find your way back from the dead.'

Greg seems altered. He's a wise man I didn't see properly before.

After a while he continues. 'Adam and Mary are prepared to let you back into our home. But you've got to be well enough for that to happen.'

I swallow and understand.

'Will you do it, Joshua?'

Finally, I manage. 'Yes.'

It's late, and hours since Greg left. What happened with him was exhausting. I hear the trolley being rolled in and then someone places a tray with my evening meal on the table. I open my eyes and thank them. I raise myself with difficulty, but I can do it. I don't want to eat but I do. Food is real. It's keeping me here on this earth. I need to come back.

I've slept so much for days, but now I lie awake for a long time. Everything Greg said is true. I think of my father – whoever he was. A man who lived in the news, in stories told and shared, and on footage online. A man who was one person to Gemma, another to Baz, Tom and all the others. It's possible the Disciples knew him better than me. He kept a copy of that photo of us together. A family. Except I'm three years old in that picture and he never took another.

'Please, Benjamin, forgive me for everything.'

He meant so much to so many people, but I got so little of him. In my mind I see him outside that store again. My heart is pounding and I've tears on my cheeks. He was calling me and I ran to him. I could've died. I see him standing there and it takes everything in me not to go to him. Not to follow. To acknowledge I'll never have what I never had. It takes everything but I leave him with the dead.

This is what my inner eye sees. The vision comes in a dream: I'm well enough to leave hospital. I walk back to the square and find the tree where I saw the nest. I look up, wondering how I'm going to get to it – I want to see the phoenix. Then suddenly, I'm high up amongst the branches and looking down. Below, walking into view, is Gemma. She's not hurt. Her body is whole: no bullet wounds, no blood. She's beautiful. I see a woman who's lived her life and made mistakes but always loved me. She's my mother. Her gaze rises to meet mine and her voice is full of joy.

'Oh, Benjamin. Look. You've got wings of fire.'

CHAPTER 42

Jess

When I get back to uni, the first thing I do is break up with Ollie. I feel cruel because he's upset, but I know it's for the best. Our feelings are too different, and I can't pretend I can love someone when I don't; Benjamin's taught me that. I want a break from seeing anyone so I can concentrate on studying and hanging out with friends – I want to have fun. It's good to be back in Glasgow. I can finally clear my head of everything that happened over Christmas.

After the call came through from the hospital, things got crazy. Dad, Aunt Emma and Theo gave me the third degree. They wanted to know everything Benjamin had said, and about Tom and Baz.

'Dad, I don't know everything, okay, I haven't seen him for weeks. But I do know he kept his promise – he didn't tell them anything about us or you.'

I tried to reassure them but they were still concerned.

'Tom knew us,' Theo said. 'He knew Dom survived and that we went to France. It took a huge effort on the Disciples' part to get us to safety. I find it hard to believe he didn't tell MI5.'

'He didn't. Benjamin was sure he didn't tell them.'

There was a tense silence. 'I think that's probably true,' Dad said. 'Nothing's happened and nobody's been here – nothing to indicate they know about us.'

'No.' Emma agreed. 'It's Phoenix they want, whatever it actually is – that's their priority.'

I sensed how jittery they were. 'And Dad's got Phoenix now,' I said, hoping that would help.

Theo and Emma grew very still.

'I'm sorry, Dad, I know I should have spoken to you before, but Benjamin told me you swapped the memory stick. It's part of why Tom beat him up so badly. It's possible he'd have killed him.'

'Jess,' Dad said slowly. 'I destroyed that memory stick.'

'Did you, Adam?' Emma asked gently. 'Really?'

'My great fear was that Benjamin would try and carry out that operation and fail. He'd screw up, or something would go wrong, and then … either they'd kill him or capture him, and that would lead them right back here. He wouldn't be able to hold out under interrogation.'

So that's why Dad did it.

'Adam,' Theo said, 'I understand why you took it, but *did* you destroy it? There really isn't any old loyalty to Gil?'

I was shocked. 'If Dad said he destroyed it, he destroyed it.'

'I destroyed that memory stick,' he said firmly. 'I have always felt loyal to Gil, and that's why I let his son stay. But the Disciples have been ripped apart. Phoenix is irrelevant. The only choice I have now is how involved I choose to get with Joshua – and seeing him move on safely.'

'My dear brother,' Emma said, serious. 'I hope that's the truth.'

I left the room. I didn't understand, it was like they didn't trust each other. Fortunately, the tension wore off and we managed to enjoy our final days together.

After that, I had some important chats with Mum. I didn't want her to think Benjamin had embroiled me in his troubles after he left. It was Gil who sat in my room in Glasgow and told me to go to him.

'And it sounds so crazy, because I don't know how much I believe in ghosts, but he was there right in front of me. And he gave me an address and that's where I found Benjamin.'

She didn't respond immediately.

'Sometimes,' she said thoughtfully, 'I thought I felt Gil's spirit here. I never saw anything, didn't smell or taste anything different, but I just sensed it in some way. Perhaps he was watching over his son.' Then after a pause she said, 'But what are ghosts anyway, Jess? Energy.'

'Energy?'

'Yes, spirit energy. A spirit energy that hasn't gone over to the other side, or a spirit energy that a grieving person won't let go of. The dead are dead, but we keep them living.'

'Is that what you think Benjamin was doing?'

'It's possible, but I wouldn't put it past Gil to hang around either.'

'Gil was a terrible father,' I whispered. 'So I can't believe he was ever watching over his son.'

'Benjamin obviously felt a lot for you, Jess, and he was in distress. So maybe Gil's ghost was the way in which *he* was communicating with you. He manifested it.'

Was such a thing possible? Were Benjamin and I really that close? I decided not to pursue it anymore.

Greg phoned every day to report on Benjamin's progress. Dad took the calls. I was scared to hear how bad he was, and then of my own feelings. Eventually Mum came to talk to me about his future.

'We're aware, Jess, that he doesn't have anywhere or anyone to go to once he's discharged from hospital, but it will take him time to recover.'

'Yes. I've thought about that. The hotel he's been staying in – it's not a very nice place.'

'So how would you feel if he came back here?'

'I've thought about that too. I feel sort of confused.'

'Yes, it's complicated,' she agreed.

'A part of me thinks that's what I want for him. But I'm not sure what it means for me. I don't know how I feel about him now.'

'That's understandable.'

'He hurt me, and …' I shrug. 'If I still love him, what do I do? And if I don't, also what do I do?'

'There's a bond between you, Jess, that's clear, but we don't want to make any decision that will hurt you.'

'No, but the reality is if we don't take him in that will hurt him.'

'Ultimately, that's his lookout.'

We were quiet. I felt very tired. Did the decision really depend on me? 'I'll be back at uni anyway, won't I? So it doesn't really matter. I won't be home for ages, and he might be gone by then.'

Mum nodded.

I let out a long sigh. 'I'll make sure I've taken all my stuff out of the attic for him.'

'He won't be up there – not initially. He'll have to be on the ground floor if he's using crutches.'

'I guess,' I say. I hadn't thought about that.

'And if, when you get back, he's still here?' Mum asked cautiously.

'I'll have got my head round it by then. Who knows, I might be glad to see him.'

'You can think about it.'

After Mum left my room I cried for a bit. I wasn't sure why. Things had happened that I had no control over and Benjamin would be back in my life. This time at least I wanted to feel I had more control over myself.

Before I left for uni I told my folks I was okay about Benjamin coming to stay. I'd even sent him a card.

'Get used to calling him Joshua,' Dad said. 'That will be important too.'

CHAPTER 43

Benjamin

The pain is less. I'm healing and manage to eat the food they give me – I can even taste it. People come and go from the ward. Visitors sit and chat by the other beds while I'm alone, but I know it won't be forever.

Adam and Mary have sent me a card: 'Get Well Soon.' It sits on the stand by my bed, and although it's the only one, it helps me feel better.

'Nobody visiting you again?' a middle-aged woman asks. She's come twice to sit with the man two beds down.

'Not today,' I say.

'Well, can I get you something then?'

'Yeah, thanks. A chocolate bar and can of drink would be great.' I motion to where I have a little money for her to use.

When she returns, she smiles. I wonder sometimes at people's kindness and remember the music festivals when I was bought food by other kids' families. I figure I'm lucky.

Jess sends me a card. The nurse brings it in and I open it carefully. There's a cutesy picture and her particular scrawl wishing me better. A smaller envelope is enclosed marked Private. I hold it in my hand but wait to read it; I don't want to be observed. I didn't treat her well. When I open it, her writing is the neatest I've seen.

I think about what she's said for a long time. I can't write back – it's just not physically possible. A part of me wants to phone her, to tell her, 'Look, I'm sorry, I don't know why I behaved like that either', but she already understands enough. A part of me feels relieved she's not seeing somebody else; another part of me feels cast out. Her letter was cold, her letter was warm. The one word she didn't use was *friend*. Maybe being friends just isn't possible – or maybe it is. At least at the moment we both have space from each other.

Greg has come to take me home with him and helps me into the car. The passenger seat is pushed back to give my leg maximum room, and there's a blanket in case I'm cold. My few possessions are in the boot.

'It'll be a long drive,' he says.

I nod. Really, I don't mind. I'll be glad to travel the miles getting further and further away from London.

He starts the engine. 'Ready to begin the rest of your life?'

'Yeah.' I smile.

Jess

'How's he settling in?' I ask Dad. We've been speaking for ten minutes but there was no way I was going to ask about Benjamin earlier. I've been training myself not to be curious. Not to get involved.

'He seems good. We've put him in Greg's room and he can make it to the bathroom on his own. I help him a bit with the shower – he's got to keep the plaster dry. But generally it's okay. And Dr Lee's got him on his list now so we should be able to get the plaster off and the pins out at the hospital here.'

'Did he say anything about me?' I'm completely ignoring my own rule.

'He said he was glad to be back here because it was a place where he'd felt happy, and he was pleased to hear you're enjoying uni.'

I'm not sure if I'm pleased or disappointed.

'Would you like to speak to him?' Dad asks.

'Not really,' I say. 'I just wanted to make sure he's okay, which he is. We'll speak another time.'

The weeks pass. Mum and Dad keep me posted on how Benjamin's improving, but there's no talk about when he'll leave. I decide not to go home for reading week. My folks would like to see me, but I'm enjoying myself in Glasgow and I don't want to deal with any feelings I have about Benjamin. Instead, I promise them I'll be home for Easter and they can pick me up at the station. I sense it would be wise to speak to Benjamin before I see him, but when I call home the words won't come. He must feel it too because then I get a letter.

Dear Jess

I'm writing this at the kitchen table you know well. I've hoped you might want to speak to me, but perhaps you said all you wanted in your letter.

I treated you badly and I'm sorry. I can't explain why I behaved like I did because it hurt you and it hurt me. I never stopped loving you, but I realise that saying that after everything I did sounds pretty shitty. I keep thinking of that old Elvis song Falcon Taylor covered where he doesn't behave well but keeps telling the girl 'you were always on my mind'. I never really got that, it's a shit excuse.

Yesterday, I graduated from Greg's room to the attic. Thanks for letting me have it – it's your room. I want to find a way to make things better, Jess. To show you I'm sorry for the hurt and confusion I caused. I realise now I'm a pretty messed-up person when it comes to girls and love, and you got caught in that mess. But can we be friends? I hope that's possible. We can put aside all that boy/girl stuff that messes things up. There were so many times when I loved just being with you. It wasn't even about the sex but the way you laugh and sing and can make me feel happy.

I hope this letter helps. Please let me know if there is anything I can do to make you feel alright about seeing me. I want to make things better. Can you forgive me?

Love

Joshua xx

I read it several times. It's hard to feel angry with someone who tells you they still love you, but they know that saying that is a bit shitty when their behaviour's been the opposite. Can I forgive him? I realise it might be easy to say you forgive someone but much harder to feel it. I don't respond or write back.

It's just before the Easter break and I'm speaking to Dad. We're about to end the conversation when I say, 'Can you do me a favour? Tell Josh I got his letter and it was a good letter.'

'I can do that,' Dad says, 'or you can tell him yourself.'

'I'll speak to him when I see him.'

Dad doesn't reply.

'It'll be fine, Dad,' I say. I don't want him to worry, and I bring the conversation to a close.

CHAPTER 44

Benjamin

I'm in the kitchen with Greg. A car pulls up outside, the gravel scrunching on the drive.

'That'll be them.' Greg walks off with a bounce in his step. Jess is back.

I look out the window and it's beginning to rain. I'd planned on going into the garden and giving them space to be together, but now retreat to my room instead. It's not that I'm nervous … or maybe I am. I don't want to mess up.

The McKenzies are good to me and I try to be good back. I've been helping Greg with the cooking and working in the garden and doing some maintenance painting. My body's getting stronger. I try not to think too much and that helps me feel better too. It also helps that we leave the past in the past. Adam and I have spoken of it only once.

A few days after I arrived, he said, 'If you want to talk about what happened, I can hear it.'

I didn't need to say anything. I understood I could keep it to myself, but I told him about Tom and Atholl and didn't spare him any of the details.

'So maybe, Adam, keeping that memory stick was the best thing you could have done. They all wanted Phoenix and the truth is I couldn't give it to them.'

'And you never will,' he said softly.

So he'd destroyed it. In a way I was relieved.

'There were two things I'd figured out about you,' he said. 'One – you were Gil's son. You'd scheme, plot and do what you thought necessary to follow your father's final wishes. Two – you were Gil's son but not Gil. There was no way you had the talent or insight to pull it off.'

'Thanks, you're telling me I was a shit Disciple.'

'I'm telling you I knew you had limited experience. You had a lot to learn, and the man who might teach you was gone.' Then after a pause he added, 'I messed up big time too when I was young.'

I felt tired again and my body was aching. 'It's time I took some more painkillers.' I stood up to go.

'Joshua, we don't need to talk about it again. But it's good to tell the truth. Once, at least.'

Sitting in my room now, I hear Jess laughing and the murmur of happy voices. The place is busy with her presence. After a while she's clattering up the stairs and goes into her room. It sounds like she's unpacking. I give her space. Half an hour later, she's coming up the stairs. I've left my door ajar.

'Joshua,' she calls out gently.

'Hey,' I say.

She pushes the door open slowly.

'Wow, your hair's grown.' She comes forward; I think she may be nervous. 'It's really long.'

We stand opposite each other.

'Hi, Jess,' I say. It's all I can manage. I think we're glad to see each other but not sure what to do.

Then she says softly, 'Can we hug?'

'That would be nice.'

We embrace. I want to tell her that feeling her body against mine is the best feeling ever. That I love the sound of her voice. That I'm glad she can still smile at me. But I don't say anything, because I'm not sure how to get that stuff right anymore. We hold each other a while.

She whispers into my shoulder. 'You may be Joshua now, but you still smell of Benjamin. I love the smell of Benjamin.'

I squeeze her tighter and then we release.

She looks at me with kind eyes. 'You're different,' she says. 'Somehow.'

'Yeah, I think I am.' Then after a pause, 'Greg … your family have looked after me. I feel a lot better. The grief is less now.'

We're quiet. I've just gone and said something intimate; you don't just say that to anybody.

'I'm glad you're wearing the necklace again.' She smiles and motions to my neck.

'Thanks for looking after it. It would never have survived if not.'

'It probably would have. It's a phoenix.'

There's a pause. She says, 'I don't know if Dad told you, but he destroyed the memory stick.'

'He told me. *That* Phoenix has gone.'

She watches me. 'And you're alright about that?'

I don't think she knows about Atholl and what he wanted. My conversation with Adam was private.

'I'm alright with that. Yeah.' It's strange. I'm telling the truth – I really mean it.

'Did he tell you about the other stuff?'

'The other stuff?'

'Yes. I know how they survived after they went over the cliff. Gil and Dominic.'

'He didn't tell me.'

She hesitates.

And suddenly, I'm not sure I want to know. 'You don't need to tell me, Jess. It's okay not to.'

She nods. I think she's relieved.

'I'm going to go down for lunch now,' she says. 'Don't stay up here too long, hiding away.'

'No. I'm not going to hide away.' I smile.

CHAPTER 45

Benjamin

I'm in the garden. It's a bright spring morning and I'm staring at a row of small pots of herbs. They should grow well once I've repotted them. It's been raining for days so the ground is soggy and my feet squelch on the grass. Jess is playing her guitar indoors and the sound drifts out through the windows. She's been composing and asking me what I think.

'It's good,' I say when she's finished a song.

'Joshua, you're not to tell me everything is good. That doesn't help me improve. You're allowed to use your critical faculties.'

'I'm using my critical faculties, Jess. You're good. The songs you sing, I like them all.'

We have a friendship. At first, I wasn't sure we'd manage it. We've had a few awkward moments but then I went to my room one day and she'd left a trail of Easter eggs.

I found her downstairs. 'You'll never guess what's happened,' I said, 'but a chocolate hen has laid eggs in my room.'

'Really? And did the chocolate hen lay big eggs or small eggs?'

'Mini eggs, but there's lots of them.' I kept a straight face. 'So many I'll never get through them on my own.'

We sat cross-legged in the attic and ate them, peeling back the wrapping and popping them in our mouths.

'Sometimes,' she said, 'with chocolate, I like to put it on my tongue and let it melt slowly.' She looked so happy I almost said, 'Sometimes, with chocolate, I like to eat it naked,' but I stopped myself. I didn't want to mess up. We can't get involved like that.

When we'd finished eating her mood altered. She said, serious, 'My father can breathe underwater, Joshua. It's how they survived.'

I was silent. It didn't sound real.

'I found out over Christmas,' she said quietly. 'Apparently, Grandpa Minster altered their genes. He did something he never should have that left his children able to breathe underwater.' She paused. 'M15 knew about it, and your father must have too.'

Still, I couldn't speak, but she needed a response. 'Okay, Jess.'

'Over the last few days, it's felt like a secret that's between us – I've wanted you to know. I'd actually like to forget it, and maybe now I can.'

We were quiet for a while then I said softly, 'We'll never fully understand what happened and I don't think we need to. Gil's dead and your father's Adam now. And … I'm happy just sitting here eating Easter eggs with you.'

Her eyes met mine. Maybe she'd wanted me to say something else, or talk about it more, but I couldn't. Slowly, she smiled and picked up an egg. She tossed it to me and I caught it.

I put on my gardening gloves and upturn a pot of thyme. I tap the bottom and shake the earth out but something else is there. It falls out wrapped in plastic. Maybe a pellet of plant feed. I look closer, but it's a small plastic bag. I unfold it, curious, peeling it open. It's a memory stick: 1TB of memory.

The world slows.

The world stops.

I'm standing in the McKenzies' garden. The sun is bright but not warm. I can taste coffee from breakfast on my tongue and I can smell the damp earth. I may have lived a hundred years, I may have lived for nineteen. None of that matters because time doesn't matter – there's only this moment.

I do not understand. Or maybe I understand everything. I slip the memory stick into my pocket and finish replanting the herbs.

When I go in everyone is getting on with their day; nothing has changed. Upstairs, in my room, I switch on my laptop. I've got one now and use it to buy the odd item, read the news and watch the occasional programme. Boring, everyday stuff. I withdraw the memory stick and look at it. It can't be real. I push it into the USB port; my hands don't even shake. The screen asks for my password. I take a deep breath and try not to think of Tom. Then I type it in, press return and the screen fills. It's there. All of it. Phoenix. I scroll through the first few pages. Shit, it's brilliant. I'd forgotten just how amazing it is.

Footsteps on the stairs and I come out of it quickly. Jess knocks on the door as I slip the memory stick back in my pocket.

'Come in,' I say.

She comes forward smiling. 'I was going to ask …'

She stops and looks at my laptop. 'Oh.'

I ignore her gaze because there's nothing to see. 'You were going to ask?'

She turns to me. 'If you wanted to come out for something to eat tonight. I'm off tomorrow.'

'Tomorrow?'

'Yes, don't tell me you'd forgotten.'

'I'd not forgotten,' I say softly. 'And of course I'd like to come.'

Then we're standing opposite each other. Her eyes hold mine – her sweet, beautiful eyes. I love her. I have the memory

stick in my pocket. And I think she can see it, what I feel inside
– at last. Fire. I can feel my own fire.

'Benjamin,' she whispers.

We lean into each other and gently kiss.

ACKNOWLEDGEMENTS

Thank you to my editor, Lesley Jones, for all she's taught me during this edit. I had no idea I had taken on such a challenge writing a book in two voices, and her help has been invaluable.

Thank you to my husband Paul for all the hours we've spent discussing Jung and myth. The Kingfisher series would not exist without you.

ABOUT THE AUTHOR

Shona Blass was born in Glasgow and grew up in London. She wrote stories before she could read, and has been writing them ever since. She studied in Manchester and London. She lives in the New Forest with her husband. *Phoenix* is her third published novel.

Phoenix is part of the Kingfisher series and follows *Kingfisher* and *Eagle Heart*.

To find out more visit: www.shonablass.com